RETURN TO ATLANTIS

RETURN TO
ATLANTIS

BOOK 2

KATE O'HEARN

ALADDIN

NEW YORK   LONDON   TORONTO   SYDNEY   NEW DELHI

ALADDIN

An imprint of Simon & Schuster Children's Publishing Division

1230 Avenue of the Americas, New York, New York 10020

First Aladdin hardcover edition January 2023

Text copyright © 2023 by Kate O'Hearn

Jacket illustration copyright © 2023 by Devin Elle Kurtz

All rights reserved, including the right of reproduction in whole or in part in any form.

ALADDIN and related logo are registered trademarks of Simon & Schuster, Inc.

For information about special discounts for bulk purchases, please contact Simon & Schuster Special Sales at 1-866-506-1949 or business@simonandschuster.com.

The Simon & Schuster Speakers Bureau can bring authors to your live event.

For more information or to book an event contact the Simon & Schuster Speakers Bureau at 1-866-248-3049 or visit our website at www.simonspeakers.com.

Jacket designed by Karin Paprocki

Interior designed by Michael Rosamilia

The text of this book was set in Adobe Garamond.

Manufactured in China 0822 SCP

2 4 6 8 10 9 7 5 3 1

Library of Congress Control Number 2022024495

ISBN 9781534456945 (hc)

ISBN 9781534456969 (ebook)

For Jill B., wherever you are—
I'm sorry I didn't do more to stop the bullying

RETURN TO ATLANTIS

1

"NO!" RILEY HOWLED. "LET US GO! MY dad needs to stay in the water!"

"Riley . . . ?"

Riley woke with a start and felt hot and disoriented. She could still feel the dream wrapped around her as tightly as her sheets were. It was terrible, and she felt so helpless.

Her mother was at her door and entered her room. She sat on the side of the bed. "It's over, baby, it was just a dream."

Riley was panting as she sat up and untangled herself. "That wasn't a dream, it was a nightmare."

"Was it Mada again?" her mother asked.

Riley shook her head. "No, I—I was with Dad and Galina. We were riding the Leviathan and having so much fun. But then the Coast Guard came. They shot the Leviathan with a harpoon and then threw nets over us to catch us. We couldn't get away. Dad was screaming and trying to stay in the water, but the men didn't care. . . ."

Her mother hugged her tightly. "I'm sure your dad is fine. That was just a bad dream because you're worried about the detectives' visit this morning."

Riley's breathing was returning to normal as she calmed down. "When will it end? Mom, they've asked us the same questions over and over again. They asked them in Florida when we arrived. And they asked them again when we got home. And now they're coming back. When will they finally leave us alone?"

"Soon," her mother said. "They have to make sure everything fits. Don't forget, your father had a large insurance policy. They could be looking for some kind of foul play. We know the truth, but they don't. They can't ever know."

"Could they think Alfie and I killed Dad and Aunt Mary?"

"I'm sure they don't think that. But there are concerns about what happened." Her mother brushed hair out of Riley's eyes. "Remember, you and Alfie were gone over six months. There are a lot of questions about your dad, Mary, and the *Event Horizon*. No one can figure out how you managed to survive alone at sea for so long. Not to mention Maggie's blood in Miss Pigglesworth's cabin. So just stick to the story, don't elaborate, and you'll be fine." She got off the bed. "They'll be here soon. Get up and get dressed; I want to talk to you and Alfie one more time to make sure your stories remain the same."

When her mother left, Riley climbed from her bed. She looked at the clock. It was almost eight, and the police detectives were due at nine. There wasn't time for a shower if she wanted to talk with Alfie about what they were going to say.

Riley never imagined that escaping Atlantis would cause so much trouble. It became a media circus when everyone heard about their "miraculous survival." All the networks, newspapers, and magazines wanted interviews with them to talk about their time alone on the ocean.

When there weren't television crews waiting to

talk to them, there were the police and investigators asking question after question, as though they somehow believed that Riley and Alfie had done something wrong. Riley's mother said that the media was always looking for a juicy story, even if they had to make one up. It was Maggie's blood in the cabin that caused the real trouble, despite it being proven not to be human. But it wasn't animal either. The investigators were especially interested in that.

The problem was they could never tell the truth—that the blood came from a leopard-woman named Maggie who had been badly wounded in a fight with a tiger-man while they were trying to leave Atlantis. And that they hadn't been lost at sea at all. Instead they'd spent over half a year on a mysterious island filled with strange people who were slowly turning into animals. Where gargoyles and mermaids were real, and a monstrous sea serpent called the Leviathan patrolled the waters around Atlantis while dangerous unicorns protected the land. . . .

"Riley!" her mother called from downstairs.

"Coming," Riley called back.

By the time Riley made it downstairs, Alfie was already there. "Hey, Shorty," he said. Alfie tried to sound casual, but he was as nervous as she was.

"Hey, Creep."

"Sit down, Riley," her mother, Beverly, said. "Let's go through it all again."

The police detectives arrived promptly at nine. Riley and Alfie had been through this so many times before. But they had to do it all again because any time there was a mysterious death at sea, it had to be thoroughly investigated.

They all gathered in the dining room and sat at the table.

"You are welcome to have your attorneys here," the lead detective said as he pulled out his tape recorder and a notebook.

Riley was about to speak when her mother said, "Do they need attorneys? Are you accusing these children of something?"

"Not at all," the female detective said. "We're just letting you know your rights."

"We don't need lawyers," Riley said, "because we didn't do anything wrong."

"Of course," the woman said. "Now, why don't you tell us what happened?"

Riley took a deep breath and started to speak. "We'd been on the *Event Horizon* for two weeks. Dad was making a record of the humpbacks we saw."

"Whales?" the male detective asked.

"No, humpback elephants," Alfie said sarcastically.

"Alfie," Beverly warned.

"What?" Alfie demanded. He stood up angrily. "We keep telling everyone what happened, but they won't believe us! A storm came out of nowhere. The ocean turned wild. Then this big sailboat hit us. It wrecked our boat and threw us all in the water. Then Riley and me managed to get aboard the sailboat, but we couldn't find my mom or Uncle Andrew. We looked, we kept looking, but they were gone. . . ."

Alfie threw himself down in the chair, put his head on his crossed arms, and started to cry. "Why won't you believe us? We didn't do anything wrong. . . ."

"It's all right, Alfie," the female detective said. "You're not in trouble. We just need to understand how you two managed to survive so long alone on the water."

"And understand about the fresh blood in one of

the cabins," the male detective said. "What was in there? It's been tested and forensic teams still can't identify it. Was it some kind of animal? We know it's not human blood."

Riley wasn't sure if Alfie was really crying or not. But if his tears weren't real, he was a great actor.

"I don't know," Riley insisted. "I—I don't think it was there at the beginning, but maybe it was. We were too busy trying to stay alive to pay attention to everything on the boat. This was the worst time of our lives. We couldn't find my dad or Aunt Mary anywhere and our boat was wrecked. When the storm ended, part of the *Event Horizon* was still stuck on the *Moon Dancer*'s bow. So Alfie and I went back into the water and salvaged as much as we could."

"But how did you two survive?" the woman asked.

"My dad always had these safety drills," Riley started. "He taught us how to survive if anything ever happened. How to fish and save rainwater. Plus we had all the supplies from the *Event Horizon*. Alfie and I even managed to get one of her sails and used it on the *Moon Dancer*. It was all because my dad taught us what to do."

"Andrew was a safety bug," Beverly said sadly. She

was seated beside Alfie with her arm around him. "He taught all of us how to work a sailboat and survive an ocean disaster. It just destroys me that after all that training, he didn't make it back himself."

"We are sorry," the male detective said. He looked at Riley again. "But how did you manage to sail the *Moon Dancer* home? That is a big yacht that requires a full crew. How did you do it with just you and Alfie?"

"That's what took us so long to get home," Riley said. "Dad had been teaching me to sail most of my life. We took our boat out several times a year and during vacation. The *Moon Dancer* was much bigger, but some of the things were the same. Because the sail from our boat was so small compared to the ones the *Moon Dancer* must have had, it took us longer to get home. Plus, the wreckage of the *Event Horizon* was really slowing us down until we finally managed to get it away from us."

Riley's mother nodded. "Not to mention they didn't have a compass or any way of following a course apart from the stars. It was a miracle they made it at all."

"That's an incredible story," the woman said. "You must have been very brave."

"We didn't have much choice," Riley said. "We wanted to get home."

"I understand," the female detective said. "So, let's just go through it one more time. . . ."

Riley felt like screaming as she and Alfie retold the fictional story of their miraculous survival alone on the ocean. There was question after question, but after telling the story so many times, Riley knew all the answers.

Finally, after three hours, the two detectives turned off the recorders, closed their books, and prepared to go.

"That really is an amazing story," the male detective said. "And the *Moon Dancer*, what a boat. Of all the lost boats in the world to find you, what were the chances that it would be her? She's a national treasure, a real record breaker."

"She's not much of a treasure to me," Riley said. "She did hit us and ruin my life."

"I'm sorry, you're right," he said.

"But what do you mean?" Beverly said. "A 'record breaker'?"

"Don't you know?" the male detective said. "The *Moon Dancer* is a classic. It's been missing for almost a hundred years. It vanished in 1929 and was never heard from again. Everyone thought she was lost. That yacht won the Blue Riband competition four times. It's . . . it's priceless. How it's managed to survive out there on its own without a crew is just amazing. I mean, apart from some algae, from what I hear, it was intact. How was that possible, alone at sea all this time?"

"I don't know," Riley said. "What's a Blue Riband?"

"It's a speed record for an Atlantic crossing. Kind of like a race. I've always loved boats and ships, and when I saw the *Moon Dancer*, I had to look her up. . . ."

"Don't get him started!" the woman detective said. "Come on, Stew, we have to get these reports in and leave this family alone."

Stew nodded. "You're right. But when you have a moment, look her up."

"I will," Riley promised.

Beverly rose. "So what happens now?"

"Now, after our report, I believe it can be officially declared a tragic accident. There won't be any further investigation; we're satisfied and can close the case." The female detective paused and said, "If I'm honest, I don't think there should have been this big an investigation in the first place. It's obvious there's been no foul play, just bad luck."

"What happens to the *Moon Dancer*?" Riley asked. "Can we keep her?"

"I'm afraid not," Stew said. "Right now she's been seized for investigation. First because of what happened to you two and the blood in the cabin. Then they have to establish rightful ownership. She's a priceless treasure, and I'm sure a lot of people are going to be fighting to get hold of her. Including the insurance company from years ago that paid out on its loss, plus the family that once owned it."

"So we'll never see it again?" Riley asked.

The woman shrugged. "I guess you could go back to Florida to look at it. But you won't be allowed back on board. It's all locked up tight until ownership is decided."

Beverly shook her head. "Meanwhile, I'm paying a fortune for it to be moored at the marina."

"I'm sure you'll be reimbursed once ownership is decided."

"Or I go broke," Beverly said, "and they take it for back rent."

"These things have a way of working themselves

out," Stew said as he finished packing up. "Our involvement ends here." He looked at Beverly. "We'll send our report to your insurance company, and they should pay out on your husband's policy. If anything, it will help pay for the *Moon Dancer*'s mooring."

"Thank you, detectives," Riley's mother said.

When the police left, Riley, Alfie, and Beverly went downstairs to where the Atlanteans were hiding. Not long after they arrived at the house, the basement was converted into an apartment for them.

"They're gone," Riley called. "It's safe to come out."

"Is everything all right?" Pea asked. The koala appeared from behind the old bar Riley's father had built but never used.

"They've closed the case," Beverly answered.

"Thank heavens," Mary said. She was also hiding behind the bar. Her spider-monkey tail twitched with irritation. "There shouldn't have been a case to answer in the first place."

"But you're considered dead," Alfie said. "We couldn't tell them what happened to you or Uncle Andrew."

"I'm just glad it's over," Mary said.

Soon Maggie appeared from her hiding place behind a secret wall. She limped back to the sofa. She was recovering from her wounds but still weak. "Are you all right?"

Riley nodded. "I am now that it's finally over."

"Where's Bastian?" Alfie asked.

"Here," Bastian called as he, too, emerged from his hiding place. Miss Pigglesworth was beside him.

Alfie looked at Bastian. "Where's the laptop? I need to look something up."

Bastian walked back into his hiding area and returned with the computer. With Mary's help, Bastian and the Atlanteans were learning to read. Within a short time, Bastian had been introduced to the internet and was now spending time on it discovering all the things he'd missed while living in Atlantis.

Alfie sat down beside Maggie on the sofa and started to type.

"What are you looking up?" Mary asked.

"Here it is!" Alfie looked at Riley. "Wow. That cop was right. The *Moon Dancer* is famous."

"Really? What's it say?" Riley asked.

Alfie started to read the first article aloud about

the sailing yacht and the four Blue Riband wins it had. The article said the yacht was built in 1890. "Hey, Bastian, look, that's you and your family. It says your dad was on it during one of the races."

Everyone looked at the screen and the black-and-white photograph of Bastian's family standing beside the *Moon Dancer*. As always, Miss Pigglesworth was there, holding on to young Bastian.

"Oh, weren't you adorable," Beverly said. "Look at you in your little sailor suit. And your parents were so dashing. I love their clothes."

"And look at the *Moon Dancer*," Mary said. "Wasn't she pretty before the Forbidden Zone covered her in algae and moss and her brass railings turned green?"

"She still is," Riley said.

Maggie pointed at the screen. "So many sails! It would take ages to make them all."

Riley counted the sails. "There are twelve. They'd be a lot better than the one we used from the *Event Horizon*. No wonder it was fast. I just wish we could have kept her."

"Why can't we?" Bastian asked. "It was my father's boat. It should be ours."

"Sorry, dude," Danny said as he came downstairs

and joined the conversation. "You're officially dead." He walked to Riley and punched her lightly on the arm. "Good job with the cops. I heard everything from my bedroom."

Alfie looked at Riley and blushed. "I'm sorry I started to cry. But that guy just bugged me with all the same questions."

"Creep, it worked perfectly," Riley said. "The detectives felt sorry for you. It really helped."

"Well, I, for one, am glad it's over," Beverly said. "Now, how about we make us a celebration lunch?"

"That would be great," Riley said. "I'll help."

Her mother nodded. "Then we can talk about getting you and Alfie back into school."

Riley looked at her cousin. "Is it too late to go back to Atlantis?"

2

IT WAS THE MIDDLE OF NOVEMBER AND a new school year had already started. Riley and Alfie didn't have to go while there was still so much media coverage of their return and the police investigation. But now that the media had moved on to a new story and the police investigation was finally over, there were no more excuses.

"Morning, Riley," her mother called as she knocked on Riley's bedroom door. "First day back at school, sweetie. You don't want to be late. Breakfast is ready. I've got to get to the hospital early, but Mary's in the kitchen with Alfie, Danny, and Pea. I've checked on Maggie and she's doing fine." She peeked her head in the door. "Are you going to be all right?"

Riley sat up. "I'm dreading this almost as much as I did the police investigation. All the kids are going to stare at me and whisper about us being lost at sea."

Her mother entered and shrugged. "You could always tell them the truth about Atlantis."

"What?" Riley cried.

Her mother grinned, leaned forward, and kissed her on the forehead. "Just kidding. You'll be fine. If they stare at you, you stare right back." She checked her watch. "I've got to go, or I'll be late. I'll see you later and you can tell me all about your day."

When her mother was gone, Riley lay back and closed her eyes. She was glad the police investigation was over, but things were far from normal.

It wasn't because Mary and Alfie's home had been sold and they were now living permanently with them. Or the fact that all the Atlanteans were in the house as well. That part of her life felt normal and right. It was when she went out with the friends she'd had before Atlantis that things started to feel wrong.

Right from the start it was awkward and strange—like she didn't belong. They had been in Atlantis six and a half months, and the changes it had made in her seemed profound and permanent. She no longer had anything in common with even her closest friend, Lisa. They had nothing to talk about. Lisa wasn't interested in what Riley went through, and Riley was bored by Lisa constantly talking about her latest shopping trip.

Riley preferred to spend her time with Bastian, Alfie, and Miss Pigglesworth, going for walks in the area and sharing the outside world with Bastian.

Like Pea, Maggie, and Mary, Bastian and Miss Pigglesworth also settled into the house instead of contacting Bastian's family. He and Danny had looked them up online and found them. There were more members of Bastian's family than everyone expected, and they were all still very wealthy. But after they read several articles about the vicious family squabbling over ownership of the *Moon Dancer*, Bastian wanted nothing to do with them. He asked if he and Miss Pigglesworth could stay. There was no need for him to ask. Like the others, he was considered family.

Maggie was also enjoying her new life. As she recovered, she quickly became addicted to TV soaps. She and Pea regularly debated what they watched.

With Riley's mother treating her wounds, Maggie was soon walking around as she healed.

Dinners were now eaten downstairs so everyone could stay together. These were lively events with a lot of laughter and deep conversations. Danny had adjusted to the newcomers well, and after school he worked with Pea to make improvements to the house and basement apartment. Pea was teaching Danny all about carpentry, which he took to like a duck to water. Soon the house was unrecognizable with the changes.

After dinner, instead of watching television, they would gather together and sing. Riley's mother and Danny were taught the songs of Atlantis, and once Danny learned them, he brought down his guitar and accompanied the singers.

It was the strangest arrangement Riley could imagine. The house was loud and filled to bursting, but she loved every minute of it. The only thing missing was her father. She knew he wasn't dead. But he may as well have been as he'd chosen to stay in Atlantis. The pain of his loss was an ache deep in her chest. She often heard her mother crying softly in her bedroom at night. But she wasn't the only one. The pain of losing her father was so great, Riley would often cry herself to sleep as well.

By the time Riley finished dressing and made it downstairs, she heard Alfie's voice coming from the kitchen.

"Mom, let me do it!"

"No, you're my baby; it's my job to take care of you."

"It's just orange juice!"

When Riley reached the kitchen, she saw Mary standing at the table. It came up to her neck, so she had to strain to pour the juice into Alfie's glass. As spider monkeys didn't have thumbs, she was having a difficult time holding the carton. By the time she poured a glass for Danny and Pea, most of the juice was on the table.

"Good morning, sleepyhead," Mary said when Riley arrived. "Would you like some fried eggs?"

Riley scanned the mess in the kitchen from Mary's attempts. "Cereal is fine for me, thank you."

Mary gave her a hug that was almost painful because of the powerful grip her aunt now had. Not to mention Mary's prehensile tail that she wrapped around Riley fully. "So, are you two ready for your first day back at school?"

Riley looked at Alfie and he shrugged.

"Not really," she answered. "If I'm being honest, I'd rather stay home with all of you."

"School sounds very exciting to me," Pea said as he spread jam on his toast. "With all those books."

Riley gave the koala a kiss on his warm, furry head and then took a seat beside him at the table. As she poured herself a bowl of cereal, she turned to Pea and grinned. "Not so long ago, a certain someone I know said they didn't like books or reading—that they'd gotten along fine without them."

Pea grinned his adorable smile. "Well, obviously, that was there, this is here. Since I've learned, I now love reading."

Miss Pigglesworth arrived in the kitchen moments before Bastian. He followed behind her, wearing one of Danny's sweatshirts and jeans. Riley still had a hard time adjusting to seeing him dressed like an ordinary teen. She tried not to stare, but he was so handsome in the modern clothes, she felt her heart flutter.

"Morning, Bastian," Riley said.

"Good morning, everyone," Bastian said brightly.

"Morning, Baz," Danny called.

"Come, come, sit," Mary said to Bastian. "Would you like some eggs?"

Bastian looked around the room. "Um, no, thank you very much, Mary, but I'll just have cereal and some fruit, if I may."

He took a seat beside Riley. "I wish I could go with you today."

"Me too," Riley agreed.

"Trust me, you don't wanna go to school," Alfie said. "If I could, I'd stay here."

Mary finally took a seat between Bastian and Alfie and reached for an apple. She turned to Bastian. "If you keep studying those books and learning, you might just catch up enough to join Alfie and Riley at school."

"That would be such fun," Pea said. "I wish I could go."

"Trust me, it's not fun," Alfie said. "Home is much better."

"I'm sure you'll have a wonderful time," Mary said.

"Don't count on it," Alfie muttered.

Now that they were all back together, Riley realized that despite being much shorter, with jet-black fur and a spider-monkey face, her aunt was still her aunt, with the same warm expressions and caring soul. Riley was grateful that her aunt hadn't chosen to stay in Atlantis.

As they sat at the table, no one dared mention the one subject that was on everyone's minds. They'd been away from the influence of Atlantis and the Forbidden Zone for weeks, yet none of the animals showed any signs of turning back to human. But could they? Riley recalled what the detective said about the blood they found from Maggie and how it had been tested and showed it was neither human nor an identifiable animal. If so, what was Maggie, or the others?

Riley realized if they had brought her father with her, he would have been in real danger. Colorado was nowhere near an ocean. He would have had to stay in Florida and be all alone. At least in Atlantis, he had Galina and Gideon.

After breakfast, Riley and Alfie left the house and walked to the bus stop. They were both nervous. This was a new school for Alfie, and for Riley, a new school year had already started. They had advanced her with her class, but it was provisional, provided she could keep up with her studies.

"I probably shouldn't ask this," Alfie said softly, "but do you miss Atlantis?"

Riley looked at her cousin. Finally she nodded. "If I'm being honest, a bit. I don't know what's wrong with me. We have everything here, but I still can't get used to being back. I miss so many things, especially Dad, Gideon, and Galina. I might even miss Lisette and the others a little bit. It just feels so different now."

"I know what you mean," Alfie admitted. "It's like Atlantis has infected us or something. I can't believe that I actually do miss parts of it."

Riley nodded. "Me too. But not Mada."

"Or the Red Moons," Alfie agreed.

The bus pulled up and all talk of Atlantis stopped. They took a seat together and stared out the window at the passing houses as the bus wound its way to their school. This was home, but somehow, it wasn't.

When the bus arrived at school, Riley escorted Alfie to the office and helped him get his schedule. He was one grade behind her, so she showed him around.

"We have the same lunch period," she said, checking his schedule. "Wanna meet up?"

Alfie nodded but didn't say anything.

Finally Riley took him to his homeroom. "This is you," she said when they stopped before a classroom. "Good luck, Creep."

"You too, Shorty," Alfie said. "See ya later."

After leaving her cousin, Riley made her way to her new homeroom. The moment she walked in, she could feel the eyes of her class resting on her. Most of her classmates were the same from last year, with only a few new faces.

Riley saw Ms. Young standing at the front of the room. She knew Ms. Young from seeing her in the school. She had a reputation of being tough but fair.

"Riley, come in," Ms. Young said.

Riley approached her new homeroom teacher and held out the document she was given in the office.

"Welcome back. You've had quite the adventure. We've been following it on the news. We're all so sorry to hear about your father and aunt, but we're grateful that you are safe."

Riley knew this was going to be hard. "Um, thank you. . . ."

Ms. Young pointed to an empty seat at a double desk beside a sad-looking girl. "You can sit there with Jill."

Riley had never seen the girl before and thought maybe she was new to the school too. She didn't even look up when Riley joined her at the two-person desk. Riley could feel the eyes of everyone in the classroom resting heavily on her. These were all kids she'd known for most of her school life. If they made her feel uncomfortable, she couldn't imagine what Alfie was going through.

Ms. Young called the class to attention and did the attendance check. A while later, the bell rang, and Riley had to go to her first class.

The whole morning was a nightmare as she moved from class to class and saw the same sympathetic expression on every teacher's face. She shared all her classes with Jill and in each room, she was assigned to sit beside her.

Riley noticed that Jill's clothes weren't the cleanest and were in desperate need of repair. Her blond hair was unkempt and dirty. If Riley was being honest, Jill had a bit of an unwashed odor about her as well.

But it was the haunted expression on Jill's face that struck Riley the most. As though Jill was carrying the weight of the world on her shoulders.

By the time the lunch bell sounded, Jill still hadn't

spoken one word to her. The teachers seemed to ignore her and didn't ask a single question.

Riley left her class and headed to the cafeteria. Just outside it, she saw Alfie waiting for her.

"Hey, Creep," she said as she approached. "How was your morning?"

"It sucked," Alfie said. "I hate your school!"

"I'm not a fan of it either. I feel like it's going to take me all year just to catch up. We weren't gone that long, but it's like they're speaking a different language now. Math is a nightmare!"

"I know," Alfie agreed. "There were some boys in my homeroom that are looking for trouble. They were making fun of me. I came this close to hitting one of them!"

"Don't!"

"I won't. At least not on my first day."

"Not ever," Riley said. She leaned closer. "No matter what they say to you, you can't. What if the school calls Mom and wants to see her, or they might even try to find your dad?"

"I'm never going back to my dad!" Alfie said angrily. "Doesn't matter anyway, he didn't want me. He left Mom and me."

"Still, you don't want that kind of trouble."

Alfie nodded. "I hadn't thought of that."

"I did. We have to be extra careful and not draw attention to ourselves."

"So, like, I'm supposed to ignore them when they cause trouble?"

Riley nodded. "For now, yeah."

"Great," Alfie said darkly. "Now I hate this school even more."

They walked into the cafeteria together and joined the lunch line. Riley and Alfie heard the not-so-quietly whispered comments about them being lost at sea and how they had probably eaten their parents to survive.

Riley tried to ignore them, but it was hard. How could this be the same school with the same students from before? Last year, she never had any trouble at all. Now she and Alfie were the butt of cruel jokes and comments.

They got their meals and found an empty table at the back of the room. The cafeteria was noisy and confusing. Nothing like the meals they had in Atlantis, where everyone was polite and they all ate together.

There was extra-loud yelling to one side of the room. Riley looked over and saw a group of boys surrounding Jill. They were teasing her, calling her "Stinky," and pulling at her torn sweater. Another boy took her juice and most of her meal. Jill just stood there, saying nothing as they bullied her.

Riley could feel knots bunching in her stomach. None of the other students did anything to stop it, and the teachers across the room either didn't notice or didn't care what was happening.

Finally, Riley stood up.

"No, Shorty, don't get involved," Alfie warned. "Remember what you said."

"I know what I said, but this isn't right." Riley walked away from the table and over to the boys. "Leave her alone!"

"Oh, look who's here. It's the cannibal!"

"Yeah, I'm the cannibal, and you should be scared. You all look like you've been eating just fine. I might try taking a bite!"

That shocked them, but only for a moment. "Go away, Cannibal. This is none of your business."

Riley caught Jill by the arm. "Come on, you can sit with us."

"Leave," one of the boys warned.

Riley felt Alfie arrive behind her. "Hey, Shorty, you think we should eat that one over there first?"

Riley looked at Alfie and nodded. "Looks good to me; we don't even have to cook him. Go get the forks."

Their comments caused the bullies to back up. "You two are sick, you know that? You're sick!"

Without another word, they drifted away.

"Thank you," Jill said softly. She turned to leave.

"You can eat with us if you'd like," Alfie offered. "We're not really cannibals."

When Jill smiled at Alfie, his cheeks went red. Riley was stunned. She's hadn't seen him react that way since he met Galina. She looked at Jill again and realized that beneath her messy hair and unwashed face, she was very pretty.

"I know you're not cannibals," Jill said. "But I don't want you to get into more trouble because of me."

"It's too late for that," Alfie said. "C'mon, let's just eat."

Jill joined them at their table, and both Riley and Alfie shared their meal with her. When Jill tried to protest, Riley said, "They've given us too much food anyway. We're used to smaller portions. . . ." She turned and looked around at all the servings on all of the students' plates. "There's too much food here, it's such a waste!"

"Shorty," Alfie warned. "Just because we had a hard time on the *boat* . . ."

Riley realized what she was saying and stopped. "Sorry, you're right." She turned to Jill. "So how long have you been going to this school?"

Jill looked down and wouldn't meet Riley's eyes. "Not long. We came here a few months ago, so only since the new school year started."

"Do you have any brothers or sisters?" Alfie asked.

Jill nodded. "I have two brothers and three sisters."

"That's a big family," Alfie said. "Until now, it's just been my mom and me. Now I live with Riley's family."

"Alfie's my cousin," Riley explained. "Where did you come from?"

"Ohio," Jill said. "My mom got a job here and we moved . . ." Her voice trailed off and she looked down again.

"Riley!"

Riley's best friend, Lisa, came over to the table.

When she saw Jill there, she frowned. "Riley, can I speak to you for a moment?"

Riley rose and walked away with her friend. Once they were far enough from the table, Lisa said, "What are you doing with Stinky? No one likes her. If you want to get back to normal, you should avoid her like everyone else does."

"Why?" Riley said. "It's not like she's a Red Cloak or something."

"A what?"

Riley shook her head. "Never mind. She's nice, have you tried talking to her?"

"Me talk to Stinky. Yuck. I don't think she's ever had a bath in her life. And look at her clothing."

Riley looked back at Jill as she talked to Alfie. "What's wrong with it?"

"Gah! Can't you see? It's torn and dirty and doesn't match." Lisa held up the bottom of her stylish jacket that she wore over her blouse. "I ripped this today in chemistry. It's trash now. . . ." A cruel grin appeared on her face. "Or maybe I should give it to Stinky."

Riley frowned. "Lisa, that's not nice. Her name is Jill, not Stinky." She lifted the bottom edge of Lisa's jacket and inspected the damage. "This is just a small tear. I can fix this for you in no time. You don't have to waste it and throw it out."

"Fix it?" Lisa cried. "No, it's ruined. I want a new one."

"But there's nothing wrong with it. A few small stitches and it'll be good as new. You'll never know it was torn."

"I'll know," Lisa insisted. "Riley, what's wrong with you? Since when do you care about saving clothing?"

Riley so wanted to scream, *Since I lived on Atlantis, where every scrap of clothing was precious!* But instead she said, "We're destroying this planet with waste. I think it's time we stop."

Ms. Young approached Riley and Lisa. "Hello, Riley, are you settling in all right?"

Riley nodded.

"Did I hear you say that you can sew?"

Again Riley nodded. "I was just telling Lisa her jacket isn't ruined, that I could fix it."

Ms. Young focused on Lisa. "Why don't you let her try? We should all try to produce less waste."

"But I don't want it now—it's garbage," Lisa insisted.

"What can it hurt to try?" Riley said.

Lisa's brow came together in a tight, angry frown. "If you want it so much, Riley, you could have just said!" She tore off her jacket and threw it at Riley. "Here, it's all yours." She stormed off in a huff.

Riley stood in shock as Lisa left. Her best friend had changed so much. She was unforgiving and snotty to people she didn't like.

"I saw what you did with Jill," Ms. Young said. "That was kind of you."

"Why didn't you stop the boys from bullying her?"

"I was about to when you stepped in," Ms. Young said. "I'm afraid poor Jill has been picked on since she arrived here. I've tried to help, but I can't spend every minute with her. Her younger brother and sister are also being bullied."

"Why?" Riley asked. "Jill seems nice."

"Oh, she's a lovely girl and so sweet." Ms. Young paused. "Riley, I know it's your first day back and that you've had a very traumatic experience, but do you think you could maybe be her friend and talk to her?"

"Me?" Riley said.

Ms. Young shook her head. "I'm sorry, I shouldn't have asked."

"No, it's not that. But why would she listen to me? Everyone here is calling me a cannibal."

"That's why. You can understand what she's going through. But you stick up for yourself. She won't. Just think about it, will you?"

"Sure," Riley said.

"Thank you. The bell's about to ring—you had better finish up."

Riley went back to her table.

"Everything all right?" Alfie asked.

Riley nodded. "Yep." She held up Lisa's jacket. "Lisa tore this today and I said I could fix it. Then she got mad at me because she'd rather have a new one. Then Ms. Young came over and we started talking about sewing."

"You can sew?" Jill asked.

"You bet she can," Alfie said. "She's had the best teacher."

"I wish I could," Jill said. "Then I could fix this." She showed a tear in her sleeve. "And maybe my brothers' and sisters' clothes. But I don't know how."

"I could show you," Riley offered. "We could do it here at school at lunch."

Jill's face lit with a big smile and her eyes sparkled. "Yes, please."

Riley nodded. "Great, we'll start tomorrow."

The balance of the day dragged on and on as Riley traveled to each of her classes with Jill. If there had been muttering about her in the morning, it was worse in the afternoon as Riley heard whisperings about her being a cannibal and how she was planning to eat Stinky. Right before her last class, she walked past Lisa in the hall, and when Riley said hi to her, Lisa turned away.

With each cruel comment directed at her, Jill's shoulders dropped even more, and her eyes stayed down.

"Ignore them," Riley said.

"How?"

"By thinking of things beyond this school. Like where you would like to go, or what you would like to do. This world has some pretty amazing places with creatures you couldn't imagine. Just think of them. Then their teasing won't matter."

Jill looked up at her with an expression that suggested she doubted it. "I had better go, my brother and sister will be waiting for me." She walked away without raising her head once.

Riley watched Jill leave and felt anger for her. They had spent most of the day together and though Jill was quiet, she seemed so nice. Yet everyone was being cruel to her just because of how she looked and smelled. Yes, her clothes needed repair and cleaning, and yes, she could use a bath and a brush of her hair and teeth. But that was nothing. In Atlantis Riley'd gone several days without bathing right after they arrived. It was hot and humid, so she must have stunk, but no one said anything.

After leaving her books in her locker, Riley left the school and headed toward the buses. She met up with Alfie. His face revealed that he'd had as bad a day as she did.

"Hi, Creep, how was your day?"

"Can we go back to Atlantis now?"

"That bad?"

"Worse," Alfie said.

"Yeah, I know what you mean," Riley said. "It's changed so much from the last time I was here. Even Lisa won't speak to me now because of the jacket thing."

"Do you think maybe you've changed and not them?" Alfie said.

"I don't think so."

Alfie laughed and shook his head. "Riley, you used to be just like them. Seriously, I mean it. You weren't as bad as Lisa, but you were pretty bad."

"No, I wasn't."

"Yeah, you were. That's why I never liked you. You treated me like your friend treated you today. You were always part of the popular group, so you never realized what was happening to the unpopular kids."

Riley stopped and looked at her cousin. Could it be true? Had she been just like Lisa? She thought back to the days before Atlantis and remembered a few occasions when she and her friends made fun of a girl in class because her shoes were worn-out.

Riley was horrified. "Alfie, I'm so sorry, I never realized. But you're right, I was just like them."

"Maybe not *as* bad," Alfie said. "And I wasn't any better. I'm sorry too."

"We can't go back to being like that. It's ugly."

"I don't think we can," Alfie said. "I think Atlantis changed us. Besides, we've got reminders at home."

Riley smiled thinking about the most special new members of the family. "Yes, we do."

They stopped talking when they reached their bus. Then they stayed silent all the way home and only spoke again when they exited the bus.

"I've got loads of homework," Alfie complained. "It's gonna take all night."

"Me too," Riley agreed. "School isn't nearly as much fun as I remember."

"I never liked school, so it's no different."

When they entered the house, Miss Pigglesworth bounded to the door and did her spinning happy dance. Riley bent down and hugged the dog tightly and laughed as Miss Pigglesworth licked her face. "I missed you too, Miss Pigglesworth."

"We've all missed you," Bastian said as he approached. "How was your first day?"

"Awful," Riley said. "How was yours?"

"Boring," Bastian said. He started to smile. "It's better now that you're home."

When he smiled at her, Riley felt her cheeks going red.

"I'd rather be bored than go to that school," Alfie added.

Mary arrived in the foyer and ran over to Alfie. "How was your first day back?"

"Mom, you really shouldn't be upstairs," Alfie warned. "What if someone sees you?" He looked around at all the open windows.

"It's fine. I'll go batty if I stay downstairs all the time. Come into the kitchen, I'll make us all some snacks."

"I'll help," Riley offered quickly.

"Me too," Bastian agreed.

After a quick trip to the kitchen, where they gathered fruit and drinks for everyone, they all headed to the downstairs apartment.

Maggie was curled up on the sofa with her long leopard tail wrapped tightly around her. When she saw Riley, she climbed slowly to her feet.

"Please don't get up for me," Riley said as she ran over to help Maggie. "You need your rest."

"I am fine," Maggie said as she rose and embraced Riley. "And getting stronger every day."

Pea came over and looked up at Riley and Alfie. "So, tell us all about your day. We've been anxious to hear."

They all sat down together as Riley and Alfie told them of their first day back at school.

"I can't believe how mean they are to Jill," Riley said.

"People can be very cruel," Pea said. "Look what the others did to us."

"Especially during the Red Moon," Maggie added. "Though I am sorry for your new friend."

"I'm not sure if she's a friend," Riley said. "Not yet, at least. I barely know her and it's impossible to get her to talk very much. But she did want me to teach her to sew so she can repair her clothes. So we're starting tomorrow." She looked at Maggie. "I just hope I'm as good of a teacher as you are."

Maggie smiled broadly. "You will be. Teach with your heart as well as your mind."

"That's nice of you to do that for her," Mary said. She was sitting down and rubbing her head.

"You okay, Mom?" Alfie asked.

Mary nodded. "Just a small headache."

"I have one too," Bastian agreed. "Right at the back of my head."

"So do I," Pea added.

"It's probably a lack of fresh air," Mary said. "I guess I'm not used to staying in all the time."

"It is an adjustment," Pea said. "I must admit, I do miss a few things—like going out in the fresh air."

"Me too," Maggie said. "But I will never regret our

decision to leave Atlantis." She looked at Riley and everyone in the room. "This family I have become part of is the most precious thing in the world to me."

"Indeed," Pea agreed. "And well worth the inconvenience of staying in all the time."

"Hi, everyone," Danny said as he walked down the stairs.

"Hi, Dan," Riley said.

"Danny," Pea said. "Join us. We were just talking about how we may miss a few things from Atlantis but have found so much more here."

Riley looked at her brother. "I've just had an idea, and I need your help with Mom so she'll let us do it."

"What are you thinking?" Danny asked.

"I think it would be great if we could take everyone out for a late-night drive. We can show them around without the risk of being seen. Maybe even go for a walk in the woods by the lake."

"What a wonderful idea," Pea said. "Another adventure, how exciting!"

Mary bobbed up and down and squeaked excitedly. "There are some beautiful places around here. We must do it; we must do it!"

Danny nodded. "I'm sure Mom will agree, especially if we finish our homework, clean up, and make dinner."

Then Alfie grinned. "And if she doesn't, we'll sneak out anyway!"

Everyone became excited at the prospect of going out together. It was only then that Riley realized how isolated Pea, Maggie, and Mary were. Bastian and Miss Pigglesworth could go out for walks anytime and only have to deal with a few comments about Miss Pigglesworth's size, but that wasn't possible for the others.

"It's all set, then," Riley said. "Tonight, we all go out together."

3

BY THE TIME RILEY'S MOTHER CAME home, the house was spotless and dinner was ready. She immediately went on alert.

"All right, what's up?" she asked suspiciously as she entered the kitchen. "You guys only clean up when you want something, or you've done something wrong. Which is it?"

Alfie and Riley were at the kitchen table doing their homework while Mary was at the stove stirring the vegetable stew.

"Nothing," Riley said innocently.

"Don't tell me 'nothing,'" her mother said as she kissed Riley on the top of the head and did the same to Alfie. "I know you. Something is up. What is it? Did you get in trouble at school?"

"Not at all; in fact, it was a good first day," Alfie said.

Riley looked at him and he raised his eyebrows. "Yes, it was," she agreed.

Her mother walked over to the stove. Mary was standing on a chair as she stirred the stew. "All right, Mary, what's up?"

Mary squeaked and waved the spoon around, splashing stew everywhere. "Nothing, Bev, everything is fine. . . . But . . ."

"Here it comes," Beverly said. "What is it?"

"Well," Mary said. "We've been talking, and later tonight, Danny has offered to take us all out for a nice drive. We're going to go for a walk in the woods by the lake."

"What?" Beverly cried. "You can't possibly think this is a good idea! What if you're seen?"

Riley rose from her chair. "I know it's a risk, but Aunt Mary, Pea, and Maggie are getting house-sick. They rarely come upstairs and haven't had fresh air since we got here. In Atlantis they were out all the time; now they're trapped downstairs."

"But it's too dangerous."

"They'll keep their heads covered with their cloaks so no one will see them. Please, Mom, we have to do this for them. It will be very late, no one will see us, and if we're stopped . . ."

Her mother dropped her head and sighed. "If I'm driving, there's no reason for us to be stopped."

"You're coming?"

"Of course, I can't let you do this alone. Besides, I could use a nice walk by the lake too."

Riley ran over to her mother and gave her a big hug. "Thank you!"

Excitement grew as everyone ate dinner downstairs.

"For the first time, I won't mind wearing my cloak again," Pea said cheerfully.

"Me neither," Maggie agreed.

"I think I need a cloak," Mary said.

"I can make one for you," Maggie offered. "It won't take that long. I made most of the cloaks in Atlantis. You would definitely be blue."

Riley looked at her mother. "Mom, do we still have Grandma's old sewing machine?"

Her mother looked at Maggie and then nodded. "Stay here, I'll be right back."

When Beverly returned, she was holding a sewing machine case and an old shirt from Riley's father. She walked over to one of the smaller tables. "Maggie, I'd like to show you something."

Maggie climbed to her feet and walked over to the table. When Riley's mother opened the case, Maggie looked at the machine. "What is it?"

Pea also came over. "Is it some kind of mechanical device?"

Riley's mother set up the sewing machine. "This was my mother's. She loved to sew." She looked up at Maggie. "Just like you, and now Riley."

"I don't understand," Maggie said. "What does that machine have to do with sewing?"

Beverly reached for the scissors from the case and cut a slit up the back of Riley's father's shirt.

"Why did you do that?" Maggie gasped. "It was perfectly good."

"And it will be again," Beverly said. "Just watch."

She threaded the sewing machine while Riley plugged it in. Moments later the two torn edges were sewn back together. Beverly handed it to Maggie. "Riley told me all about the fine work you do, but if you want to save a bit of time, perhaps this could help."

Maggie's mouth hung open, revealing her sharp predator teeth. The whiskers on her face twitched and her eyes were wide. "This is magic!"

"It's called a sewing machine," Riley said. "Have you never seen one before? Before Atlantis, I mean."

Maggie couldn't tear her eyes away from the small stitches the machine made. "I do not recall my life before Atlantis."

"Me neither," Pea said as he leaned closer to the machine and turned the wheel that made the needle go up and down. "This is so clever. I wonder who thought of it?"

"I don't know," Riley said.

"Perhaps we could look it up on the computer," Bastian offered.

Riley turned to him and grinned. "Sure, I'd like to know too."

"Great idea," Alfie said, not particularly interested.

"Can you imagine how much time it would save if we had something like this in Atlantis?" Maggie commented.

"It wouldn't work there," Riley said. "There's no electricity."

"What a shame," Pea said.

Beverly said, "In the past they used to have sewing machines with treadles. You pump them with your feet and the needle works. You don't need electricity. They are antiques now, but you can still get them. They would work fine in Atlantis. I might just get one here for the fun of it."

Maggie was still studying the line of sewing. "Look at the stitches—they're perfect. May I try it?"

"Of course," Beverly said. "You may have it if you like. We could get you some patterns and fabric and you could keep sewing. But only if you want to."

Maggie was speechless as she looked at Riley's mother. Tears came to her feline eyes. "This is the most wonderful gift. I—I don't deserve it."

"Of course you do," Beverly said. "It's only been gathering dust upstairs. My mother would have been thrilled to see it working again."

"I—I don't know what to say," Maggie said. She threw her powerful leopard arms around Beverly. "Thank you."

Riley felt her throat tighten. "Maybe once you learn how to use it, you could teach me how to make clothes."

"I would love to," Maggie said.

"Isn't this the perfect night?" Pea said. "First this, and later a trip outside. It couldn't get better."

They all watched Maggie learn to use the sewing machine. With each strip of fabric she joined together, her confidence grew, and she grinned.

Finally Maggie looked over to Mary. "I should be able to make you a cloak before we leave, if you want one."

"I don't suppose you could make a coat with a hood?" Mary asked.

"Not before this evening," Maggie said.

Mary nodded. "Then a cloak will be fine, as long as I have the choice to wear it. Thank you."

"No one's ever gonna make you wear one, Mom," Alfie said. "Not here, not anywhere."

While everyone settled down in their chairs, Riley and Maggie got to work making a cloak for Mary.

Riley marveled at how Maggie worked the fabric without patterns or instructions. She just cut it. Within a short time, Mary had a cloak. It wasn't blue like Maggie said. They didn't have any blue fabric. Instead a floral sheet was cut up and made into the cloak.

By the time Maggie finished, it was almost ten.

Everyone put on their cloaks or winter coats and went into the garage. They all climbed into the SUV and started out.

"This is so thrilling," Pea said as he peered out the car window. He was standing on Bastian's lap and pointing at everything. "Look at all the lights!"

As they drove, Riley explained everything they were seeing. From the houses to the library—that especially excited Pea—and then the shopping center. Bastian explained to Pea and Maggie what it looked like inside.

"I should love to see that," Pea said.

"I wouldn't," Maggie said. "It sounds far too busy for me. I am happy at home."

"Me too, now," Riley agreed. "I don't like a lot of the things I used to."

"I'm sure it will take time to readjust," Beverly said from the front. "You were in Atlantis a long time."

Riley doubted she'd ever adjust. Things were just too different now.

Finally they made their way out of town, and buildings gave way to trees. After a while, they pulled into a deserted parking area at the edge of the woods and climbed out of the car. Pea was back in his blue cloak, but the hood was down. He walked in a circle. "The trees are so different here." He looked up. "But our old friends the stars are the same."

Bastian opened up the rear hatch to the car for Miss Pigglesworth. But when the dog leaped out, she landed on the ground and then fell.

"Miss Pigglesworth!" Bastian cried. He went over to her and helped her up. "Are you all right?"

Miss Pigglesworth whined and barked softly.

"Me too," Bastian agreed.

"What is it?" Danny asked. "Is she all right?"

"She still has her headache," Bastian said. "So do I."

"Me too," Pea said. "But I thought it was the excitement of going out." He turned to Maggie. "What about you?"

Maggie nodded. "To be honest, my head is hurting."

"Right at the back," Mary said, pointing to the back of her head.

Beverly frowned as her doctor's mind clicked into action. "So you all have headaches?"

When the Atlanteans nodded, Alfie added, "I've had a slight headache all day. But I thought it was stress from school."

"So did I," Riley admitted. "But it's not really bad now. I took some aspirin and it seemed to help."

"This is very interesting," Beverly said. "I might look into this later, especially if you all have the same type of headache. I'm thinking it could be your new diet or the change in the water. It could even be the pollution levels. There must be so many differences between Atlantis and here."

"But we didn't get sick or have problems when we first went to Atlantis," Alfie said.

"Yeah, probably because it's much cleaner there," Riley added.

"Whatever it is," Pea said, "a silly headache is not going to ruin my evening. You said there was a lake?"

"You betcha," Danny said. "Come, it's this way."

Danny turned on his flashlight and led the group through the trees. Riley kept her eyes and ears open, listening for the sounds of people. Even though there were no cars in the lot, it didn't necessarily mean that there were no people here.

After a short walk, the trees opened up, revealing a beautiful, smooth lake that reflected the stars and moonlight shining down.

Maggie raised her head, closed her eyes, and

inhaled deeply. "The air is intoxicating here. It smells so sweet."

Miss Pigglesworth treaded into the water and barked softly.

"How can you do that?" Riley called to the dog. "It's freezing out."

"Not if you have fur," Maggie said. She took off her cloak and treaded into the cold water. "Oh, it's delightful. Pea, you must try this."

"Thank you, no," Pea said. "I prefer to stay dry."

Riley walked up to the water's edge and dipped her fingers in. The water was biting cold. Instead she sat down on the damp ground and smiled as Miss Pigglesworth and Maggie enjoyed their swim.

Bastian settled down beside her—close enough to be touching her. "It is lovely here."

Riley felt her cheeks flush as he looked at her. She quickly turned away. "It sure is. It's even prettier in the summer, or when it's snowing. Every winter we come here, and when the water freezes, we go skating."

"What is skating?" Bastian asked.

Riley almost reacted to Bastian not knowing about skating, but then she realized it never got cold in Atlantis. "In winter the temperature drops, much colder than it is now. The lake turns to ice. So we wear skates and play." She went on to describe skating.

"That sounds delightful," Pea said. "I should like to try that."

"We will," Danny promised as he sat down. "There're a lot of things you can try when winter comes." He looked over to Riley. "Wait till they see snow for the first time!"

They all settled down before the lake, just enjoying the peace and quiet of nature and chatting softly. After a while Miss Pigglesworth emerged from the water and shook herself off, spraying water everywhere.

While everyone stood and complained, Maggie came out of the lake and playfully did the same. "I needed that," she said as she reached for her cloak. "It did wonders for my head."

Moments later, they heard screaming echoing across the lake. Riley walked closer to the water's edge to listen in case someone was in trouble, but then the screaming was followed by loud laughter.

"I think we'd better get going before they come closer," Beverly said.

With great reluctance, they made their way back to the car.

"Maybe we can do that again?" Pea asked hopefully.

"You bet!" Danny said. "I haven't been out to the lake since before Dad . . ." His voice trailed off and he looked away.

Riley knew what he meant. The last time they came here was right before spring break when Riley went with her father, Mary, and Alfie on their trip. It felt like a lifetime ago, and everything had changed.

The return journey was a lot quieter than on the way. Everyone hated to go back to being locked in the house. But it was the only way to keep the Atlanteans safe, and that was the most important thing of all.

4

THE RINGING OF HER ALARM DREW
Riley from a deep, dreamless sleep. The moment
she awoke, she remembered the previous night and
the fun they all had at the lake. Seeing Bastian, Pea,
Maggie, and Miss Pigglesworth enjoying themselves was wonderful. She also recalled the starlight
reflected on Bastian's dark hair and the smile on his
face when he looked at her. . . .

Shaking her head, she climbed from her bed, and
she noticed the headache was still with her. It wasn't
bad, but it was there. Considering what time she had
gone to bed, she wasn't shocked to be feeling it.

Riley was the first to arrive in the kitchen, which

was a surprise. Normally Mary was the first one up, followed by her mother and Pea. Instead she set the table and put the coffee maker on.

By the time the others arrived, breakfast was ready, but there was barely time to eat and say goodbye as Riley raced around gathering sewing supplies to take with her to school.

When she and Alfie climbed on their bus, they found a seat together but didn't speak much on the way to school. Riley noticed Alfie rubbing the back of his head.

"Another headache?"

"Same one," Alfie said.

"Me too," Riley agreed. "I took a couple more aspirin this morning, but they're not helping much." She looked at her cousin. "Do you think it's stress? I mean all of us living together and worrying about— you know."

"I guess it could be," Alfie said.

They stopped speaking and focused on looking out the window. The day was dull and gray, and the forecasters said it was going to rain or perhaps even snow. One thing was for sure—it was getting colder.

When Riley arrived at her homeroom, she saw

Jill already seated at the double desk they shared. Once again her hair was an uncombed mess, her face needed to be washed, and her clothes were filthy. Riley wondered how Jill's mother could let her go out looking like this.

Jill looked up and smiled shyly as Riley sat down.

"How are you doing today?" Riley asked.

"All right," Jill said softly. "And you?"

"I was up late last night with friends, and now I'm really tired."

"Was it fun?"

Riley thought back to the moment Miss Pigglesworth and Maggie came out of the lake and shook off the cold water, soaking everyone. She smiled at the memory. "Yeah, it was."

Riley was aware of the others in the class staring at her—as though she shouldn't be speaking to Jill. She looked over at several girls, but they turned away quickly and started to giggle. Maybe it was the lack of sleep, but this really annoyed her.

Each class in the morning brought more of the same. Even from some of the students she had known most of her life. It was like she'd never had a past with them—had never been friends with them. She was only gone a few months; how could things have changed so quickly?

Riley was never more relieved than when the lunch bell sounded. Just as they rose from their desks, Jill asked, "Riley, do you remember what you said yesterday? That you might teach me how to fix my clothes?" She lowered her head. "I mean, I understand if you don't want to. You have friends to see. . . ."

Riley nodded. "I brought my sewing kit. It's in my locker. Meet me in the cafeteria and we can get started after we eat."

"Really?"

Riley saw the joy in Jill's face and couldn't help but smile. "Really. I'll meet you there."

Riley left Jill and walked to her locker. Putting her books inside, she reached for the bag containing the threads, needles, and scissors. She was just about to close the door when Lisa appeared beside her.

"I really need to speak with you."

"Sure," Riley said.

Lisa frowned. "Riley, everyone is talking about you—and not in a good way. It's bad enough that they're calling you Cannibal, but you're not helping yourself by talking to Stinky. I'm telling you for your own good: if you want to be my friend and have things go back to the way they were, you have to stop talking to her. Maybe even ask the teacher to change desks for you."

"What?" Riley said.

"You have to stay away from Stinky," Lisa said. "She's not good for your reputation."

Riley could hardly believe what she was hearing. She and Lisa had been friends for most of their lives, but she never realized how cruel and small-minded Lisa was. With her head aching, Riley couldn't keep her anger under control.

Finally she slammed her locker door shut and exploded. "I'm not the problem here, Lisa, you are! I never realized how judgmental you are. Maybe I was that way, too, before the accident, but I've changed. I hope I never go back to being that way again. It's ugly and mean—you're ugly and mean!"

Lisa gasped. "I'm not ugly! I'm just trying to help you fit in again. But you won't if you keep acting like this and talking to Stinky!"

"If fitting in means being like you and everyone else who's picking on Jill, then forget it. I don't need that kind of friendship in my life!"

Riley didn't wait for Lisa to answer. Instead she shoved past her and got away from Lisa as quickly as she could.

When she approached the cafeteria, she saw Alfie was there waiting for her. His expression suggested he'd had as bad a morning as she had.

"Hey, Shorty," he said. "What's wrong? You look like someone just stomped on your brownie."

"I'm so angry! I just saw Lisa. I can't believe we used to be friends." She told Alfie about her conversation. "All morning the kids have been looking at me and laughing because I'm sitting with Jill and talking to her."

"Ignore them," Alfie said. "I am. In my classes they're still calling me a cannibal."

"Me too." Riley took a deep, calming breath. "I guess we'd better go in. Jill is going to be waiting for us." She took a second breath, steeled her shoulders, and walked into the cafeteria.

Almost immediately the teasing started again.

"Are you sure I can't hit them?" Alfie asked as he glared at a group of boys calling out names.

"No. You told me to ignore them, and now I'm telling you. Besides, soon they'll be like the TV and magazines that don't want to talk to us anymore. They'll find something else to occupy their time."

"Like a fresh victim," Alfie said darkly.

"Exactly."

Riley and Alfie collected their meals and walked over to the same table at the back that they had sat at the previous day.

When Jill entered the cafeteria, once again the calls and teasing started.

"Stay here," Alfie said. "I'll be right back."

"Alfie, no, you can't get into a fight."

"I'm not going to. At least I'll try not to. But I'm not going to let them steal Jill's lunch again."

Riley watched her cousin walk over to Jill and escort her to the counter to collect her meal. Despite being frightened for him, Riley couldn't have been prouder. He, too, was a different person than the one he'd been before Atlantis. A much better person.

Despite the calls and cruel remarks from the same troublemakers as the day before, no one made a move on Alfie or Jill, and they arrived back at the table without incident.

"Thank you, Alfie," Jill said shyly.

"No problem," Alfie said.

While they ate, Riley and Alfie tried to get Jill to talk about her family, but Jill avoided the subject. When they finished, Riley said, "Let's go into the library and find somewhere quiet where I can show you how to repair your clothing."

Jill's face lit with gratitude as they got up. Making it to the library, they found a place to sit down. Just as Riley opened her bag of supplies, Jill pulled out a small green shirt with a tear on the side seam. Not only was it torn, it was also filthy.

"Isn't that a little small for you?" Alfie asked.

Jill shook her head. "It's not mine. It's my sister's top; she's only three."

Alfie started to laugh. "I know that—I was just teasing you."

Jill lowered her head and smiled. "Sorry."

Riley found thread in her bag that was close to the same color as the top and threaded the needle. She tied a knot in the end and then showed Jill how to carefully match the torn edges together and make small stitches to hold it. As she worked, Riley thought back to her first day learning to sew with Maggie as a teacher. She hoped she could be as good and as kind of a teacher as the leopard-woman had been.

After a few stitches, Riley handed the top to Jill. "Now you try. It's simple if you don't let it intimidate you."

Riley guided Jill's hand through her first unsure, uneven stitches. "That's it," Riley encouraged. "Nice and tight. Don't worry about how it looks right now. It's function over fashion."

When Jill finished the repair, Riley then showed her how to tie off the thread. Jill's face beamed with joy. "I did it! I really did it!"

"You sure did," Alfie said. He looked at Riley and smiled. He mouthed the word *Cool* to her.

Jill reached into her bag and pulled out another piece of clothing. It looked like boys' pants; these were for someone around Alfie's size. "Can we do one more?"

"Sure," Riley said. "This time you start it. Just thread the needle again and tie a knot in the end like I showed you. But remember, you need that knot or it will all come apart. I learned that the hard way."

With Riley there to guide her, Jill made a second repair. Her stitches weren't even or particularly neat, but with practice she would get it, just like Riley had.

The school bell sounded the end of the lunch

period, and Riley started to pack up the supplies. She caught Jill eyeing them enviously. Looking at the state of her, Riley guessed Jill's family didn't have a lot of money. So maybe they couldn't afford sewing supplies.

Riley finished packing the bag and handed it to Jill. "Here, this is for you. A reward for being a great student."

Jill gasped. "I—I can't take it. It's too much."

"No, it's not," Riley said. "Please, take it, there are several colors of thread in there and more needles and the scissors. You can practice at home tonight and if you like, we can do it again tomorrow."

Jill's face turned bright red, and she looked like she might cry. Finally, she looked up at Alfie and back to Riley. "Why are you being nice to me?"

"What?" Alfie said.

"Why are you being so nice? Everyone here hates me and my family."

"We don't hate you," Riley said. She looked at Alfie and then back to Jill. "I don't know if you've heard what happened to Alfie and me, but we've been through something really dangerous. It—"

"Shorty," Alfie warned.

Riley looked up at him and realized he thought she might tell Jill about Atlantis. But she wasn't going to. To Jill she said, "Being alone out there on the water and wanting to come home so much changed us. Alfie and I had to work together, to get along no matter what, if we were going to survive. Now that we're back, we see things differently. And how badly some people treat others—it's wrong."

"It wasn't always this way for me," Jill said. "Back in my old school, I had friends. But after we moved here and my mother . . ." Jill stopped.

"What happened to your mother?" Alfie asked.

Jill shook her head. "Um, nothing. Um, the bell just rang, we'd better get back." She got up, took the sewing kit, and ran toward the library door before they could ask her any more questions.

Alfie watched her go. "She's got some serious problems."

"Don't we all," Riley said. "I bet she doesn't have a talking koala living in her basement or a leopard for a sewing teacher."

"She might already have a leopard for a sewing teacher," Alfie said. When Riley frowned, he laughed. "We don't know what you would have turned into."

Finally understanding, Riley nodded. "Who knows, I could have become a rhino like Kevin."

"Nah," Alfie said, and laughed. "You'd probably be a warthog!" He punched her lightly and started to run into the hallway, making snorting pig sounds.

Back in the classroom, Jill was even quieter than usual. She hardly said a word to Riley all afternoon, apart from thanking her again for teaching her to sew and for the sewing supplies—but then she said a hurried goodbye and ran to find her brother and sister.

Riley watched her go. Jill wasn't being rude; she was sure of it. It was more like she was scared. Really scared. But of what? What happened to change things?

The rest of the week and all the following week was the same, with Jill being distant and untalkative. At lunch, while Riley and Alfie waited for her, Jill never turned up. They had no idea if she'd brought her lunch or didn't eat at all.

When Thanksgiving week arrived, Riley hoped to speak to Jill to clear the air before the holiday. But Jill was absent from school every day.

"Don't worry about her," Alfie said as he sat

beside Riley on the bus home. "Let's just enjoy Thanksgiving—it's been another really long week, even though it's only been three days."

Riley nodded. It had been. And despite the aspirin she was taking, her headache wasn't fading. Alfie's too. The one thing she was looking forward to was heading back out to the lake later that evening.

When they arrived home and walked through the door, the greeting was the same. Miss Pigglesworth bounded up to them with her tail wagging. Bastian was right behind her, and as always, he asked about their day.

There were smells coming from the kitchen that were making Riley's mouth water.

"Who's cooking?"

"It's Maggie," Bastian said. "She said she wanted to contribute more and learn to use modern appliances. Mary and Pea are in with her making a start on Thanksgiving dinner. I don't know what they're making, but it smells delicious."

"Maggie's in the kitchen?" Riley gasped. "What if someone sees her through the window?"

"We've closed all the blinds," Bastian said. "They're safe."

They made their way into the kitchen and the moment they opened the door, the aromas made Riley's stomach start to growl. On the kitchen table was a stack of chocolate chip cookies large enough to feed half the school. A cake and two pumpkin pies were sitting beside it.

Maggie was at the stove stirring a pot. It was from there that all the delicious smells were coming. She was standing in all her leopard glory as her long tail hung down but twitched at the very tip. Mary was at the counter kneading dough for bread. Pea was also working on his sweet rolls at the table.

"Wow," Alfie said. He walked over to his mother and gave her a kiss. "This place smells awesome."

Riley approached the stove and kissed Maggie on her fur-covered cheek, then peered down into the pot she was stirring. "That smells yummy."

Maggie offered Riley the spoon to sample the stew. "Thank you, my sweet. Now, tell us, how was your day?"

"All right." Riley tasted the stew, and it was the best she'd ever had. "This is amazing. We'd be rich if you could bottle it and sell it."

"Yeah, Maggie would look so cool on the label," Alfie said.

"I hardly think it's that good. It's not the same as on Atlantis, but I am making do with what I have here."

"Our Maggie is quite the cook," Pea called. "I have always loved her stew."

Riley went over to Pea at the table and kissed his furry head. "How was your day?"

"The same," Pea said. "But in a good way. Though I do have a new project for Danny and me to start."

"Oh?" Alfie said. "What's that?"

Pea grinned. "It's a surprise. You'll have to wait and see."

Maggie turned from the stove. "Riley, was Jill in school?"

Riley reached for a warm cookie and took a bite. There was an explosion of chocolate deliciousness in her mouth. "No, she wasn't in all week. I don't get it, everything was fine—we were having fun sewing, and then bam, she stops talking to me and now she's vanished."

"I'm sure she has her reasons," Mary said.

Bastian went to the refrigerator and pulled out the

juice. Then he poured drinks for everyone. "Maybe you should ask her what's wrong."

Riley sat down at the table and took a second cookie. "I planned to today, but she wasn't there. It's just so strange."

"Well, you gotta admit, she is a bit strange," Alfie said. "Not in a bad way, but I mean, she never bathes or brushes her teeth. And her hair is always a mess."

"You can't judge people by their outer appearance," Mary said. "Maybe there's a reason why she doesn't."

"Maybe," Alfie said. "I really like her; I just wish she'd talk to us."

"Talk to who?" Danny entered the kitchen. "Wow, so this is where the party is. What's happening?"

"We were bored," Mary said. "So we decided to start Thanksgiving early."

Danny went to the stove and picked up a spoon and stole a mouthful of the stew. "Oh wow, that's really good." He took another spoonful. "But you know, this isn't really Thanksgiving food. Where's the turkey and stuffing?"

"This is our own special Thanksgiving," Mary said. "Atlantis style."

Danny stole another mouthful of stew. "This is so good. . . ."

"You'll ruin your appetite," Maggie said, but then secretly handed him another spoonful.

"We were just talking about Jill," Riley explained. "She's still not talking to us and I'm wondering why."

Danny took a seat at the table. "Is her last name Decker?"

Riley nodded. "How'd you know?"

"Because there's a Sarah Decker at my school. We're in the same music class. She plays violin really well, but she's like your friend Jill—her clothes are filthy and a bit torn, and I think the only time she showers is after gym. She's being picked on, too, so she doesn't talk to anyone."

"That's very curious," Pea said. "Have you tried talking to her?"

"Me?" Danny shook his head. "No, I play guitar and that's across the room. Besides, she doesn't seem to want to talk to anyone."

"Perhaps you should try," Mary offered. "She sounds like she could use a friend."

"I guess," Danny said.

Riley asked, "Are you scared your friends will turn

on you if you talk to her, the way they've turned on me at my school?"

"No, that's not it. She just keeps to herself."

"Liar," Riley teased.

Danny broke off a piece of cookie and tossed it at Riley.

"Hey," Mary snapped. "I didn't spend all afternoon baking those so you two could have a food fight. If you have enough energy to fight, you can both peel carrots and potatoes for dinner."

"Sorry," Danny said to Mary. "I have a lot of homework to do. Besides, Riley should do it."

"What?" Riley cried. "Why, because I'm a girl?"

"You said it, not me! We're all equal these days, haven't you heard?"

"Dan, we all work together in Atlantis," Bastian said. "There are no specific jobs for men or women. It's based on ability."

"That's my point," Danny said. "I hate cooking and burn everything, whereas Riley is a great cook. So, she should do it because she has the ability to."

"You don't need to be a great cook to peel potatoes," Mary said.

"No, probably not," Danny said as he picked up a

cookie. "But it helps." He grinned, tossed one more piece of cookie at Riley, and then dashed out of the kitchen.

Mary shook her head. "That boy is impossible!"

5

DINNER WAS AS DELICIOUS AS THE AROMAS suggested, and Maggie was asked to cook more often. If she could blush, she would have. Instead she promised to make her stew again.

It was such a treat having everyone upstairs and eating in the dining room. Granted, all the curtains had to be closed, but it was much nicer than the basement, and Riley was so happy to have those she cared for most all around her in more comfortable surroundings.

After everyone finished, Danny volunteered to do all the dishes, as if to prove that he knew that everyone should help in the kitchen. Then they all settled down together for a while before getting ready to head back out to the lake.

At ten that night, the Atlanteans donned their cloaks, and everyone piled into their large car. Because it was the night before Thanksgiving, the roads of Denver were busier than usual, and Pea couldn't stick his head out the window. But he seemed equally joyful at watching the cars, buses, and trucks driving past them.

Riley watched him and couldn't help but smile. Pea had to be very old to have completed his transformation—although spending time in the Forbidden Zone had accelerated it. But still, for all his age, he was looking at the world with eyes wide and filled with childlike wonder.

The traffic soon thinned as they moved farther out of town and toward the mountains. When they reached the woods, they parked in the deserted lot, climbed out, and turned on their flashlights.

"How can it be colder than before?" Bastian commented as he zipped his coat up tighter. "It hasn't been that long since we were last here."

"Depending on elevation, winter arrives quickly in Colorado," Beverly said as she pulled on her scarf.

"Especially here in the mountains. I'm surprised it hasn't snowed yet."

"How delightful!" Pea squealed. "I've read all about snow and would like to see it for myself."

"You will," Riley promised. "Then we can make a snowman together."

"A man made of snow. Won't that be wonderful!" Pea said eagerly.

The koala's enthusiasm was infectious as they all entered the woods and strolled toward the lake. The air was cool and fresh and smelled of pine.

There was one problem with the chilly wind, though. It bit into Riley's forehead and made her headache more irritating. Despite that, the walk through the woods carried all her worries away.

When they reached the lake, they heard an owl hooting in the distance. Pea looked around. "Maggie, doesn't that sound just like the owls in Atlantis?"

"It certainly does," Maggie said.

"You know, I'd have liked to see Atlantis," Danny said. "I know a lot of it was awful, like how you were treated and having to wear cloaks and all, or the Red Moon. But some of it sounds really cool."

"Some if it was," Riley admitted. "Now that I'm away from it, I realize how everyone there worked together. There didn't seem to be any theft or violence. People shared everything and weren't really mean to each other—except maybe Kerry."

"Yeah, but that's because she was jealous over Bastian," Alfie said.

"No, she wasn't," Bastian argued.

"I'm afraid she was," Pea said. "But generally speaking, everyone shared there."

"That was because we didn't have much," Maggie added.

"We didn't need much," Pea said. "Mind you, if someone didn't get along, they would be given the memory berries, and that would restore the calm."

"But that's artificial peace," Beverly said. "It's taking away freedom."

Maggie paused. "True. But it did work most times. And on an island like Atlantis, we needed to get along, as there was nowhere else to go."

"It sounds like you miss it a bit," Danny said.

"Do I miss it?" Maggie asked. "I must admit that although there are some aspects of Atlantis that I do miss, being here with all of you has been the happiest time of my life, and I wouldn't trade that for the world."

"Me too," Pea said.

Miss Pigglesworth barked, and Bastian nodded. "We agree."

The owl hooted again, and Pea nodded. "He really does sound the same."

They strolled slowly around the water's edge. Danny was holding a stick and dipping it into the cold lake. "I wonder how Dad is."

Riley nearly gasped. This was the very first time her brother had mentioned their father. He was rarely spoken of at home. It was just too painful.

"I'm sure he's having the time of his life," Beverly said.

Riley heard the pain and bitterness in her mother's voice. "Mom, considering how no one has changed since we got back here, if Dad had come with us, he'd be in a lot of trouble."

Her mother smiled and put her arm around Riley. "I know. But it's still hard."

"It sure is," Mary agreed.

As they continued around the lake, Miss Pigglesworth stopped and woofed. She started to growl softly.

Maggie turned and looked in the direction they came from. "She's right. There are others here."

Riley felt her stomach clench. There were no Red Cloaks, but there were wild animals, or worse—people. "What is it?"

Maggie's feline ears tilted. "It is boys. Several of them."

Everyone looked around. The lake was before them, and the boys were coming from the direction of the parking area. There was very little time to decide what to do.

"Mary, grab Pea; you're faster at climbing than he is," Maggie said. "Let's get up into the trees. We can't let them see us." She turned to Riley. "We'll be here if there's trouble. You're not alone."

"Just be careful," Beverly said.

Mary wrapped her prehensile tail around Pea and lifted him off the ground. Then she ran toward the closest tree. With a graceful leap, she was soon up in the canopy of pine.

Maggie was equally agile as she went down to all four feet and practically leaped halfway up a tree.

Miss Pigglesworth's growl deepened and the hair on her back rose.

"It's all right, Miss Pigglesworth. They're probably out walking just like us." Bastian tried to sound calm, but Riley could see the concern on his face. What else had Miss Pigglesworth said to him?

A moment later, several boys in their late teens and early twenties arrived. They were laughing and staggering. It was obvious that most, if not all, were drunk. Some were still holding beer cans.

"There they are," one slurred. "Hey, sorry about your car. We had a bit of an accident."

"Yeah, accident," another said, and they all laughed.

"What did you do to our car?" Danny demanded.

"It's your fault," one of the boys said. "You shouldn't have parked in my spot."

"Tell us what happened?" Beverly asked.

"Well," the boy who must have been the leader said. "Here's the thing. Everyone around here knows I park in that spot, but you took it. So I had to move your car."

They all burst into drunken laughter. "Yeah, he moved it . . . ," one called.

"If you've damaged our car, you're gonna pay for the repairs," Danny challenged.

The leader called, "Hey, check the 'tude on him." He walked closer to Danny and suddenly didn't seem so drunk. "Watch your mouth, kid. Nobody talks to me like that."

"I just did," Danny said.

"Daniel, stop," Beverly warned. She looked at the boys. "Let's go see what you've done."

"We ain't going nowhere, lady," the gang leader said as he took a step closer. He was completely sober.

Miss Pigglesworth's growl deepened.

"Look at the size of that dog!" one of them warned. "It looks like a wolf."

Bastian stepped forward, beside Danny. "She doesn't like strangers. You had better go."

"Not yet," Alfie insisted, joining Danny and Bastian in standing up against the boys. "They can't leave until we've seen what they've done to our car."

"Don't worry about it, Alfie—I have insurance," Beverly said. "They can go now."

"You're not telling us what to do, are you?" the leader threatened.

Riley could see things starting to change. The strangers weren't drunk at all; they'd been pretending to be so they could get close. She looked around and realized they were surrounded. There had to be at least eight of them.

Miss Pigglesworth bared her teeth and started to growl again.

"I told you, she's very protective. Get out of here before it's too late," Bastian warned.

One of the boys pulled out a knife. "She takes one step toward me and I'm gonna cut her."

Riley looked up into the trees. Any minute now, Maggie was going to move. Riley moved closer to the leader. "Please, just go. We don't want any trouble."

"Riley, get back," her mother warned.

"Yeah, *Riley*, get back," the gang teased in unison. The leader pulled out his knife. "I want all of your phones and wallets—now."

"Hey, um, Mike," one of the boys called. "Let's forget it. Let them go. They don't got nothing we need."

Mike turned quickly. "Shut your mouth, Josh, we're doing this."

Riley looked at the boy, Josh. He was older than Danny and appeared terrified. But that didn't stop him from holding up a knife in his shaking hand.

Beverly shook her head. "You can't just hit our car and then rob us."

"Oh, we're not just going to rob you," Mike said as he looked at the others, and they all started to laugh menacingly. He took one step closer to Beverly and formed his hand into a fist that he smacked against his other hand. "We're gonna get some boxing exercise as well."

Before his next step, a ferocious roar filled the air.

Riley was stunned by the sound. Back on their last day in Atlantis when Maggie and Mada had fought in the fog, Riley hadn't heard Maggie's feline voice because Mada was roaring too loudly. But with the quiet of the night, Maggie sounded just like a lion.

The boys froze and looked around. "What was that?" one of them called.

Riley stole a glance over to the trees. Maggie continued roaring but was still high in the canopy.

Miss Pigglesworth barked and growled. Then Bastian looked wildly around and said, "It must be the monster that's hunting this lake! Riley, you know, the one you told me about!"

Riley instantly knew what Bastian was doing. "Yes, yes, the Denver Lion!" She held her flashlight aloft and shone it into the trees, away from Maggie's area. "I read that someone's released a big cat in the woods. It's been seen going after picnickers! We all have to get out of here!"

"Do I look stupid?" Mike challenged.

"Yes, if you don't think we're all in terrible danger," Danny said.

The roar sounded again. This was followed by a loud crashing through trees and a heavy thud. Maggie was now down on the ground. The roar turned to heavy growling and snarling that was getting closer.

"Riley, over there," Beverly said. "Shine your light over there; I saw something moving in the dark."

Riley moved the flashlight and it landed on Maggie. Her leopard markings seemed almost neon in the flashlight's beam. She was on all fours and unrecognizable as her mouth was open in a snarl and showing her predatory teeth. Her eyes glowed the iridescent green-gold of when light catches an animal's eyes in the night.

"Oh man, it's true!" one of the boys cried. "It's not a lion, it's a jaguar! It's gonna kill us."

"No, it ain't!" Mike shoved Danny down to the ground. "It's gonna kill them. Everyone, run!"

Maggie roared again. The sound was chilling and caused goose bumps on Riley's arms, even though she adored Maggie. Then Maggie leaped forward and charged the departing gang members.

Miss Pigglesworth also moved. She ran forward and leaped up on Mike's back, knocking him to the ground. Then she put her mouth over his exposed neck and her growling increased.

"Don't move," Bastian warned, "or she'll bite down!"

As the other gang members fled, Riley's family ran up to Mike. Danny rose and kicked the knife from Mike's hand. He picked it up and held it aloft.

"Hey, that's mine!" Mike snapped. But when he did, Miss Pigglesworth's growls increased.

Bastian said, "You make one move and she'll bite you!"

"Call her off!" Mike shrieked.

"No way," Alfie said. He looked at Riley. "Help me go through his pockets."

Riley frowned. "We're going to rob him?"

"No, dummy, we're going to see if he has any identification."

While Riley checked one side of Mike's jacket, Alfie tried the other.

"I got his wallet," Alfie said. He opened it up and took out Mike's driver's license. Holding the flashlight, he read, "Michael Peterson, I'm sure the police will be very interested in meeting you."

Without his gang behind him for support, Mike started to whimper. "Please, please, call off your dog. Don't let her hurt me!"

"Why should we?" Alfie said.

Danny nodded. "Yeah, you guys were about to hurt us."

"No, no, we weren't, we were just fooling around. We do it for fun."

"It wasn't fun for us," Riley said. "How many other people have you attacked?"

"None!" Mike spat.

Miss Pigglesworth snarled.

"You'd better tell us the truth," Bastian warned. "Miss Pigglesworth knows when someone is lying, and she hates it."

"Okay, okay, a few," Mike said. "We do it for kicks and cash."

"That's enough," Beverly said. "Miss Pigglesworth, everyone, let him up."

Miss Pigglesworth released Mike's neck and backed up. But her teeth were still bared, and she growled, ready to strike if he tried anything.

When Mike sat up, he looked wildly around. "Where's that cat?"

"It's probably eating your friends," Alfie said.

"No!" Mike started to climb to his feet, but Miss Pigglesworth barked and snapped at him.

"Don't move," Bastian warned. "She does not like you very much."

"Just keep her back!" Mike cried.

"We will if you behave yourself," Riley said. "Now show us the damage you've done to our car."

"You're worried about your car when there's a monster out there?" Mike gasped. "We have to get out of here before it kills us!"

"Not until we've checked our car," Danny said.

Mike climbed to his feet and walked toward the cars. Before leaving the area, Riley looked to where her aunt and Pea were in the trees. She held up her hand and motioned for them to stay and wait. Then she followed the others.

The damage was worse than they expected. The back end had been crushed in by Mike's vehicle hitting it several times. All the windows were smashed, and it looked like they'd kicked the doors and dented them badly.

"Why would you do this?" Beverly demanded.

"You took my spot," Mike said.

"That is the stupidest answer ever!" Alfie said. "You don't own this place."

"We practically do," Mike said. "This is our lake where we hang out."

"Hang out and attack people," Riley added.

Another roar sounded, followed by screams coming from the trees. Riley wondered what Maggie was up to and hoped she stayed safe. The gang did have knives.

"It's coming back!" Mike panicked and tried to run to his car, but Miss Pigglesworth blocked the way and growled at him.

"Don't move," Bastian warned. "She's really not happy with you."

"Call her off!" Mike cried. "I need to get to my car."

"You want to hide in your car," Alfie said. "But look what you've done to ours. No windows, no way of protecting ourselves. You'd be happy if that cat came here and killed us."

"I wish it would!" Mike shouted.

Beverly pulled out her cell phone and started to

take pictures of the damage to her car, as well as a photo of Mike standing beside it. Then she took pictures of Mike's car, his license plate, and the damaged front end.

Suddenly the other gang members burst from the trees, crying, "It's coming—we gotta get out of here!"

Beverly took their photos as they ran up to their car and climbed in.

"Go on," Beverly said to Mike. "Get out of here before there's more trouble. But don't for one minute think that you're getting away with anything. You'll be hearing from the police shortly."

"You people are messed up!" Mike cried as he ran to his car. "I hope that cat kills all of you!" He gunned the engine and tore out of the area, with the car spitting gravel at them.

Maggie arrived at the group just as the other car pulled away. She stopped and stood up. "Is everyone all right?"

Riley ran to her and hugged her tightly. "We are because of you and Miss Pigglesworth. Thank you!"

"You don't have to thank me," Maggie said, hugging her back.

"Yes, we do," Beverly said. "I have a feeling those

boys were planning something terrible for us. I'm sure the police will be very interested in my photos."

"And Mike's wallet," Alfie said, holding it up. He handed it to Beverly and then trotted toward the trees. "I'm going to get Mom and Pea."

Riley was trembling as she suddenly realized something. "I bet it was them," she said. "Do you remember last time we were here? We heard screaming and then laughter."

Danny nodded. "It must have been them attacking someone else."

"I wish I had known," Maggie said. "I could have helped them."

Bastian was shaking his head. "I don't understand. Why would they do this?"

"Because they're jerks," Danny said.

Beverly sighed and turned to Maggie. "I don't know why they did it, but what I do know is that this night could have turned out much differently if you hadn't been here."

Alfie, Mary, and Pea arrived moments later. Alfie was carrying Maggie's cloak.

"Thank the stars you are all right," Pea said. "I felt so helpless in the trees watching those boys with you."

"I was going to come down," Mary said. "But Pea wouldn't let me." She looked at the koala. "You might be small, but you're very strong."

Pea nodded. "When I have to be."

"I'm glad you didn't," Alfie said. "If they'd seen you, too, there's no telling what could have happened."

"But they saw me," Maggie said. "Could this be trouble for us?"

Beverly shook her head. "I don't think so. When the police find them, they won't listen to their story about a big cat. They'll be more interested in their knives and the other people they've attacked. Still, I think we should see if the car drives, and then get everyone home. After that, I'm going to the police."

"Do you think you should?" Riley said.

"Absolutely," her mother said. "Those boys are dangerous. Who knows how many people they've hurt in the past, or will hurt if we don't report them?"

"I'm going with you to the police, Mom," Danny said.

"All right," Beverly agreed. "Let's just get everyone home first; then we can go."

Despite the damage to their car, it did start.

After they brushed out all the broken glass, they climbed in.

The drive home was quiet and cold as all the windows were gone. Because of the damage to the car, Beverly drove especially carefully so she wouldn't draw any more attention than necessary. There were a few curious stares from the other vehicles passing them, but no one saw the occupants of the car with their hoods pulled up tightly.

Once they made it home, everyone settled in the basement apartment with hot cocoa while Beverly and Danny left for the local police station.

They all stayed together watching television and trying not to think about what could have happened.

"It's my fault," Pea said softly. "We went out because you knew I wanted to."

"No, Pea," Riley said. "It's not your fault; it was theirs. They did this, not you. And maybe because we were there, we've saved other people they might have attacked."

Pea rubbed his chin. "I didn't think of it like that."

"It's true," Mary said. "Who knows how many people they've already hurt, let alone would have hurt in the future."

"Or even worse," Alfie said, "they had knives and seemed ready to use them."

Maggie remained quiet during the conversation. Riley looked over to her and saw that her eyes were haunted, and she wouldn't look at anyone.

"Maggie, are you all right?"

Maggie nodded but didn't say anything.

"What is it?" Riley asked.

"I—I—" Maggie started to shake.

It was then that Riley saw the tears sparkling in Maggie's eyes. She rose from her chair and took a seat beside the leopard-woman. Then she took one of Maggie's hands. "Tell me what's wrong."

Maggie sniffed. "I'm so scared. . . ." Her shoulders shook.

"It's over. We're all fine and safe at home," Mary said.

"It's not that," Maggie said, and sniffed. "I—I liked it."

"Liked what?" Riley asked.

Maggie lowered her head and stared at her hands, which were more like paws with sharp claws. "I enjoyed chasing those boys. When they ran, it triggered something in me. I wanted—no, I *needed* to chase them." She turned her sad eyes to Riley. "I'm terrified that I've become just like Mada. That I'm losing the last of my humanity and becoming a wild predator that wants to hunt."

Riley couldn't believe what she was hearing. Maggie was the gentlest person she knew, besides Pea and Mary. "Maggie, listen to me. You are *nothing* like Mada. Nothing! He is a dangerous killer; you're not. The fact that you're even questioning yourself proves that you're still a thinking, caring person and not a predator."

"But I am a predator," Maggie said, weeping. "I wanted to hunt them."

"No, my dearest friend," Pea said softly. He left his chair and padded up to Maggie. "What you are is the most wonderful, compassionate person I've ever met. Dear lady, you might have wanted to hunt them, perhaps kill them, but only because they were threatening your family. If they had just been playful boys running around us, would you have come down from the tree?"

"I—I don't think so."

"What was triggered in you wasn't a predator's nature. It was your loving, protective nature. You chased them away to keep us safe. We all know you could have caught them easily, but you didn't. You just chased them."

"Pea's right," Riley said. "It would have been so much worse if you hadn't been there."

"You don't understand, I liked it." Maggie continued to weep.

"I truly believe that what you liked," Mary said, "was the satisfaction of protecting your family. You must never feel shame in that."

Miss Pigglesworth started to whimper and whine.

"Miss Pigglesworth did a lot more than you did," Bastian said. "She actually put her mouth around Mike's neck and would definitely have done more if he'd tried to hurt any of us." He looked over to Riley and Alfie. "She said she really wanted to bite him hard, because he was threatening us."

"Maggie," Riley said. "I trust you with my life. You mean everything to me. Maybe you scared yourself because you enjoyed the chase. And maybe that is from the wild cat in you. But you, *Maggie*, the human part of you, stopped yourself before you did anything. What you are to me is the best of both. I never felt scared once, knowing you were there.

Please, don't compare yourself to Mada. You are nothing like him."

Alfie nodded. "I wasn't scared at all because you were there."

Riley squeezed Maggie's hand and tried to reassure her, but she knew Maggie. Being faced with her wild side scared her. Knowing how deeply Maggie felt things, it would take her a long time to recover, if she ever did.

"Besides," Riley said, "how many dangerous predators do you know that are addicted to soap operas?"

Maggie actually smiled. "I guess you are right."

"Indeed," Pea agreed. "Though I doubt we'll ever agree on *General Hospital* when *The Young and the Restless* is so much better."

This time, Maggie chuckled softly. "Oh, I don't think so."

The mood lightened as Pea purposefully engaged Maggie in a heated debate about the soaps. His favorite versus hers. The tactic worked perfectly, and though Riley didn't like any of them, she was relieved to see Maggie become more animated.

The long night dragged on as they waited for Beverly and Danny to return from the police. It was nearly dawn when they did.

More cocoa was made and served as Beverly sat down and explained, "It was worse than we imagined. That gang has been terrorizing people at the lake for months. They've seriously injured so many, but the police just couldn't trace them."

"Yeah," Danny added. "The police staked out the lake all summer, but they never caught them. I mean, it is a big lake to patrol, and they would strike at different areas."

"So now what?" Alfie said.

"Now," Danny answered, "they know who their leader is, and they have the photos of most of them."

"What about the car?" Pea asked.

"We have a police report for the insurance company, so that shouldn't be a problem. Though there is one small point of concern."

Riley's mother and her brother exchanged looks. Finally, Danny nodded.

"What?" Mary asked. "What aren't you telling us?"

"Well, the police searched our car and we found out that Mike's gang has taken our details from the glove compartment. They know who we are and where we live. The police think they might try to come after us."

Miss Pigglesworth barked and whimpered. Bastian said, "Miss Pigglesworth says that won't be a problem. If they come here, she will take care of them."

"So will I," Maggie added softly.

"And me," Pea offered. "I'm small, but I'm scrappy."

Beverly smiled. "Thank you. But I'm not worried about that. What I'm worried about is that the police are going to patrol our area more often and have a car stay out front for a few days."

It took a moment for this to sink in. Then Riley said, "Oh. So they're going to be watching us."

"Watching *over* us," Danny corrected.

"Isn't that the same thing?" Riley asked. She looked at the Atlanteans. "That means no more coming upstairs for a while."

"Or trips to the lake," Beverly added. "Not until Mike and his gang are caught."

"So they commit the crimes," Alfie said angrily, "but everyone here is put in prison."

"For the time being, yes," Beverly said. "I'm sorry, but this is a really dangerous gang. Worse than we imagined. There's no telling what they might try. Especially now that they know we've involved the police."

"Do the police really think they might try to get revenge?" Mary asked.

"We don't know what they could be planning," Beverly said. "They'd be foolish to come after us. But it could happen. We just have to be careful."

"We'll be fine," Pea said brightly. "It will be like an extended Red Moon. The wildlings are out there, and we are safe inside. It won't be fun, but we'll manage."

Now that her mother and brother were home, Riley felt the heavy weight of exhaustion pressing down on her. "I can't keep my eyes open." She got up. "I know it's almost morning, but I'm going to bed."

"We all should," Mary said. "It's been a long and dreadful night."

Before leaving, Riley went over to Maggie and kissed her on her furry cheek. "Please don't worry about what happened. We love you and trust you completely. You are family."

Maggie put her arms around Riley and held her tightly. "If those boys do come back, I promise you, they will never harm anyone here. If it means me releasing my inner predator, rest assured, I will."

• • •

It was almost noon on Thanksgiving Day when Riley rose. Everyone in the house was quiet and tired. She saw Alfie peering out the front window and joined him.

"Are the police out there?" Riley asked.

"Yep," Alfie said. "Your mom took them some coffee and cookies earlier. They said they're going to be here all day."

"That's so sad," Riley said. "It's Thanksgiving; they should be with their families."

"I know," Alfie agreed. "They also asked us to stay inside all weekend."

"I'm too tired to do anything else anyway."

Alfie nodded glumly. "I guess it means I actually have to do my homework."

Everyone in the house spent the entire holiday downstairs either watching television together or, for Riley, having Maggie teach her more about making clothing.

When Monday arrived, the police were still with them. Riley and Alfie waved at the two officers in the car as they left the house and headed to the bus stop.

"I wonder how long they'll be here," Alfie asked.

"I don't know. But I wish they'd go away. Mike

and the gang would be nuts to come to our home. Even without knowing about Maggie, they know how dangerous Miss Pigglesworth is."

They stood at the bus stop and Riley rubbed the back of her head. "My headache is worse. I think all this stress is getting to me," she mused. "That, or maybe I need glasses or something."

"Then I do, too, because I still have mine," Alfie said. "And Mom said hers is getting worse."

When the bus came, Riley sat quietly looking out the window at the dull gray day. It was cold and miserable. Winter was definitely knocking on late autumn's door.

After saying goodbye to her cousin, Riley headed to her homeroom. With the events of Wednesday night filling all her thoughts, she'd forgotten about Jill and her odd behavior. Entering her homeroom, Riley saw Jill was back and seated at her desk.

When she sat down, Jill didn't even look up. This time, Riley didn't care. She had her own problems to deal with.

Ms. Young came in and called everyone to order. While she went through the attendance list, Jill slid a note to her. When Riley accepted it, she looked over.

Jill's eyes were red and puffy, and she looked like she'd been crying.

Riley opened the note and read the simple message: I'm sorry. She reached for her pen and scribbled, For what? Then she slid the note back.

Jill read the message and wrote a quick response. When she slid it back and Riley read it, Riley gasped. I know what happened to you at the lake. I'm so, so sorry.

A million thoughts flashed through Riley's mind. How could Jill know what happened? Did others? The possibilities were limitless, and none of them good.

Finally, Riley leaned over to Jill. "We have to talk."

Jill wouldn't look at her. She just sniffed and nodded.

When the first bell sounded, Riley got up and waited for Jill to get up as well. While everyone left the room, Riley leaned closer. "How do you know about the lake?"

Jill's chin started to tremble. "My brother told me."

"Your brother? How could he . . ." Riley paused and had a terrible thought. "Your brother was there, wasn't he? He was one of the guys who attacked us."

Jill kept looking down as tears trickled down her face. Finally she nodded.

Riley gasped again. This was huge. "Have the police caught him?"

"No," Jill said, and wept. "He left us."

Riley reached for Jill's arm. "Now we really have to talk. Come on. . . ."

There was no hesitation or resistance in Jill's body. She did as she was told and walked beside Riley out of the classroom. "Let's go to the library. We can talk there."

"What about math class?" Jill asked.

"We're going to be late."

They reached the library and, as Riley hoped, there was no one inside. The librarian nodded to them from her desk on the other side of the spacious room.

"Let's sit over there where we won't be heard."

When they sat, Riley leaned closer to Jill. "Okay, tell me everything. What happened on Wednesday night, and how did your brother know it was us?"

Jill sniffed as tears streamed down her cheeks. "Josh knew your names because I told him about you and Alfie and how nice you've been to me—and that you stopped the bullies from picking on me. And he knows you were teaching me to sew. He said he heard your mother call you Riley. She said 'Alfie' as well, and he realized who you were. He said he tried to stop Mike, but he couldn't."

Riley remembered Josh and how he'd told Mike to forget about attacking them. She nodded. "He did try. But Jill, your brother had a knife."

"I—I know . . . ," Jill wept. "But Riley, he's not bad, not like Mike and the others. He was doing it for us."

"I don't understand," Riley said.

Jill's shoulders started to shudder as deep sobs shook her. "We—we're not supposed to talk about it."

"I'm sorry, but you'd better, because your brother and his gang wanted to hurt us. If that big cat hadn't been there, I'm sure they would have."

"He told me about the cat. He said someone released a jaguar or something into the woods and that it chased them."

Riley nodded. "If it hadn't been for that cat, things would have been much worse for my family. Now, you have to tell me, what's going on?"

Riley could see Jill was torn and debating what to do. Finally she said, "Our mother ran away."

"What do you mean, 'ran away'?" Riley said.

"Three months ago, our mother left. There was a

note saying she was sorry, but she wanted her—her old life back from before us. She took all the money and left us alone. She said we should go to the police, and they would find us new homes and families. . . ."

Riley could hardly believe what she was hearing. How could a mother abandon her children? "Do you know where she went?"

Jill was now crying too hard to speak. She just shrugged.

"What about your dad?"

"He—he left when I was young. I don't remember him. I don't even know his name."

"Do you have any other family? Aunts or uncles? What about grandparents?"

"It's just us."

Riley put her arm around Jill and held her until the tears trailed off. Finally, Jill said, "I'm so sorry about Josh. He joined the gang so he could get us money for food. My brother Pauly and me have paper routes, and my sister works at a burger place after school and weekends. We've sold everything in the house but our clothes and beds—even our toys are gone. But it's just not enough. They've shut off our power and water because we couldn't pay. That's why we are always dirty. The landlord doesn't know yet; we keep telling him that Mom is working all the time. The school's tried to reach Mom, too, but Sarah pretends to be her on the phone. But I'm sure the school is going to send someone out one of these days. Then they'll find out the truth and put us in foster care. What if they separate us?" She turned her tearful eyes to Riley. "Please don't tell. My family is all I have."

Riley realized that their time in Atlantis was nothing compared to what Jill's brothers and sisters were going through. "Jill, they're going to find out eventually. Can you pay your rent?"

Jill shook her head. "Not really. But now that Josh is gone . . ."

Riley nodded. "Where is he?"

Jill's chin started to go again. "I swear I don't know. When he came home and told us what happened, he packed a bag. He said he had to go because the police were after him." She turned to Riley sadly. "What are we going to do?"

"I don't know," Riley said. "But I have to tell my mother."

"No!" Jill cried. "She'll tell on us."

"No, she won't," Riley promised. "Believe me, my

mom is great at keeping secrets. And she's a doctor. Have any of you seen a doctor since your mom left?"

Jill shook her head. "We've never had enough money for us to see a doctor."

Riley gasped. "Never, in your whole life?"

When Jill shook her head again, Riley asked, "What if you get sick?"

"We talk to the pharmacist."

"They're not doctors," Riley said. "Please, Jill, trust me. My mom won't tell. But I know she'll want to help, just like I do."

"But if Sarah finds out I told you, she'll be really angry."

"I understand, but it's better to have her angry and get you what you need. Think of your little sister."

"I—I don't know," Jill said.

"Please, let me help. I mean, to start, we could do your laundry for you and repair some of your clothes. And we can get you some food."

"I can't ask you to do that."

"You're not asking, I'm offering."

Jill started to cry again—this time, Riley could see it was from relief. She reached out and embraced the frightened girl. "Let's head back to class."

Jill nodded. "I want to go to the bathroom to wash my face first. I don't want anyone to know I've been crying."

"Good idea," Riley agreed. "Let's go."

At lunch, Riley found Alfie and told him briefly what Jill had told her.

"Her brother did that to us?"

"No—I mean, yes, but Josh was the one who told Mike to stop. He ran away from Maggie with the others."

"And now you want to help her?"

"Don't you?" Riley asked. "Alfie, this is Jill. Now we know why she's always dirty and hungry. We have to help her."

Alfie considered for a moment. Then he nodded. "You're right."

Riley let out her breath in relief. The old Alfie would have said something cruel and not wanted to help. The new Alfie was much better.

"There she is," Alfie said as Jill entered the cafeteria. He rose and walked over to her. Then he escorted her into the line to get some food.

Riley suddenly realized the school lunch might

well be the only meal Jill ate all day. What had she been eating while she stayed away? And what about the rest of her family? How were they eating? They weren't old enough to be on their own but didn't want to separate either.

As Jill and Alfie walked back to the table, there was the usual name-calling from the same kids in the cafeteria. But no one made a move against them. They sat down and started to eat.

Riley pulled out a pen and opened one of her books. "Jill, may I have your address, please? I know my mom will want to help."

Fear rose in Jill's eyes, but then it calmed as she gave Riley her address. "You promise you won't call the police?"

"Us? Are you kidding?" Alfie said. "It's bad enough that they're parked outside of our house now."

"Why are they at your house?" Jill asked.

"Because of Wednesday night," Riley said. "Mike and the gang wrecked my mother's car. The also broke into it and stole stuff from it, including our house details from the glove box. The police are sure Mike is going to come back to get revenge because our dog attacked him and then we told the police about him."

"Have you met him?" Alfie asked.

Jill shook her head. "No, Josh said he's bad news. He doesn't like him and wouldn't let him come to our house. Josh didn't tell us what your dog did."

"Probably because Mike didn't tell him," Riley said. "Considering how Mike was crying like a baby, I'm sure he wouldn't want his friends to know."

"I hope they don't come to your house," Jill said.

"They're in for a big surprise if they do." Alfie grinned. When Riley looked at him and frowned, he added, "I mean, with those police cars out front."

They finished their meal and, when the bell sounded, headed off to their afternoon classes. When the day finally ended, Riley told Jill she would most likely see her later. Jill's eyes became haunted again and Riley realized she was still worried because she'd talked about her family. Riley took her hand. "It'll be all right, I promise."

Jill didn't look convinced.

Making it home, Riley and Alfie walked past the police car parked out front. The two officers inside waved at them and smiled.

When Riley and Alfie waved back, Alfie said, "I wonder how long they'll be here."

"I don't know, but I wish they'd go. I'm so worried they might see something in the house and try to come in."

"Me too," Alfie agreed.

They went inside and immediately noticed the change. No one was there to greet them. Even Bastian and Miss Pigglesworth were missing.

"We're home!" Alfie called.

Riley and Alfie walked over to the door leading to the stairs to the basement. But when Alfie tried the handle, he found it locked. He looked at Riley. "This door didn't have a lock on it."

"It does now," Bastian called from behind the door. They heard a *click* and then the door swung open. "We're being extra careful."

When they made it down into the basement apartment, Riley saw Maggie, Pea, and Mary on the sofa. Maggie was asleep.

"Have you eaten anything today?" Riley asked.

Mary shook her head. "We didn't want to risk going up and being seen. Being hungry is making my headache worse."

Riley felt her temper start to flare. Not at anyone here, but at Mike for the trouble he and his gang had caused.

"I've eaten, but it hasn't helped," Riley said as she rubbed the back of her head. "First Alfie and I will make you something to eat, and then we can talk."

After making a load of sandwiches for everyone, Riley and Alfie carried them downstairs. When they made it back, Maggie was awake but didn't look very well.

"Are you all right?" Riley asked.

Maggie nodded. "I'm just tired. How was your day?"

"Interesting," Riley said.

While they ate, they discussed Jill and her situation.

"Oh, the poor dear," Mary said. "We must do something."

"What kind of person would abandon their children?" Maggie asked. "I just can't imagine. They must be so frightened."

"They are," Riley said. "Jill cried so hard when she finally told me. She's feeling guilty because of what her brother did."

Pea nodded. "We can't allow our anger at Josh's involvement in the gang taint our compassion for those children. It's too bad we can't get them to Atlantis. They would never want for anything there."

Riley nodded. "I was thinking the same thing."

"Since that isn't an option," Mary said, "the first thing we need to do is get those children over here for a good meal and a hot bath. Then we can get their power, heat, and water back on."

"What?" Alfie cried. "Mom, we can't bring them here! What if they see you?"

"They won't," Mary said. "We'll stay down here with the door locked. I, for one, will gladly give up a bit of freedom if it helps those children."

"Me too," Maggie said.

"So would I," Pea agreed.

Riley looked at Bastian and he shrugged. "I'm happy to stay down here with Miss Pigglesworth, so they can have my bed."

"Then it's decided," Mary said.

Riley looked at her aunt. Mary was always very loving. But since she'd transitioned into a spider monkey, her maternal instincts were especially active. When Mary heard about Jill's family's situation, those instincts were put into overdrive.

"I do want to help," Riley said, "but I won't endanger you. Ever."

"You won't be," Maggie said. "We're content down

here. And perhaps more so, knowing we're helping children."

"Absolutely," Pea agreed.

By the time Riley's mother made it home from work, Riley, Alfie, and Danny had carried some of their camping equipment from the garage. There were cots and extra sleeping bags.

Riley expected her mother to insist that Jill's family go to a hotel, but she surprised Riley by agreeing. Though she added, "They can stay here a night or two, but this isn't the solution. Those children are not old enough to take care of themselves. They'll need help."

"Mom, I promised Jill we wouldn't call the police or social services. She's terrified that the family will be separated."

"They will separate them," Mary said. "There are very few foster homes that will be prepared to take on five children at once."

Beverly sighed. "Well, we'll worry about that later. Right now, let's go see them."

Riley went with her mother in their new rental car and drove over to Jill's house. It wasn't far, but it was a world away. The neighborhood was rough and there were several boarded-up homes. Half the houses on Jill's block were dark.

Riley was counting down the numbers on the houses. Finally they reached twenty-nine. "There," Riley said. "That's their home."

Her mother leaned forward and peered out the cart window. "There are no lights on."

"Their power is shut off, remember? Jill said they are using candles. Heat and water's off too."

"That is criminal," Beverly said. "Especially in this cold. They can't stay here. Come on, let's get in there."

Riley took a deep breath, dreading the next few minutes. Jill said her older sister, Sarah, would be angry. Riley just hoped she wouldn't be too mad.

They walked together up to the front door. Riley knocked several times. From behind the door she could hear movement and hushed whispers.

"Jill? It's me, Riley. My mom is here too. We want to help."

There were more soft sounds, but the door remained closed.

"Please," Beverly said. "We haven't called anyone. It's just us. Please open the door."

After another moment, the door opened. Jill was standing in the dark with a young girl of two or three in her arms. There was the faint glow of candlelight from the room behind her.

"Riley, it's not a good time," Jill said.

"I'm sorry, but we have to get in there." Beverly pushed past Jill. "I would like to see Sarah, please."

A moment later a girl older than Jill arrived. Danny had said she was in his school and looked as unkempt as Jill. Added to that was the furious expression on her face.

"We don't need your help," Sarah said sharply as she lifted their youngest sister away from Jill. "Now do you see why I told you not to tell anyone? They're going to separate us."

Beverly shook her head.. "We only want to help. I'm a doctor. Riley has told me what's happened and that none of you have ever seen a doctor. I would like to check on you all."

"We're fine," Sarah said defensively.

"No, you're not," Beverly said. "I hate to be cruel, but you smell awful, and your clothing is filthy. You haven't washed and I'm sure you're not eating properly. There is no heat in your house, and that's not good for this little one."

"We eat," Sarah said. "When I can bring home food from the restaurant."

"Have you eaten tonight?" Beverly challenged.

Sarah hesitated. Soon a girl and boy arrived and stood behind Sarah. The boy looked to be around eleven and the girl a little younger, perhaps eight or nine.

"No, we haven't," the boy said. "And I'm starving. Jill said you're going to bring us some food?"

"Yeah, I'm hungry," the young girl said.

"Pauly, Robbi, be quiet," Sarah snapped.

Beverly leaned closer to Sarah and lowered her voice. "I know you're trying your best to keep your family together—and you're doing a wonderful job. But part of being a responsible adult is knowing when to ask for help. And you all need help. So why don't you go pack up a few bags of clothing and come with us. You can spend the night at our house. Have a hot meal and a bath. We can do your laundry too. Then I can check out your brother and sisters."

Sarah hesitated.

"Please," Jill said. "Chrissy hasn't eaten anything all day."

"Please, Sas," Pauly begged.

"Please," Robbi called.

"It's all right, Sarah," Beverly said. "I'm not going to call anyone. We just want to help. Come home tonight so we can talk and perhaps make some plans for you."

Sarah appeared so much older than her young age. She was exhausted from taking care of her family.

"Just for tonight," Riley added.

"Please," Pauly and his younger sister begged.

Finally, Sarah nodded. "Just one night." She looked at her siblings. "Pauly, Robbi, go pack some clothing to wash." Then she looked at Jill. "Go get some of your clothes. I'll pack up some of Chrissy's things and my clothes." She turned back to Beverly. "Will you hold on to Chrissy for a bit? We'll be ready to go soon."

Beverly accepted the youngest child. "Take your time, we have all night."

Just over an hour later, they were all driving back to Riley's house. Little was said in the car, though when Riley looked into the mirror to the back seat, Jill nodded to her and smiled. Riley nodded back.

When the car pulled into their driveway, Beverly pressed the button that automatically opened the garage door. While they waited, Sarah looked at the police car parked on the street and became wild with fear. "There are police here! You said you didn't call them."

"Calm down," Beverly said. "I didn't call them. They're here because we were attacked on Wednesday night. . . ."

"Attacked?" Sarah paused. "Oh yeah, Josh told me. I'm really sorry."

"It's not your fault," Beverly said. "But the police are worried that Mike and the gang might come after us. So they've posted a car out front for a few days for our protection. I don't like it any more than you do."

Sarah nodded. "I understand, and they're right. Mike's no good; he might come here."

"Do you know him?" Riley asked.

"Yes," Sarah said. "But I wish I didn't. He's really scary and dangerous."

"That he is," Beverly agreed.

When the garage door closed after them, they climbed out and headed into the house. Beverly took off her coat and said, "How about you all take baths first and when you're done, we can eat. Meanwhile, I can get started on that laundry."

Jill, Robbi, and Pauly didn't look happy about this, and Riley could see they were very hungry. "I can lend you some of my clothes while yours are in the wash." She looked at Pauly and said, "You can wear some of Alfie's clothes."

Just then Alfie appeared and was introduced. "Sure," he said to Pauly. "You can have some of my clothes."

While Beverly and Sarah carried the dirty clothing to the laundry room, Riley and Alfie escorted Jill, Pauly, Robbi, and Chrissy upstairs to start to get clean.

It seemed like ages before everyone was back downstairs and in the dining room eating the first full meal they'd had in ages. The Decker family tried not to tear into their food, but it was obvious they were starving.

Now that Jill was clean, Riley could see just how pretty she was. With her hair still wet, she reminded Riley of Galina, the siren from Atlantis. Thinking about her mermaid friend and how much she missed her nearly brought a tear of sadness to Riley. Instead she sighed heavily and watched the family they were helping.

Chrissy was seated beside Sarah, and it was touching how Sarah made sure Chrissy ate before she took a bite of food.

When the meal ended, Beverly took her medical bag into the kitchen and each child was invited in for her to check over. Despite their ordeal, they were generally in good health, if not a bit thin from lack of food and good nutrition.

After that, while the washing machine was kept busy, everyone moved into the living room to watch television.

Riley sat with Jill and noticed how long Sarah was staying in the kitchen with her mother. She was anxious to hear the outcome of their discussion. Jill was, too, as she kept looking at the closed kitchen door.

When Sarah emerged, her eyes were red and puffy, and it looked like she'd been crying. But she was smiling. She came up to Jill. "Beverly says we can stay here a few days while she helps us with our house, getting the services turned on again."

Riley was glad to hear that, but at the same time, she worried about the others downstairs. It wasn't fair that they should be locked away. But what choice did they have? There was no way they could ever let Jill's family know about the Atlanteans.

When bedtime arrived, Beverly insisted that Sarah, Robbi, and Chrissy take her room as it was the largest, while Jill stayed with Riley in her room. Alfie invited Pauly to share his room. Beverly said she would be happy on the sofa. It was tight and the house was full to bursting, but they managed.

Bastian and Miss Pigglesworth remained downstairs with the others. But once everyone went to bed, Riley's mother promised to take meals down to the Atlanteans and that Bastian and Miss Pigglesworth could come up so they could go for a walk.

Riley noticed that her new friend fell asleep the moment her head hit the pillow. Perhaps it was the hot food or warm bath, but none of their guests stayed awake long.

With Jill deeply asleep, Riley checked the clock. It was barely ten. She got up and treaded softly out of the room. She made it to the kitchen to help her mother prepare food to take downstairs.

"Can I help?" Riley said.

Her mother jumped, but then smiled. "You should be in bed."

"I can't sleep. I'm worried about the others."

"Me too," Beverly said. "I don't think Maggie is particularly well."

Riley's stomach tightened. She'd seen Maggie earlier and had the feeling something was wrong. "Is it her headache?"

Her mother nodded. "It's getting worse and she's becoming very tired. So are Pea and the others." Her mother looked at her. "How are you feeling?"

Riley didn't want to alarm her mother, but her own headache wasn't leaving either. "I've still got my headache and so does Alfie. Mom, could it be because we left Atlantis? That we're still adjusting to being back?"

Her mother nodded. "Bastian's also off. He's going to let me draw some blood. I think I should try you and Alfie too. I can't risk taking any from the others after what happened with Maggie's blood from the *Moon Dancer*. The last things we need are awkward questions we can't possibly answer."

Just then Bastian and Miss Pigglesworth walked quietly into the kitchen. "Hi, Riley," he said, smiling. "I thought you'd be in bed."

Riley shook her head. "I wanted to see how you were all doing."

"We're fine, thank you. Just a bit hungry."

"I'm taking care of that," Beverly said. She looked at Riley. "Why don't you and Bastian go for a quick walk with Miss Pigglesworth? When you get back, we can take this food down to the others."

Miss Pigglesworth whined softly and licked Riley's hands.

"She says she's missed you," Bastian said. "We all have."

"I feel the same," Riley said. "I'm sure it won't be for long."

"Go on, now," Beverly said. "But be careful."

Riley and Bastian went to the front door and pulled on their coats. When they opened the door, Bastian gasped. "What's that?"

Riley looked up. "It's snowing." There was a dusting on the ground, and the air was still as the large flakes drifted down.

"That's snow?" Bastian held out his hand and grinned like a child when snow settled on it and then melted.

Riley smiled at his enthusiasm. "Guess winter's here."

Bastian looked up at the sky. "Pea is going to love this." When he looked back at her, his eyes were sparkling. "I've really missed seeing you."

Riley flushed. "I've missed you too." They walked out into the snow. At first Miss Pigglesworth lifted up her paws, as the wet snow was unfamiliar to her, but soon she was treading happily.

Bastian paused and hesitantly reached for Riley's hand. "I wanted to ask you if I could maybe . . ."

There was something in his eyes that made Riley's heart pound faster. "What's that?"

Just as Bastian was leaning down closer to her and Riley was sure he was going to kiss her, a voice shattered the moment.

"Is everything all right?"

It was one of the police officers from the car. His window was down, and he was looking at them. "It's a bit late for you two to be out."

Bastian cleared his throat and straightened up. "I'm sorry, officer—"

Riley smiled as best she could. "We've been playing and lost track of time. We're just going for a quick walk around the block."

"How about you stay in your yard," the officer said. "I don't want to alarm you, but we've heard reports that Mike and some of his gang might have been spotted not too far from here."

This caused a knot in Riley's stomach. "Are they coming this way?"

"Don't think so," the second officer inside the car said. "Don't you worry, we're here for you. But to be on the safe side, please just keep to your yard."

"We will," Bastian promised.

With their walk cut short, Miss Pigglesworth did what she had to do, and they returned to the house. Before entering, Riley waved at the officers.

"Can this get any stranger?" Riley asked softly when they entered the warm home again. "Jill's family here, you guys locked in the basement, and now Mike and the others are in the area."

"I know it's not easy," Bastian said. "But we're all right downstairs. Mary is thrilled that you're helping the others. They heard one of the young girls laughing and now they all want to meet them."

Riley's eyes went big. "They're not coming up?"

"No, they won't," Bastian said. "But I never realized how much Pea and Maggie love children. I guess it's because there aren't many in Atlantis."

"Probably," Riley agreed.

They made it back into the kitchen and when they entered, Riley and Bastian received a shock. Chrissy was seated at the kitchen table, stroking Pea's head, and talking animatedly to the koala.

Beverly was at the stove stirring a pot.

"Mom?!" Riley cried.

"I know, I know," her mother said calmly. "Pea came up for some juice for Maggie and then Chrissy walked in. She can't sleep because it's a strange house."

"It is quite all right, Riley," Pea said softly. "I'm sure this enchanting child won't be believed if she tells the others."

Riley frowned and her mother said, "Chrissy thinks Pea is a talking teddy bear."

Chrissy's face was beaming as she continued to chat with Pea. Riley couldn't understand half of what she was saying; Pea just nodded and laughed.

When the meal was prepared, Beverly said to Riley and Bastian, "Would you start carrying that downstairs? I'll take Little Miss back up to bed."

But when Beverly went to lift Chrissy, she started to cry and reach for Pea. "Teddy . . ."

Pea climbed down from the chair and walked over to her. "Time for bed, Chrissy," he said kindly. "I have to go to bed too. But I will see you soon."

"Sleep with Teddy," Chrissy wailed.

"No dear, not tonight," Beverly said. "Teddy needs his rest."

"Chrissy?" Sarah called. "Where are you?"

Pea dashed under the kitchen table just as Sarah shoved open the kitchen door and ran inside. When she saw Chrissy with Beverly, she calmed. "I'm—I'm sorry, I was asleep, and she slipped away. I hope she hasn't caused you any trouble." She reached for her little sister and took her from Beverly.

"She's no problem at all," Beverly said. "Sarah, this is Bastian and Miss Pigglesworth. They're staying with us, too, and have an apartment downstairs."

Sarah's eyes landed on Miss Pigglesworth. "This is the dog Josh told us about. She really is big!"

Miss Pigglesworth trotted over to Sarah and sat before her. Sarah was fearful as she raised Chrissy out of reach of the dog.

"She won't hurt you," Bastian said. "She's very nice and loves children."

Chrissy leaned down and reached out her hand. Miss Pigglesworth licked it and sent her into a fit of giggles. Then Chrissy said, "Where's Teddy? I want Teddy."

"Teddy's not here," Sarah said.

"Yes, he is," Chrissy insisted.

"Bastian and Miss Pigglesworth got in late tonight,"

Beverly explained quickly. "So I'm just making them something to eat. Then it's off to bed with all of you." She said to Sarah, "Do you want me to take Chrissy back up?"

"No, thanks, I got her." She looked around. "I'm sorry she got away. I'll block our door."

"No problem," Riley said. "It must be hard for her, being in a strange place."

"She'll be fine," Sarah said. "Good night, everyone."

When Sarah left carrying Chrissy, Pea peeked out from beneath the table. "Well, that was fun."

"Not the word I'd use," Riley said. She pulled away a chair and helped Pea climb from beneath the table. "Are you all right?"

"Meeting Chrissy has helped me feel much better," Pea said.

While Riley assisted Pea up onto one of the chairs, she felt his fur wasn't just warm, it was hot and damp. "Mom, does Pea feel hot to you? Or are my hands still cold?"

Beverly came over and felt Pea's head and then stroked down his back. "You are warm. How are you feeling?"

"I must admit that I have felt better," Pea said.

"This might make you feel better," Bastian said. "It's snowing out."

"Is it?" Pea said.

Bastian nodded. "There are big white flakes falling from the sky."

Riley expected Pea to jump out of the chair and try to go out. Instead he stayed put. This scared her. "Yes," Riley said. "And if it keeps up, we can build that snowman."

"That will be fun," Pea said. "Oh dear, I completely forgot why I came here. Maggie isn't well and is asking for some juice."

"I'll get it," Riley said. She pulled out glasses and poured juice for everyone. "I'll take this down to Maggie and Mary and tell them dinner is on its way."

"I'll come with you," Pea said. When he started to walk, he staggered a bit and then toppled over.

"Pea!" Riley cried.

She and Bastian ran to Pea and helped him get up.

Pea was chuckling with embarrassment. "I'm not sure what came over me. I was so dizzy. It's this headache."

Bastian reached down and lifted Pea in his arms.

"I am quite capable of walking now," Pea said.

"And I am quite capable of carrying you. Those stairs are steep. It's safer this way."

Pea didn't put up much of a fight. As Bastian carried him forward, Riley looked at her mom.

"I'll submit your blood tomorrow," her mother said. "I just hope it will show us what's happening to everyone. Otherwise we may be in trouble."

6

RILEY WOKE BEFORE JILL. HER FRIEND was sleeping soundly beside her. Checking the clock, she saw it was an hour earlier than when she normally got up. It reminded her of all the days she woke early in Atlantis to watch the sunrise. Then she would go for walks and spend time with Galina.

It amazed her how much she still missed the mermaid and Gideon. They were a world away, but their memories remained fresh and had not faded into a dreamlike state as memories often do.

Unable to get back to sleep, Riley rose and dressed. She padded softly out of her bedroom. There were sounds from the kitchen, so she wasn't the only one up.

When she entered, she found her mother working with Bastian at the kitchen table. Her medical bag was open, and she had her blood-drawing kit out.

"Morning," Riley said.

"Good morning, Riley," Bastian said. His tone was softer than usual, and he looked flushed and warm.

Miss Pigglesworth was lying on the floor beside him but barely lifted her head. Riley bent down and stroked the dog and felt her fur was as warm as Pea's had been.

"Mom, I think Miss Pigglesworth has a fever too."

"They all do," her mother answered. Then she looked at Bastian. "You'll feel a sharp scratch. But it won't hurt for long." She brought the needle closer to Bastian's arm.

"It's all right," Bastian said. "If it can help, take as much as you need."

After several vials were filled, Beverly extracted the needle and put a bandage on the injection sight.

"You're next," she said to Riley. She put her hand on Riley's forehead. "How are you feeling?"

"Not great," Riley said as she took a seat. "I'm getting pretty tired of this headache."

"You're warm too," her mother said. She reached

for her digital thermometer and did the test. "Yep, you've got a slightly elevated temperature as well. Not as bad as the others, but it's there."

Her mother's brows knit together in a deep frown. "Something is definitely going on with all of you. It's not good. I'm putting a rush on these blood tests."

"Do you think we should stay home from school?" Riley asked.

Her mother shook her head. "Whatever this is, I'm sure it's not contagious. Danny and I are fine. This has something to do with Atlantis; it's just not clear what. Hopefully the blood tests will let me know."

By the time Alfie got up, Bastian and Miss Pigglesworth had already departed to the basement apartment. Riley went with him and checked on everyone. After her visit, she was even more frightened. Everyone downstairs was feeling weak and hot. Their headaches were getting worse too.

"Any idea what's wrong with us?" Alfie asked as he sat at the table giving a blood sample. "Have you seen Mom? She doesn't look good. I'm getting scared."

"So am I," Riley's mother admitted. "Fevers can cause a headache and the weakness."

"But what's causing the fevers?" Riley asked.

"They are our immune system's way of fighting infection. Considering what you've told me about Atlantis, it could possibly be malaria or some other tropical disease. Hopefully these blood tests will let me know."

"If it's malaria, wouldn't we have gotten sick in Atlantis?" Alfie asked. "But no one ever did."

"I don't know," Beverly answered.

"When will we get the results?" Riley asked.

"Sometime today. Then we can start working on a treatment."

There was something in her mother's eyes that frightened Riley even more. "What is it, Mom? What aren't you saying?"

"Well, I'm just worried about medications for Mary and the others. They aren't human anymore, but they're not full animals either. I have to look into something that can work on all parts of them. But before we can even start talking about that, we have to diagnose the problem."

Further discussions were cut off as Jill and the others came down for breakfast. Jill and Danny entered the kitchen together and saw Beverly putting the blood tests into her bag.

"Is everything all right?" Jill asked.

"Sure," Riley said. "Alfie and I have had a headache for a while, and Mom's checking it out."

Danny looked at her with questioning eyes. Riley shook her head quickly. Danny also knew the others weren't well. But they couldn't discuss it. "Yeah, you faker," he teased. "You just don't want to go to school."

Riley looked at Alife. "I think he's found us out."

As more of Jill's family entered the kitchen, all discussion of the blood tests was stopped and a noisy, excited breakfast started as Pauly went straight for the cereal. "Wow, dinner and breakfast. This is great."

He and Robbi had two portions of cereal each. When Sarah entered, she was carrying Chrissy. Beverly immediately went over and lifted her out of Sarah's arms. "Have a seat and get yourself something to eat; then you and Danny can head out. I'll take care of Little Miss."

Sarah shook her head. "Thank you, but I should stay home with Chrissy."

Without missing a beat, Beverly said, "Don't you worry about her. Bastian is home today, and I should be back early. Chrissy will be well cared for."

Chrissy was glancing around the kitchen. "Where's Teddy?"

Sarah sighed tiredly. "I told you, Chrissy, Teddy isn't here. He's at home." She turned to Beverly. "She won't stop talking about her 'teddy bear.' I've never seen her so obsessed."

"No, he here," Chrissy insisted.

Riley looked at her mother. "Should I get her one of my stuffed animals?"

"It's all right," Sarah said. "She gets like this. She'll have forgotten by tonight." Then she looked at Beverly. "If you're sure it's okay to leave her . . ."

"Of course it is," Riley's mother said.

Just as quickly as the insanity of breakfast started, it was over, as everyone gathered their books and headed to the bus stop. The snow was still falling, but the flakes were smaller and not really sticking.

"Your mother is so nice," Jill said softly as they all waited for the bus.

"She's awesome," Pauly said. "I haven't eaten this much in so long, I think my stomach forgot what food is."

Robbi hadn't said much for most of the walk to the stop, but then she said, "I wish she was my mom."

Riley looked at the three of them and wondered what their life was like. What was their mother like? "Yeah, she's pretty good."

"Where's your daddy?" Robbi asked.

"Don't ask that," Jill said quickly.

"He's in the ocean," Riley answered. She looked at Jill and shrugged.

Alfie nodded. "Yes, he's swimming with all the fish and mermaids."

"I love mermaids," Robbi said.

"Me too," Riley agreed softly.

When they arrived at school, there were actual gasps in the class as Jill walked in with Riley. She was clean and her hair was combed, her teeth brushed. She was wearing some of Riley's clothes and looked beautiful.

But the morning dragged for Riley as she and Jill walked from class to class. At lunch, she wasn't particularly hungry and noticed that Alfie was much the same. His face was flushed, and she knew that he, too, had a slight fever. They were both feeling . . . off.

It was just as well that Jill wasn't teased at lunch— Riley didn't have the energy to take on the bullies.

Like the morning, the afternoon seemed endless.

Riley spent more time watching the clock than she did looking at the front of the class. She waited for each minute to pass so that she could get home and perhaps hear what her mother had to say about the blood tests.

When the afternoon bell finally rang, Riley practically ran for the door. Jill was with her but seemed to be moving too slow. Riley didn't want to say anything, but she needed Jill to speed up. They had to get home so she could check on the others. But that would have to wait because of their visitors.

The snow was falling heavier again as the bus dropped everyone off. Making it home, Riley waved to the police in the car again and smiled when they waved back.

"How long are they going to be here?" Jill asked nervously.

"They said a few days," Alfie answered. "I wish they'd go now. They're freaking me out."

"Us too," Robbi said.

They entered the house and found Chrissy in the living room, lying against Miss Pigglesworth on the sofa. Bastian was in an armchair, sleeping soundly. Riley looked at him sitting there in his jeans and sweatshirt with his dark hair falling down into his eyes. She felt her heart flutter. Her cheeks were already warm, but seeing him there, they went redder.

"Bastian?" Riley said as she touched his arm. His skin was hot to the touch. Riley looked at Alfie. "He's really hot."

"So is Miss Pigglesworth," Alfie said as he pet her.

"Who is this?" Jill asked.

Riley was so worried about Bastian, she'd completely forgotten that Jill, Pauly, and Robbi were standing there. "Um, Bastian is our friend. He lives here too. But he hasn't been feeling well lately."

"Just like you," Jill observed.

Riley nodded. "But Bastian and Miss Pigglesworth are worse. My mom is hoping to find out what's wrong."

Bastian finally opened his eyes. "Oh, Riley, you're home early."

Riley checked her watch. "No, we're not. It's almost four."

"Really?" Bastian said. He sat up. "I—I must have fallen asleep. It's just this headache. And I feel so peculiar."

Riley introduced Bastian to Jill, Pauly, and Robbi.

"We didn't see you yesterday," Jill said.

"I—I've been working." Bastian started to stand up, but then fell back into the chair.

"Bastian!" Riley cried.

"I'm all right," Bastian said. "I'm just dizzy."

Looking at him, she could see he was far from all right. His face was flushed with fever, and he was weak. This made Riley want to check on the others. She looked at Alfie. "Would you stay here with everyone? I'm going to go check on, um, something downstairs."

Alfie nodded. "We'll stay here."

While Alfie and Bastian kept the others occupied, Riley went to the basement door. It was unlocked. She ran downstairs and found everyone sleeping. Maggie and Pea were on the sofa together and Mary was curled in a chair.

"Mary," Riley said as she gently shook her aunt's arm. "Mary, wake up."

"Hello, dear," Mary said sleepily. "Is Alfie all right?"

"We're fine; it's you we're worried about." Riley felt Mary's black, furry forehead and could feel the heat. Her fever was climbing. "How are you feeling?"

"Head hurts," Mary said. "Very sleepy . . ." She wouldn't open her eyes.

Before, Riley had been concerned about the Atlanteans. That worry now turned to fear. Something was seriously wrong. Pea and Maggie were as difficult to rouse as Mary. And when they did wake, they, too, wouldn't open their eyes.

By the time Riley made it back upstairs, her mother was walking through the front door. She was two hours early and the expression on her face was grim. "Where are they?" she whispered.

Riley pointed to the living room. "In there with Bastian and Miss Pigglesworth. Bastian is hot and dizzy. Do you have any results?"

Her mother nodded and motioned her into the kitchen. When they were alone, she said, "Riley, it's not good. Yours, Alfie's, and Bastian's blood isn't normal. Its makeup has changed completely, and there are things in there I don't recognize. The lab didn't either. They are asking a lot of questions about where the blood came from."

"Will they find us?"

Her mother shook her head. "No, I didn't use your names. I used old patient numbers and identifiers. But there are odd markers and chemicals in your blood that are unrecognizable. Bastian's results are even stranger."

Riley felt her throat constrict with fear. "So what's wrong with us?"

"I don't know," her mother said. "The only thing I can say for certain is it's not a virus or bacterial infection. But after that . . ."

Riley was almost afraid to ask. "Mom, are we still, um, human?"

Her mother's eyes answered before she did. Finally, she shook her head. "I don't know. Whatever Atlantis did to you, it changed your blood chemistry. There was one thing that I saw in the results: some of your red blood cells are exploding."

"Exploding?!" Riley cried.

Her mother nodded. "Some rare blood cancers will do that."

"Atlantis gave us cancer?" Riley gasped.

"No, I don't think so. But it did change you. I just don't know how or what's happening now."

"Bastian really isn't well. He's so sleepy and weak. And the others downstairs are worse. Mary won't even open her eyes. She's awake, but not awake."

"I'll get my bag," her mother said.

Within a short time, Beverly had checked on Mary, Pea, and Maggie. Then she came upstairs and examined Bastian. They all had the same symptoms: headache, fever, and extreme fatigue. Their heart rates were slower, but not dangerous yet, and their blood pressure was down.

By the time she finished with Bastian, Danny and Sarah were getting home from school.

"I just don't know," Beverly said as she put away her stethoscope. "It could be so many things."

"Maybe you should take him to the hospital," Sarah suggested as she stood back with Danny, looking at Bastian.

Everyone in Riley's family said, "No!" at the same time.

"It's—it's against his religion," Danny said to her.

Riley knew that whatever was wrong with Bastian and the others was also happening to her and Alfie. It was much slower, but it was happening. What had Atlantis done to them? Had it infected them? When would it stop? Could it stop? There was only one thing she could think of, and it was unthinkable.

"Mom, can I see you in the kitchen?"

Her mother nodded. "We should start dinner anyway."

"Can I help?" Jill offered.

Beverly nodded. "That would be lovely. Just give us a moment."

Riley's feet felt like lead as she followed her mother into the kitchen. When they were alone, she said, "I think we have to take them back to Atlantis."

Her mother gasped. "Riley, we can't! We have no way of doing it, and even if we did, how could we find it again?"

"I don't know," Riley said. "But Mom, they're getting worse. I'd hoped that the blood test would show something. . . ."

"It did," her mother said. "That Atlantis changed you."

"I know. And whatever is wrong with the others is happening to Alfie and me too. Not as bad, but we're getting worse. I think we have to go back."

"Riley, what you're suggesting . . ."

Riley nodded. "What choice have we got? We're not getting better, we're getting worse. I'm just so scared that they're going to die. Can you tell me they aren't?"

"I—I . . . ," her mother said.

Riley shook her head. "I really thought that taking the others away from Atlantis was saving them. But Mom, I think we're killing them."

7

JILL DID HELP MAKE DINNER, AND SARAH and Pauly did the dishes right after. Bastian remained upstairs but was too tired to eat. Instead he rested in the living room with Miss Pigglesworth right beside him. When Riley secreted some food downstairs, no one wanted to eat.

Riley didn't mention to the Atlanteans that they were considering going back to Atlantis. Not until they were sure it was the only way. But even if they wanted to, how were they supposed to find it again?

When she told Alfie, she expected him to call her stupid or some other name. Instead he nodded and said he'd been thinking the same thing. That if leaving Atlantis had made them sick, maybe returning there might be the cure.

So he looked up the *Moon Dancer* and saw that it was now under federal seizure order until the legalities of insurance and ownership were sorted out. Who would own the *Moon Dancer* after the court case was uncertain? The only thing they did know was that it wouldn't be them.

"We have to rent another boat," Alfie said softly. "A big one."

Outside, the snow flurries turned heavier, and the weather forecasters said it was going to be the first big storm of the season. The news stations were already talking about school closures. It also meant that Jill's family couldn't go back to their home as there still wasn't any heat, electricity, or running water.

With the way Riley was feeling mixed with her fear for the Atlanteans, it was all getting to be too much. Her small, nagging headache was turning into a beast. Not to mention the slow but steadily increasing fever. When the aspirin stopped working, she said her "good night"s and went to bed early. Hours later she didn't even feel Jill arrive and climb into bed beside her.

A loud shout woke Riley from the deep sleep. "It's over there!" the voice warned. When she sat up in bed, she heard loud banging.

Jill was sitting up beside her. "I think the police are shooting at someone," she said fearfully. "What if it's Mike and his gang? What if Josh is with them and they shoot him? Are they going to kill my brother?"

Riley threw back the covers and reached for her robe. Jill did the same. Then they heard her mother's voice in the hall outside their room.

"Is everyone all right?"

"Yes," Danny called. Then they heard knocking. "Riley and Jill, are you okay?"

"Yes," Riley called. "What about the others?"

Riley and Jill made it to the corridor outside their bedroom. Sarah was holding Chrissy in one arm and Robbi's hand in another. Alfie appeared with Pauly. "There was shooting!"

Everyone jumped when there was knocking on the front door.

"All of you stay up here," Beverly said. She took the stairs down. Moments later they heard the front door open, and voices.

Riley couldn't hear what was being said, but the

tone was very serious. The front door closed. "You can all come down now, it's over."

"Mom, what happened?" Danny asked.

They all gathered in the living room. Bastian was awake and seated beside Miss Pigglesworth as Beverly explained what the police told her.

"They saw something big moving around the area. They think it was a bear. It's unusual for one to be so close to a built-up area, but not impossible. They think they hit it."

"They opened fire?" Alfie cried. "What if it wasn't a bear? What if it was someone walking their dog or a jogger or some poor drunk trying to get home?"

"Even if it was a bear, why shoot it?" Riley added. "Why not just scare it away? Or call in someone with a tranquilizer gun or something?"

Beverly shook her head. "I don't know. They said it was big and that by the way it was moving, they were frightened it might have rabies or something. I'm sure they wouldn't have shot at it if they didn't have a good reason. The police officers think they hit it. But with the snow coming down so heavily, they can't be sure. They're checking the area but don't expect to find any-thing. For now, everyone is being told to stay inside."

Riley looked up to the hall clock; it was almost three in the morning. "I'm making cocoa. Anybody want some?"

When everyone agreed, Riley and Jill walked into the kitchen to start. Miss Pigglesworth followed them but then went to the back door and began scratching at the glass.

"All right, Miss Pigglesworth," Riley said as she walked into the dining room to let her out. "You heard what Mom said—don't go looking around. Stay close to the house. If it is a bear and it's been shot or has rabies, it could be really dangerous."

Miss Pigglesworth ran outside but a moment later rushed back in and started to bark loudly. Bastian staggered out of the living room and ran to the door. Wearing only his slippers, he charged into the snow. He reappeared at the door—his face was a picture of fear. "Riley, I need your help!"

"What is it?" Riley called.

"Get Alfie and the others." Bastian moved to run out again.

"Bastian, wait. What's out there?"

"The police didn't shoot a bear," Bastian called. "They shot Gideon!"

8

IN JUST HER ROBE AND SLIPPERS, RILEY charged across the snow-covered backyard to a large lump in the middle. She threw herself down beside the immense gargoyle. "Gideon, are you all right?"

"Riley," Gideon said, gasping. "That man, he—he . . ."

"He shot you," Riley said. "Can you stand?"

"I don't think so. He—he used lead. It's poison for me."

"We'll help you," Bastian said.

Alfie was beside Riley in a moment, followed by Danny.

"Gideon!" Alfie cried.

"Quiet, Creep!" Riley hushed. "The police might

hear you and come around. We have to get him inside and remove the bullets."

"This is Gideon?" Danny choked as he stood staring at the gargoyle.

"Yes," Riley said. "Now help us!"

They struggled to half carry Gideon to the house. Just as they reached the threshold to the door, Riley realized that Jill, Sarah, and their whole family were standing there, watching the immense gargoyle being helped in. Their eyes were wide with terror.

"Jill, everyone, it's all right," Riley said quickly. "This is Gideon, he's our friend. He's saved our lives so many times. Please don't be frightened, and help us. He's very heavy."

Pauly was the first to move and started to pull the dining room chairs out of the way. A moment later, Sarah and Jill joined him.

"I'll get my bag," Beverly said as the doctor in her came forward. "Robbi, close the doors and all the curtains in the house. We can't let anybody see."

"Riley," Gideon said, and gasped. "There is no . . . no time. You . . . you must get everyone back to Atlantis, or—or . . ."

"I know," Riley said. "We're dying."

"What!?" Danny cried.

Gideon said a few more garbled words, then his wings went limp and he collapsed. The weight of the unconscious gargoyle was more than they could carry, and everyone fell down with him. When he hit the floor, it actually shook.

It was only then that Riley saw the dark gray blood on his back and in his thick tail. His wings were torn as well. "Mom, he's bleeding. He said they shot him with lead and it's poisonous to him. We have to get the bullets out."

"We will," Beverly said. She looked up at Danny. "Go get some clean towels." Then she looked at Riley. "Go get the emergency medical kit—we're going to need all the bandages we can find."

Riley ran past Jill and dashed into the kitchen to get the medical kit. When she returned, all of Jill's family was standing back, looking fearfully at the massive gargoyle.

"I need more room," Beverly said. "Move the table away."

Everyone came forward and shifted the dining room table. When it was moved, Jill asked Riley, "How do you know that . . . that . . . thing?"

Riley snapped, "Gideon is not a thing! He is a gargoyle and one of the nicest people on the planet. You'd be lucky if he considered you a friend."

"I'm sorry, Riley," Jill said, "but he looks so scary."

"Well, he's not. He's kind and gentle."

They stood back and watched Beverly examine Gideon. "It looks like they shot him several times. I've got to get the bullets out, but I don't know his physiology. I might do more harm than good."

"Gideon!" Pea appeared at the entrance of the dining room. His fur was wet from the fever, and he was staggering. He came forward and fell beside Gideon's head. "Gideon, what has happened to you?"

"Teddy!" Chrissy cried when she saw him. "There's Teddy!"

Sarah, Jill, and the family looked at Pea in wonder. When Mary appeared behind Pea, she pushed past Jill. "What happened to him?"

"He was shot by the police," Riley said. "They thought he might be a bear."

Riley looked up at the gaping mouths of Jill and her siblings. Mary and Pea's appearance wasn't the best timing. But they cared deeply for the gargoyle and must have heard them talking about him.

"Riley and Alfie, please take Sarah and her family into the other room. I think it's time we explain what's happening," her mother said.

"I want to stay for Gideon," Riley said.

"Me too," Alfie said.

"We'll take good care of him," Pea said weakly. "Take the children away; they shouldn't see this."

Riley looked at Jill's family. Robbi and Pauly were watching with fear in their eyes. Chrissy was too interested in Pea to care, but still, they were all too young to see what her mother was doing for the gargoyle.

With her family—including Bastian, Pea, and Mary—working with Gideon, Riley and Alfie herded the others out. "Come on, we'll tell you what's happening. But this is a huge secret."

They were reluctant to leave the dining room but finally made it to the living room.

"Who are they?" Sarah asked. "What are they?"

"They are our family, and we love them," Riley said. "Please sit down. This is going to be hard to believe. . . ."

The long night passed slowly as Riley and Alfie explained everything about their time in Atlantis and all the things they experienced there.

"Gideon saved my dad and Aunt Mary. We couldn't have made it home without him," Riley said. "He means everything to me."

"They all do," Alfie added.

Sarah was shaking her head. "I have to believe it, because they're right there in the dining room. But it's so hard to believe. So Pea, Mary, and Miss Pigglesworth used to be people?"

"They still are," Riley said. "They're just not human anymore. There is one more that you haven't met." She looked at Jill. "Her name is Maggie and she's the one who taught me how to sew. She's still downstairs. She probably won't come up because she's worried she'll frighten you."

"Why?" Jill asked. "What is she?"

"She is the sweetest woman there is," Riley said. "But—but she's also a leopard."

"Your brother saw her," Alfie added. "She was the big cat that stopped Mike and the others from hurting us."

Sarah gasped. "That was real?"

Riley nodded. "Maggie is wonderful. But she's sick. They all are—"

"*We* all are," Alfie corrected.

"You have headaches and fever," Sarah said.

"We think it's because we left Atlantis," Riley said. "It changed us somehow, and maybe we can't survive away from it. The others who lived on Atlantis longer are much sicker. That's probably why Gideon came here—he wanted to warn us."

"I heard," Jill said softly. "You said you're dying?"

Riley nodded. "Maybe. All I know is something is very wrong with all of us and we're getting worse. I'm afraid that we have to go back."

"You're leaving?" Jill said.

Alfie shrugged. "Probably. Aunt Beverly is a great doctor, but even she doesn't understand what's happening to us."

Riley added, "She sent our blood to the lab, and it's all messed up. They're asking a lot of questions that Mom can't answer. So she's not sending in any more samples, and we have no way of knowing what's wrong."

"I don't want you to go," Jill said. "You're my best friend."

Riley was shocked to hear that. She liked Jill, but she never imagined that Jill cared that much for her. "I don't think we have a choice."

"Are you going to take your boat?" Jill asked. "The one you came on?"

"The *Moon Dancer*?" Riley said. "No. It's a priceless treasure and a lot of people are fighting over it, so we can't use it—even if we wanted to."

"Do you want to go back?" Jill asked.

Riley and Alfie looked at each other and shrugged. It was a sobering question. Riley thought for a moment about her life here, compared to the life she had in Atlantis. While she was living there, she'd often thought it wouldn't be bad if her whole family was with her.

"I don't know," Riley finally answered. "It really is beautiful, and the people are so friendly. It's a simple life there, but it's not perfect and it does have its problems."

"Yeah, a lot of problems," Alfie said. "Like Red Moons, Red Cloaks, Memory Berries, the Forbidden Zone . . ."

Riley nodded. "Mada is terrifying; he's like a tiger-man and he hates us. There's no electricity, no internet or anything like that. It's all very basic. But every night they all gather around a big fire and tell stories and sing."

"And there's no poverty or hunger," Alfie said. "Everyone shares everything."

"Did you have fun there?" Robbi asked.

Again Riley and Alfie looked at each other. Did they? Finally Riley said, "Yes and no. I mean, if our family was there, it would have been a lot of fun. But for Alfie and me, we were worried about finding my dad and Alfie's mom and getting home. There's also a lot of hard work to do. But there were some amazing people, like this really big rhino named Kevin. He's so adorable, and my best friend was a mermaid named Galina. She was awesome—we used to laugh so much."

"Mermaid?" Jill gasped. "For real?"

"Yep," Alfie said. "And the talking gorilla named Jeff. He was really cool."

"That place sounds amazing," Pauly said.

"Part of it was," Alfie said.

Riley nodded. "There are some things I would change if I could. But I think it was a good life there."

"It sounds like you do want to go back," Jill said.

"I don't know," Riley said. "But I'm so scared for the others. If anything happened to them because we stayed . . ."

"But I don't know if we can find it again," Alfie said. "I mean, we don't even know where it is. I think Atlantis needs to find us."

Riley couldn't bear to think about it. Her head was pounding, and she was too frightened for Gideon to sit still. She got up. "Stay here. I'm going to check on them."

When she made it to the dining room, Mary was there and held up her hand. "Don't come closer, Riley, it's not pretty. Your mom has already removed three bullets from him, but she's having trouble with the fourth. We've managed to get him on his side, but the bullet's deep in his chest."

Riley walked over to the kitchen window and peered out beyond the blinds. It was still snowing, but it was looking lighter. "Mom," Riley called. "When the sun rises, Gideon will turn to stone. I don't know how it works with bullets. But when his wing came off if we didn't have it in place . . ."

"It's all right, Riley," Pea said gently. "I've told her. We're almost finished."

"Got it!" her mother said. "Let's just close him up. I've done all I can."

"You have done more than anyone else here could

have," Pea said. "I am grateful to you for your wonderful skills."

"Don't thank me yet," Beverly said. "Gideon has a long way to go. I've never operated on a gargoyle before. I just hope he doesn't get an infection."

Pea patted Gideon's arm. "He is a strong one. You have given him the best chance."

Riley returned to the living room.

"How is he?" Alfie asked.

"Mom took four bullets out of him. They're bandaging him up right now. But it's almost dawn—he should change any minute now."

"Change into what?" Jill asked nervously.

"Because Gideon is a gargoyle, he turns to stone during the day. Gargoyles are only alive at night."

"He's turning to stone?" Pauly asked.

Riley nodded. "That's why there aren't many left in the world. In the olden days, people hunted them and broke them during the day when they were weakest. So the only remaining gargoyles are in Atlantis."

When the daylight arrived, Riley and Alfie went back into the dining room. They were followed by Jill's family. Her mother was there, sitting back on her heels. Gideon was lying on the floor but was now solid stone.

"Simply amazing," Beverly said. She touched Gideon's arm. "How is this even possible?"

"Pure magic," Pea said. "Gargoyles are such wonderful creatures. But for all of their strength, they are so very vulnerable."

"I believe it," Danny said.

"We must watch over him today," Pea continued. "To keep him safe from breakage."

"Pea and Mary," Riley said. "This is Jill and her family. Sarah, Pauly, and Robbi. You already know Chrissy."

"It is wonderful to meet you," Pea said softly. "Even under these tragic circumstances." He looked at Danny. "Will you help get me back downstairs? I don't feel well and can't make it on my own."

"Of course," Danny said. He bent down and picked Pea up.

Alfie reached for his mother. "Come on, Mom. Let's get you to bed."

"I'm fine," Mary said. But she looked far from fine. She didn't fight as Alfie picked her up and carried her toward the stairs.

"I'm coming with you," Riley said. "I want to check on Maggie."

"Can I come?" Jill said.

"Us too," Pauly and Robbi added.

Riley looked at her mother and Beverly shrugged. "They've met everyone else, so why not Maggie?" She looked at Jill's family. "Just remember, Maggie is not well. I don't want any of you to be frightened of her—she really doesn't need that added stress."

"We won't be," Sarah promised.

Riley said to her mother, "I'll just check on Maggie and be back. I think we need to talk."

"Go on, I'll make some coffee and start breakfast."

Introducing Maggie went better than Riley expected, as Jill and her family were enchanted by her. When Maggie met Chrissy, holding the little girl seemed to make her feel much better.

Chrissy giggled in her arms and called her Kitty as she petted Maggie's feline face.

Despite the successful introductions, Riley couldn't help but notice how weak Maggie was becoming. She suspected that Maggie was perhaps the oldest among them and was suffering the most, or it could have been the injuries she suffered in her fight with Mada leaving her weaker. Whatever the cause, she was much worse than Pea and Mary and could barely sit up.

While Jill and the others remained with the Atlanteans downstairs, Riley and Alfie headed back up. They were both feeling rough and exhausted, but this was too serious to delay.

By the time they made it back to the kitchen, her mother and Danny were in the middle of a heated argument.

"Mom, we have to get them back to Atlantis," Danny insisted. "Now!"

"It's not that easy," Beverly said. "We can't just pick up and go. We have responsibilities. I have responsibilities. What about my patients, my practice?"

"You have patients here. They're downstairs and they're dying!" Danny insisted. "What about Riley and Alfie? And Bastian and Miss Pigglesworth, they can barely move and have no strength. We have to get them back before it's too late. I—I mean I'm sure Gideon wouldn't have risked coming here if it weren't serious."

Riley saw the fear in her older brother's eyes. She

felt it too. Not so much for herself, but for Bastian and the others. Now they had the added worry of Gideon.

"Mom, Danny's right," Riley said. "We're all getting sicker. My head feels like it's splitting open and I'm so hot. You're an amazing doctor, but even you don't know what's wrong with us. You can't help us."

"But how do we do it?" her mother asked. "How do we even find Atlantis? It's not like it's on any map. It was an accident that you found it the first time."

"We have to try," Riley said. She looked at her brother and Alfie. "But if we go back, I don't think we can return here again."

Her mother was standing at the counter holding a frying pan of eggs that never made it to the stove. She looked at Riley, Danny, and Alfie. Finally she nodded. "You're all much more precious than this stupid house or my career. All right. I don't know how we're going to do it, but somehow we're going to find Atlantis."

9

THERE WAS NO OTHER DECISION THAT could be made. It was obvious that everyone who'd been in Atlantis was getting sicker the longer they stayed away. But how would they find it? Atlantis was shrouded in mystery and completely hidden. If it didn't want to be found, it wasn't going to be found.

After Mary and Pea were settled back downstairs and Gideon had been covered in blankets, everyone gathered in the living room. Even though this was a family discussion, Sarah asked if she and her family could sit in. There was no point in saying no—they already knew the family's biggest secret.

"We'll have to buy a motor home to get everyone

down to Miami safely," Beverly was saying. "We have your dad's insurance money. I was saving that for your education, but that's not going to happen now. Then we'll have to rent a boat. After that, we have to hope and pray that we can find Atlantis."

Sarah looked at everyone and cleared her throat loudly. "Um, Riley, you said that you and Alfie were originally taken off your boat because Atlantis needed children, right?"

"Yeah," Riley said.

Sarah glanced at her family. "Well, do you think it will help you find it again if there were more children on board the boat? Like maybe five or six more?"

Riley frowned at first, then realized what Sarah was saying. "You want to come with us?"

Sarah turned to her brother and sisters, and they all nodded excitedly. "Yes, we do."

"No," Beverly said. "You have family here. Your mother . . ."

"No, we don't," Sarah insisted. "In just the past few days, you've been more of a mother to us than she ever was."

Beverly shook her head, "Sarah, I don't think you realize what you're saying. Atlantis is a world away.

It is a one-way trip—you've seen how the others are becoming ill because they left it. It means that once we go, there is no coming back. What if your mother wanted to find you? She wouldn't. You'd never see her again."

"Our mother doesn't care. She never has. From the moment Chrissy was born, Mom wouldn't do anything for her. If I didn't feed or change her, it wouldn't happen. She only thought of herself. That's why she left. She wanted *her* life. We were holding her back."

Jill nodded. "She told us to go into foster care. What kind of mother does that to her own children?"

"Yeah," Pauly said. "And she took all the money and just left us. She's the reason Josh joined Mike's gang, so he could pay the rent."

Jill turned to Riley. "Please let us come with you. We need to stay together, but if we don't go with you, they'll find out and separate us. At least in Atlantis we can still be a family."

Riley looked at her mother. "I don't know if they'll let us back. Or if they do, Beresford might not let us on the *Queen*, and we'll have to find a new place to live."

"If Atlantis needs children, they should say yes to all of you."

Everyone turned and saw Mary standing there. She was unsteady on her feet and leaned against a chair. "I came up because Maggie is worse. Beverly, would you come downstairs, please?"

Riley's stomach clinched. "What is it?"

"Her fever is spiking," Mary said. "We can't wake her up."

Beverly got up. "I'll get my bag. Danny, get some ice; Riley, Sarah, and Jill, wet some towels with cold water and bring them downstairs. Bastian, you and Miss Pigglesworth stay here and rest. Alfie, make sure he doesn't move."

"I will," Alfie said. There was fear in his eyes.

Riley, Sarah, and Jill ran upstairs and into the bathroom and grabbed a load of bath towels. Riley turned on the shower and soaked them with cold water. Riley handed one to Sarah, and she darted out of the bathroom. Then Riley soaked another and handed it to Jill, who followed her sister. They did this several times until they were told to stop.

Riley went downstairs and saw that Maggie had been laid out on the long sofa. Riley's mother placed the wet towels on Maggie, then wrapped the ice cubes Danny brought in another wet towel and placed it on Maggie's head.

"She's burning up," Beverly said. She looked back at Riley. "We don't have any choice now."

"Choice about what?" Pea asked.

Riley walked over to her dear friend and knelt down beside him. "We have to take you back to Atlantis."

"What?" Pea said. "No, we can't. I don't want to be alone. They'll make me wear my cloak again."

"You won't be alone," Riley said. "We'll be with you. And if they try to make you wear your cloak, then we'll find somewhere else on the island for all of us to live where you won't have to. We could build a nice house, just like yours."

"You—you're going back too?" Pea asked.

Riley nodded. "We don't want to lose you. Besides, Alfie and I are both sick too. Not as bad as you, but we are."

"We're all coming," Jill added.

Pea's face immediately brightened. "All of you? That would be wonderful."

Riley turned to Jill. That hadn't been decided yet,

but by the looks on their faces, Jill's family was determined to go whether Riley wanted them to or not. But when she thought about it, it would be nice to have them there and to give them a real home.

"We can talk about that later," Beverly said. "Right now, we must get Maggie's fever down. Danny, the towels aren't enough. Go get one of the big kitchen pots, fill it with snow, and bring it down here."

All talk of leaving stopped as they worked to break Maggie's fever. After several pots full of snow were poured on the wet towels, the fever broke, and Maggie started to shiver.

"That's enough," Beverly said as she pulled the wet towels away from Maggie and wrapped a blanket around her. "But let's keep those towels handy. This might only be a short reprieve. Her fever could come back."

After a while, Maggie's eyes fluttered open. "Wh- what happened? Why am I wet?"

"Your temperature shot up and we had to cool you down," Mary said.

Beverly added, "You're doing better now. How is your head?"

"Pounding." Maggie struggled to sit up, but Riley

pushed her shoulders down gently. "Not yet. Just relax. There's nowhere to go and nothing to do while it's snowing out."

"Snow?" Maggie said.

Riley pointed to a pot full of snow they were waiting to use. "This is snow. When you're feeling better, we can show you more."

"It's wonderful stuff," Pea said. "But very cold."

Maggie turned to Riley. "How is Gideon?"

Riley looked at her mother before answering. "He's resting." Riley hesitated, then said, "Maggie, he came here to tell us something."

"What was that?" Maggie asked.

Riley inhaled deeply and finally said, "He says we have to go back to Atlantis."

"Why would he say that?"

"I think you know why," Mary said. "Atlantis changed us more than we knew. The longer we stay away, the sicker we're becoming. . . ."

"But I don't want to leave you." Maggie reached for Riley's hand and started to get upset. "You're—you're my family. I can't go back there."

"Yes, we are family," Riley said. "That's why we're all going back together, and things won't be the same.

If we have to, we'll create our own community for the others, like Kevin and Jeff. You won't have to wear your cloak again."

Maggie was weak, but she couldn't rest until she fully understood what was happening. When Riley explained everything, she settled down.

"When shall we go?" Pea asked. "Obviously when Gideon is better, but that could be this evening if he heals like he normally does."

"We should go as soon as possible," Beverly said. "Before you all get much worse. But we have to make some arrangements first. Not to mention gather supplies. I want to make sure we have enough to get us started, whatever happens there." Beverly got up. "So it won't be tomorrow. Right now, all of you must hold on and stay strong."

"We shall try," Pea said.

While the Atlanteans stayed downstairs, Riley and the others returned to the living room.

"How is Maggie?" Bastian asked softly. He was frowning from the headache.

Riley understood how he felt; her head was aching too. "She's a bit better. The fever broke. Now she's resting. But she and Pea weren't thrilled with the idea of going back to Atlantis until I told them we were all going."

"Maggie is so sweet," Jill said as she and Sarah's sister sat down. "Now that I know her, it seems impossible that Josh and the others were scared of her."

"Maggie can be formidable when she needs to be," Beverly said. She started flitting around the room and going through drawers. "What did I do with it?"

Riley watched her mother tearing through the room. She was opening every drawer in the desk. "Mom, what are you looking for?"

"My address book."

"Why?"

Finally her mother found it. "Got it!" She looked at Riley. "I have to make a call to check on something." Then she looked at Alfie. "Would you get your laptop and open it up? We're going to need to order a few things. We'll compile a list when I come back."

Right before she left the room, Riley called, "Mom, who are you calling?"

"Tony Zamora!"

"Who?" Bastian asked.

"Isn't that the guy from the port in Miami?" Alfie asked.

Riley nodded. She looked at Jill and her family. "Tony is the dockmaster where we kept our boat. I've known him most of my life. Which was a good thing, because he was really shocked when we arrived on the *Moon Dancer*, but Mom was able to calm him down."

Alfie nodded. "You should have seen his face when the tow boat brought us in. I thought he was gonna have a heart attack."

Sarah frowned. "Did he see everyone? I mean, Pea and Maggie and Mary?"

Riley shook her head. "Nope. We'd called Mom before we got back to Miami, and she arranged everything with the port. Then when night came, we managed to sneak everyone off the boat."

"That was before the police and Bastian's family got involved," Alfie said. "Now everyone's fighting over the boat. But if Aunt Beverly is calling Tony, she might be telling him what's up."

"She won't tell him," Danny said. "Mom's too careful about that. She's probably going to arrange for a rental boat."

Jill frowned. "If the *Moon Dancer* was owned by Bastian's parents, shouldn't it go to him?"

"It should," Riley answered. "But we can't let

anyone know that Bastian is back. He was gone many years and should be a really old man, but he's not."

"No, I just feel it," Bastian said.

Miss Pigglesworth raised her head, whined a bit, then lay down again.

Riley didn't need to know what she said. She knew Miss Pigglesworth, like the others, was in big trouble.

Riley's mother returned to the room. "Well, that's the first job done. I explained to Tony that we need to rent a boat and he's reserved one for us."

"Did you ask about the *Moon Dancer*?" Riley asked. "Is she still there?"

Her mother nodded. "Yes, it's still there, but they've put a federal seizure warning sign on it, and it's chained to the dock. The court case is being heard in two weeks, and that will decide the fate of the *Moon Dancer* and whether it stays there or is moved by the declared owners. He said the fight is getting nasty and that a lot of people are trying to claim it. It's all very sad."

"It is," Bastian said. "But I don't care. What I care about is getting the others to Atlantis."

Riley nodded. "I don't think Maggie, Pea, or even Mary have much time." She didn't look at Bastian. It was tearing at her heart to see him and Miss

Pigglesworth looking so ill. The thought of losing any of them was beyond consideration.

"Maybe we don't have to rent a boat," Alfie said. He turned toward the dining room. "If Gideon flew here, he could probably fly back. Then maybe he could carry us to Atlantis one or two at a time."

Everyone turned toward the statue lying on the dining room floor. He was covered in blankets, but stone-still. No one had been in there all day, for fear of accidentally hurting him.

"That's if he wakes," Riley said sadly. "What if Mom didn't get all the bullets out? Gideon said lead was poisonous to him. . . ."

"Don't, Shorty," Alfie said. "Gideon will be fine."

Beverly got up and returned to the desk. When she sat down again, she had a pad of paper and a pen. "I'm sure I removed all the bullets and that Gideon will be fine. But even if he can carry us two at a time, we need to take some supplies. Perhaps more than he can carry. I really think that we should use a boat. Besides, having Gideon with us might just help us find Atlantis."

The balance of the day was spent compiling a list of what they thought they would need in Atlantis. When they finished and saw how much they had, Riley gasped. "We need a big truck to get all this to Florida!"

"We can't take a truck," her mother said. "First thing on Monday, I'm going to find us a motor home. So that will limit what we can take."

"Not if we take a car as well," Danny said. "We can pack it full, and I can drive us."

"Danny, you haven't had your license very long, and it's a long way."

"I've got my license too," Sarah offered. "Danny and I could share the driving." She paused and looked at everyone. "That's if you'll let us come with you. And I really hope you will."

"Please?" Jill said. "There's no one here for us. I promise I'll help with Maggie and Pea and Mary." She looked at Bastian. "I'll help with you and Miss Pigglesworth."

"Me too!" Robbi said while Pauly nodded.

Riley looked at her mother and shrugged. "It might help us get there if the mermaids see more children on the boat."

"I'm just worried about your mother," Beverly said to Sarah and the others. "And then there's the issue of your brother."

Sarah lowered her head. "I promise you, our mother doesn't care about us. As for Josh, I'm hoping we can find him, and he could come too. He's really not bad. He was just robbing people to help us. He never did anything wrong before Mom left."

"Maybe he didn't want to hurt people, but he did," Beverly said. "He was part of the gang that terrorized the lake area. I know you love your brother, but we have the safety of everyone here to consider. We can't risk letting him know where we are or what we're doing."

"But—" Sarah started.

"I'm sorry to sound hard," Beverly said. "If you really want to join us in Atlantis, that's fine. But Josh isn't coming. If you can't accept that, I understand. You can stay here at the house as long as you want. I'll make arrangements with the power company and water, so you won't have to worry about them being shut off. Everything we leave behind is yours to keep or sell."

Tears sparkled in Sarah's eyes and trailed down Jill's face. Riley remembered how she felt when they were first in Atlantis and told they would never see their family again. It was terrible, so she understood how Jill's family felt.

Sarah looked at her brother and three sisters before

turning to Riley. "Do you really think the people in Atlantis would accept us and give us a home?"

Riley nodded. "I do."

Alfie said, "Everyone in Atlantis would love you guys. Kids are treated the best."

"It's true," Bastian said. "We were always fed first, before everyone else. Always given the best of everything. You would find a good home there."

Beverly added, "This is a big decision—perhaps the most important of your life. Take your time and think about it. Because I told you already—once we go, there is no coming back. There won't be any TV, cell phones, or even electricity. We will be completely cut off from the rest of the world. That will be a huge adjustment."

"And," Riley added, "you must know that eventually you will turn into an animal. It won't happen for a really long time, but it will happen."

Pauly looked at his sisters. "We've been living without electricity for months anyway. At least in Atlantis, there'll be food."

"And turning into an animal won't be so bad," Jill said as she sniffed back her tears. "I mean, Pea, Maggie, and Mary are really nice."

Sarah steeled her shoulders and wiped away her

own tears. "I have to think of my family and what's best for them. Staying here means losing everything and being separated. But if we go, we can stay together. There is no decision to be made. We need to come with you if you'll let us."

"Of course," Beverly said. "If you all agree, then that's fine with me."

"We all agree," Jill said.

Beverly focused on her list again. "So we'll have a car and the motor home. I can probably rent a trailer to tow behind the camper as well. I want to make sure we have plenty of medical supplies."

"There was a doctor there," Alfie said. "He fixed up my leg really good after the alligator bit it."

"You were bitten by an alligator?" Jill gasped.

Alfie nodded. "We were in the Forbidden Zone. It might have been Susan." He turned back to Beverly. "They have these leaves that he uses, and everything heals."

"That's all well and good. But I trust modern medicine and I'm taking as much as we can. So, Alfie, warm up that laptop. We have a lot of ordering to do. Everything has to be here in a week because after that, we're leaving for Atlantis."

10

WHILE ALFIE AND JILL STARTED THE PRO-
cess of ordering what they could from the list, Riley
went downstairs and told everyone what was happening. After that, she and Danny headed upstairs
to start going through their clothes and what they
would and wouldn't take.

Having lived in Atlantis, Riley knew how precious
clothing was and that every piece mattered—but
only if it was functional. Fancy, frilly clothes were
pretty but would wear out far too quickly.

With her bed covered in useful clothing, she pulled
out a suitcase and started to pack. When that was
full, she used heavy trash bags. While she worked,

Riley realized, much to her surprise, that she was getting excited at the thought of going back. Deep in her heart, she knew that despite having been home for several weeks, she still wasn't adjusting. But if her whole family was in Atlantis, she was sure they would all be very happy.

Riley kept a close watch on the clock and window, waiting for sundown. The snow was tapering off, but the gray sky above hid the sun's movement. Finally, unable to wait any longer, she headed downstairs.

The first thing she did was close all the curtains in the house. Then, one by one, everyone gathered in the dining room. Danny and Riley helped Maggie come up from downstairs while Alfie carried his mother and Sarah carried Pea.

Pea sat down beside Gideon's large head and stroked his stone brow. "Come back to us, Gideon. You are loved and needed."

Riley was standing beside her mother, holding her hand tightly. "Please, Gideon," she whispered softly.

"How long does it usually take after sunset?" Danny asked.

"I don't know," Pea admitted. "The only time I saw Gideon turn was back on the beach when we held his broken wing in place. But that was a break. This is different. Here he's been poisoned by lead."

"And last time, it was right after a Red Moon," Bastian said. "The sky was really dark, and it was raining. So we couldn't tell."

"Indeed," Pea agreed. "All we can do now is wait."

And wait they did. Alfie was near the glass doors leading outside. He pulled the curtain back. "It's dark out. Why hasn't he changed yet?"

"It could be the poison," Pea said.

That comment chilled Riley to the bone. She'd been worried about Gideon all day and had tried to convince herself that everything would be all right. But now that the sun was down, her fear surfaced. What if he didn't come back to life? To think of Gideon dying because he was trying to save them was unbearable.

"Wait," Maggie said. "I hear something."

All eyes turned to Gideon. Riley left her mother and bent down beside Pea. She touched the gargoyle's stone arm.

"Can you feel anything?" Beverly asked.

Riley was about to answer no when she thought she felt something. "Wait, maybe . . ." Her heart was pounding so hard she was sure everyone could hear. "Come on, Gideon, you can do it!"

The stone beneath Riley's hand started to warm. "Pea, do you feel that?"

"Yes!" Pea cried. "Gideon is coming back!"

As they had done on the beach so long ago, they got up and moved away from the gargoyle as his pale gray skin darkened and took on the glow of life. But unlike the time on the beach, it took much longer for Gideon to wake.

It was almost a half an hour after the first trace of movement started that Gideon was alive and lying on the floor. His breathing was ragged.

"Danny, go get some cushions for his head," Beverly said.

She crouched down beside him, and with her stethoscope ready, she checked Gideon over.

"Well?" Riley asked.

"His heart is beating, but it's slower than last night."

Gideon groaned.

"It's all right, my friend," Pea said as he returned to the gargoyle's side and stroked his face. "We're all feeling a little rough."

"Pea," Gideon mumbled. "Are you all right? What about Maggie, the others?"

Pea chuckled softly. "We are fine; it is you we're all worried about."

"Pea, listen to me," Gideon said. "I found an ancient text in—in the Crucible. It—it spoke of what happened to those who left Atlantis. I—I'd never read that book before. It is bad. Very bad. . . . Then I started to feel you all getting sick and knew it was true. I had to come. To warn you that you must—"

"Return to Atlantis, yes, we know, and we are," Pea finished. "We will be leaving in a few days. You, my friend, are coming with us. For now, just relax and rest."

That comment seemed to calm Gideon as his breathing steadied. He tried to lift his head, but he was too weak.

"Don't try to move, Gideon," Beverly said. "You are safe here. I am Riley's mother, Beverly."

Danny arrived with two pillows, and they had to struggle to lift the gargoyle's head to put them beneath it. Gideon finally opened his eyes. "Andrew is a good friend," he said. "He has been so worried about all of you. He—he asked me to bring him here. But I could not. . . ."

"We'll see Dad soon," Riley said. "Is there anything you need to help you heal? Some food or something?"

Gideon took a moment before he answered. "Thank you, Riley. Just—just time. And perhaps a bit of water, if I may."

"Of course." Riley ran into the kitchen and returned with a glass of water and paper straw. She knelt beside the large gargoyle and pressed the end of the straw to his lips. "Here, Gideon, drink."

Gideon frowned at the straw, then used it to take a long drink of water. The glass was empty in two long gulps. "Thank you."

"Are you warm enough?" Bastian asked. "Would you like more blankets?"

"I am comfortable, Bastian, thank you," Gideon said. "Perhaps I will rest for a moment." Gideon's eyes closed again, and he drifted off to sleep.

"Let's let him rest," Beverly said as she ushered everyone out of the dining room.

"He's super polite, isn't he," Sarah said.

"And not scary anymore," Jill added.

Riley smiled. She remembered how frightened she'd been of Gideon the first time she saw him.

Now she loved him dearly. What she didn't love was how weak he was. After he awakened from his broken wing, he was back to normal. But not now. "Do you think he'll be all right?" she asked Pea.

"Of course. Gideon is strong. He's weak now, but so are we all. I am sure he'll recover quickly."

Jill said, "Gideon said he could feel that you were getting sick. How?"

Pea grinned. "Gargoyles are magic. Once they open their heart to someone, they are linked forever. Sadly, I am not magic and can't feel him. But Gideon can feel us." Pea looked over to Alfie. "Riley said you were ordering supplies to take back?" When Alfie nodded, Pea said, "I would like to add a few things to that list, if I may."

"What would you like?" Alfie asked.

"More books," Pea said first, and then he looked at Danny. "If we must build a new home for all of us, we'll need more tools."

"Oh yeah," Danny said. "Maybe even a gas generator so we can use electric drills and stuff."

"That won't work," Alfie said. "There's no gasoline on Atlantis."

"There must be some way we can generate electricity," Danny said. "I'm going to look it up."

Before heading back downstairs, everyone settled in the living room. Riley had her arm around Maggie and helped her walk. The leopard-woman was so frail now, it was like she was aging as well as being sick.

"Are you all right?" she asked fearfully.

"Yes, Riley, I am fine," Maggie said. "My headache is still with me, but I'm sure that will pass when we make it back."

"I sure hope so." Riley checked where her mother was before whispering, "Because I feel rotten. I'm hurting all over and my head is ready to explode."

Maggie stopped and looked at Riley. "You must hold on. We'll all get back there soon."

"I will if you will."

"That is a promise," Maggie said softly.

Gideon recovered slowly over the following nights. The damage to his wings healed, but he remained far too weak to be able to fly. As it was, he needed help getting down the stairs to join the other Atlanteans. It also meant they would have another passenger on their journey to Florida.

The one thing the family celebrated was the departure of the police car posted outside their home.

Though there was an investigation into the shooting, since the bear wasn't found, the police believed it returned to the woods.

The snowstorm passed, and by the end of the week, a brand-new motor home was parked in their driveway. It was an eight-sleeper with plenty of storage space that was being quickly used up by the supplies that were arriving.

With the days ticking down, they decided that they would leave right after the last of the supplies arrived. While they waited, clothing was organized, packed, and repacked into the motor home and trailer. Canned and long-shelf-life food was purchased, and Beverly used her medical license to order more medical supplies, including bandages, antibiotics, disinfectants, and surgical equipment. Riley tried to explain to her mother that they weren't needed, but her mother wouldn't budge.

With the roads clear, the deliveries started to arrive. Very soon, the living room looked like it was Christmas Eve, with packages piled up in one corner. Two items of special interest were the antique treadle sewing machines. They were in working order and were a special surprise gift for Maggie.

There was also a load of heavy-duty fabric for work clothes, as well as boxes of sewing needles, thread, scissors, and buttons.

"I hope we make it to Atlantis," Beverly said, inspecting the large pile. "Otherwise we're going to have to sell the house to pay for all of this. We've already used up your father's insurance money. I'm putting the rest on my cards."

"I know it's a lot," Riley agreed. "But I think we're practically ready to go." She didn't add that she hoped they left soon. If it was possible, she was feeling worse and was starting to suffer dizzy spells. Just before bed the previous evening, she'd fallen in the bathroom and bruised her elbow hitting the floor. If her mother knew, Riley was sure she'd start to panic.

"All right," Beverly said, rubbing her hands together. "Let's get this into the vehicles so we can see how much room we'll have left."

Riley joined the others carrying the supplies into the garage to be packed into the car or the trailer. As she worked, she felt another dizzy spell coming on, but she hid it as best she could. However, with the dizziness came nausea, which almost made her sick. She had to stop to keep her lunch down.

"Riley, are you all right?" her mother asked. "You're looking pale."

Riley said lightly, "Just a little dizzy. Do you mind if I take a break?"

"Why don't you go upstairs and lie down for a bit? We're almost done here."

"I think I will," Riley said. She took a deep breath and forced herself to keep walking into the house. When she reached the stairs, she stopped at the top and sat on the step, waiting for the dizziness to pass. Her heart was racing, and she felt extra hot.

Finally the spell passed, and Riley stood again. She walked down the hall and saw Sarah and Jill in her mother's bedroom, gathering their clothing together.

"I wish we could take it all," Jill was saying, holding up a pretty top.

"One bag each, those are the rules," Sarah said.

Riley felt a bit guilty. She was taking a lot more. But then again, she was going to share her clothes with the others in Atlantis—and the clothes Jill was taking were actually hers anyway.

Making it to her own room, Riley lay down. It was only supposed to be for a few minutes. But moments later, she was in a deep sleep.

Riley awoke to Jill's urgent voice and her hands on Riley's arm, shaking her lightly. "Riley, please, wake up."

"I'm awake," Riley said sleepily. "What's wrong? Is Maggie all right? What about Gideon?"

"They're fine. I mean, Gideon is still stone, but he seems okay. It's Sarah, she's gone. I told her not to, but she wouldn't listen. She snuck out without telling anyone to try to find Josh."

Despite her pounding head, that woke Riley right up. "She did what?"

"She said she just couldn't go without him, and she had some ideas where he could be. Then she said she was going to go home to get her violin and all the extra strings she had."

Riley sat up but swooned as dizziness overwhelmed her. She fell back down into the pillow. Closing her eyes, she waited for the room to stop spinning. "Have you told my mom?"

"No, I don't want her to throw us out."

"She wouldn't do that," Riley said. "But she's not going to be happy, that's for sure." Riley opened her eyes again, and when there was only one Jill in her vision instead of three, she sat up again carefully and looked at the clock. It was almost four. She'd slept for three hours. "When did she leave?"

"Right after you went to bed. She said she'd only be gone an hour. But that was hours ago. I'm so scared something has happened to her."

Riley wasn't sure if it was the headache or the news that was making her feel the worst. It was hard to focus and move. "We need to tell the others. I'm still dizzy. Would you help me up?"

Jill stayed by Riley's side as they walked down the hall to the stairs. Riley had to take each step one at a time until the dizziness passed. Her head was getting worse. If this was how she felt, she realized how terrible it must be for the others.

Making it to the living room, Riley saw her mother organizing the last of the items. Danny, Alfie, Robbi, and Pauly were still taking things to the trailer attached to the motor home. Chrissy was seated in the corner, playing with one of Riley's old dolls.

"This goes in the back of the car," Beverly was saying to Pauly as she handed him a package.

"I'm taking these to the motor home," Danny said, lifting a box. "Alfie, can you get that box?"

Riley noticed how pale and sick Alfie looked.

He must be feeling as bad as she did.

"Hey, look who's finally awake," Alfie teased. "Nice trick for getting outta work, Shorty."

"Sorry, I didn't mean to fall asleep," Riley said. She looked at her mother. "Mom, I think we have a problem."

Danny paused. "You okay, Riley?"

Riley nodded. "It's not me. It's Sarah. She snuck out to look for Josh and to get her violin. She hasn't come back."

Her mother paused and straightened up. She sighed heavily. "How long has she been gone?"

Jill's chin quivered. "Three hours. She said she was just going to check a couple of places for Josh and then go home. She was going to come right back. I—I'm so sorry. I tried to stop her."

Beverly looked at her. "Did she know where Josh is?"

Jill shook her head. "Not really. But we know a couple of places he hangs out. We had to sell our phones, so he doesn't have one. And Sarah said after she had to sell everything else she owns, she couldn't go without her violin."

"Everyone, this doesn't change anything," Beverly said, "You guys, keep packing. I'm going to take the car and see if I can find her."

"Mom, where are you gonna look?" Danny asked. "She could be anywhere."

Beverly looked at Jill. "Do you know where your brother hangs out?"

Jill nodded and said, "I promise, she won't do anything to hurt you or the others. She just wanted Josh to come with us." Jill's tears started to flow.

"It's not your fault," Beverly said as she came over to Jill. "But you must understand, there is more at stake than just us. If anyone were to find out about the Atlanteans . . ."

"I know," Jill said. "That's why I begged her not to go."

Riley's mom hugged Jill to reassure her. "I'm sure it will be fine. Come on, let's get going." She looked at everyone. "Just keep packing, we'll be back soon."

"Do you want me to come with you?" Riley asked.

Her mother shook her head. "No, you stay here and check on the others downstairs. Tell them to get ready to go."

Riley paused. "When are we leaving?"

Her mother didn't miss a beat. "Tonight, just as soon as Gideon wakes and we bring Sarah back."

11

JUST AFTER SUNDOWN, GIDEON STIRRED
and then woke fully. He was much better than a few
days ago but still weak from the shooting. Riley was
helping those downstairs gather what few things they
had left to pack.

"Tonight?" Pea said. "That's so sudden. I hoped
we had more time. How will I find out what happens
on my soaps?"

"I'm sorry, Pea, but it's going to have to stay a mystery," Riley said. "Maybe you could write your own
stories with the characters and make up your own
endings."

Pea's furry head tilted to the side. He nodded.

"You know, I might just do that. But I'll need to take some paper with me. Are you sure you've packed all my books? What about pens and pencils?"

"They're already on board," Riley said.

"And the fabric?" Maggie asked softly. "And all the extra sewing supplies?"

Riley nodded. "All loaded, plus Grandma's machine. We'll have to work it by hand."

"I'm sure the others in the sewing hut will appreciate everything," Maggie said.

"I wish we had more time to prepare," Mary said. "I feel like I haven't brought enough."

"I know it's sudden," Riley said. "Mom's just being careful because Sarah went out."

"Caution is always the better choice," Gideon said. "As I brought nothing, I need nothing to take back— except all of you."

Pea was seated beside Gideon. "When we get back, I should very much like to see the Crucible and all the books."

"You shall," Gideon said. "We have thousands of books; I haven't read them all. So with what you are bringing and what we have, I doubt you will ever run out of things to read."

"That's if Beresford and Lisette don't try to burn our books," Riley said. "I expect they're going to be really mad at us because we left."

"I don't believe you have anything to worry about," Gideon said. "They are not bad people, just a bit misguided."

"Misguided?" Riley choked. "Gideon, they gave Alfie Memory Berries to make him forget everything."

"Yes, they did," Gideon said. "But I still do not believe it was with malicious intent. They thought they were doing their best for him. Perhaps now all of you can teach them another way."

"Maybe . . . ," Riley said. Before she could finish her sentence, she heard the front door open. This was followed by a scream from Jill and then loud, angry voices.

Riley started for the stairs, but Gideon stopped her. "No, don't move," he said softly. "Wait and assess the situation."

A moment later, her mother called, "Riley, would you come up here, please? Sarah, Josh, and their friends are here."

Every instinct told Riley to run. The way her mother phrased it, she knew that Mike and his gang were in the house.

"It's got to be Mike," Riley whispered. "The guy who attacked us in the woods."

"Perhaps I should go up," Gideon said.

"No, not yet," Riley said. "We don't know if they have weapons. What if you're shot again?"

"I will not let fear for myself endanger you," Gideon said. "Go up first, but I shall be on the stairs waiting if you need me."

"And me," Mary said.

"I will be there too," Maggie said as she struggled to her feet.

Riley nodded and walked to the stairs. Her feet felt like lead as she took each step. Just as she reached the door, she heard Mike say, "Nice place you got here, lady."

She heard her mother say, "If you leave now, I won't call the police."

"We ain't goin' nowhere," Mike spat.

When Riley made it upstairs, one of Mike's gang members was waiting for her. He held a knife in his hand. "I heard voices. Who else is down there?"

"No one, it was the TV," Riley said.

He waved the knife. "Get in the front room."

Riley walked into the living room and saw her

mother standing before Mike. Sarah was farther back with Jill and her brother Josh. Sarah was crying and had the start of a large, angry bruise forming on her cheek. Josh's face and arms were covered in older bruises as he held his sisters protectively. His eyes were downcast and by the expression on his face, he was feeling very guilty.

Bastian was on the sofa beside Alfie and Danny. Miss Pigglesworth was sitting up and growling softly.

"Hey," Mike ordered. "Shut that dog up, or I will."

Bastian reached out for Miss Pigglesworth. "Please, be quiet."

Miss Pigglesworth whined once, then became silent.

Robbi, Pauly, and Chrissy were across the room. Chrissy was weeping softly.

"Why are you doing this?" Riley's mother said. "Wasn't it enough that you ransacked our car and then wrecked it?"

"No, it wasn't," Mike said. "We had it good until that night with you. Now the cops know who we are, and we can't go back to our apartment or the lake. We've been stuck in Josh's dump, but it's cold and dark."

"So what do you want here?" Beverly asked.

"You cost us a lot of money. So now you're gonna make it up. Get your debit card—we're gonna make a withdrawal!" He started to laugh, and his gang laughed with him. Everyone except Josh, who was shaking his head.

"It won't do you any good. I've got a limit; all you can get is two hundred a day."

"That'll do for a start," Mike said. He looked around the room. "You got some nice stuff here. I might just help myself."

"Just take what you want and go," Beverly said.

"Oh, we'll go. But when I say we're ready."

A sound came from the stairs leading to the basement. Riley realized Gideon was moving. His weight was causing the wooden stairs to creak. Everyone turned to look at the hallway outside the living room where the basement entrance was.

Mike became furious and struck Riley's mother across the face. "Why didn't you tell me there was someone else here?" He turned to one of his gang. "Stan, go check it out."

The gang member who had ordered Riley into the living room moved to the stairs. He disappeared through the door to the basement. This was followed by a strangled cry, and then silence.

Mike looked at the other members of his gang. "Derek, Leroy, go check on Stan."

"I wouldn't do that if I were you," Beverly warned.

Mike raised his knife to her. "Why not? Who's down there?"

"Your worst nightmare," Riley said. "So just leave now before it's too late."

Mike nodded to his two buddies. "Watch yourselves, but go check it out."

The two held up their knives and entered the stairwell. There were choked screams and then thudding that sounded like something heavy falling down the stairs.

"I'm warning you," Riley said. "Go now before it's too late."

"Shut your mouth, kid," Mike threatened as he flashed his knife.

Despite the weapons all the gang held up, Riley felt no fear. She didn't know whether it was the terrible headache and dizziness making her bold, or knowing that Gideon and the others were close.

The heavy tread on the stairs started again.

"Too late," Riley muttered.

Gideon appeared at the top of the stairs. The immense gargoyle had to stoop to get through the doorway. He stood up tall in the hallway and turned toward the living room.

Maggie arrived beside him. She was standing upright but snarling angrily.

Riley watched Mike's reaction to the gargoyle and leopard. The two other gang members dropped their knives and tried to run for the windows, but then Maggie leaped forward. She crossed the distance in three long strides and knocked them away from the windows.

"You aren't going anywhere!" she growled.

Mike's jaw was hanging open. He looked from Gideon to Maggie and back to Gideon again. "Wha—wha—" was all he could manage.

When Gideon entered the room, Mike lunged at him with the knife. With lightning speed, Gideon spun around and knocked Mike over with his thick, long tail. Then he darted over and lifted him high in the air. "Foolish boy. You should have left when you had the chance."

"Put me down!" Mike cried, struggling in Gideon's grip. "Please, put me down."

"Danny, Alfie, close the curtains," Beverly warned.

As they moved to close the curtains, Maggie stood up again and shoved the gang members. "You two, over there with Mike."

Their eyes couldn't have been any wider. "You— you talk. But you're a . . . you're a . . ."

"I'm a very angry leopard," Maggie said. "I believe it was a mistake that I didn't kill you in the woods."

Riley knew how sick Maggie was and that she must be using all her reserves to go after the gang. The leopard-woman pulled back her lips in a tight snarl that revealed all her sharp teeth. Even to Riley, Maggie was a terrifying sight.

Gideon lowered Mike to the ground and shoved him closer to his friends.

"This is im-impossible," Mike stammered as he kept looking back to Maggie and then to Gideon. "You're not real—you can't be real."

"Oh, we are very real," Gideon said as he moved forward and loomed over the gang leader. "And I am more than a touch *disappointed* at how you have ter-rorized this family that I care so deeply for."

"We . . . we . . ." Mike stopped speaking as Gideon loomed over him. Finally he whimpered, "Please don't kill me."

"Tell me why I shouldn't," Gideon hissed. "For all the harm you have done to so many people, you certainly deserve it."

Riley was stunned by Gideon's harsh words. She had only ever known him to be gentle and kind. But like Maggie, he was surprisingly menacing. Despite that, she was sure he wouldn't really hurt them. Just scare them.

"I swear we will never do it again," Mike wept.

"You said that before, when Miss Pigglesworth was threatening to bite your neck," Bastian said. "But you've still come back to hurt us."

"No—no," Mike sputtered. "We weren't going to hurt you."

"Liar!" Gideon roared. "I can see into your soul, boy. I know full well what you were intending to do. But this family is under our protection."

"I—I—" Mike sputtered again.

"What?" Gideon barked. "What do you say for yourself?"

Riley looked over to the two remaining gang members. They were shaking with terror. Then she had a thought that might ensure Mike and his gang never hurt anyone again.

"Gideon, I have an idea," she said. "You know how

you can track people once you've met them? Now that you've met Mike and his gang, you'll know if they've done something wrong. And if they have, if they break their promise, you can punish them then."

Gideon shook his head. "No, that's not good enough. My rage must be satisfied—now!"

"Riley's right," Beverly said. She walked up to Gideon and placed her hand on his arm. "There are children here. You don't want them to see this."

Gideon glanced over to Jill's family and saw the fear on their faces. His shoulders dropped a bit. Finally he looked at Mike. "You should be punished for your crimes."

"We will be! We'll turn ourselves in to the police," Mike offered. "Anything you say, but please don't kill me."

"How do we know you'll do it?" Beverly asked.

"I will, I swear I will," Mike cried.

"Do not trust him, Beverly," Maggie said. She moved closer to Mike and put a clawed finger under his chin and peered into his eyes. "This one is a talented liar."

"No, no, I'm not!" Mike cried. "I'll do it, I'll call the police right now."

"No, you won't," Beverly said. "But I do have an idea that will work for all of us." She looked at Maggie. "Keep them here, I'll be right back."

Beverly returned several minutes later holding a long, coiled-up rope. "Danny, Pauly, go into the dining room and grab some chairs."

Within a few minutes, Mike and the two gang members were tied securely to the dining room chairs and were gagged so they couldn't talk or shout. Then Danny and Alfie took more rope downstairs and tied the three gang members up down there.

When they returned, Mary and Pea were with them.

Mike and the others' eyes were wide as Pea stood before them. The koala was unsteady on his feet, but despite how he was feeling, Pea had strength enough to wag his finger at them. "You are all very nasty boys, and only bad things will happen to you if you continue on this path. If you do not change, Gideon will be the least of your worries."

Riley couldn't help but smile as Pea scolded the gang. He seemed fearless as he stood before them. Across the way, Josh was still standing back with Sarah and Jill. His eyes were wide and staring as they watched Gideon and the others.

Riley walked over to them and faced Sarah. "What happened?"

Sarah started to weep. "I'm so, so sorry. When I got to the house, I found Mike, and everyone was living there. And when I wouldn't tell Mike where we were staying, he got so angry he hit me. Then Beverly and Jill came, and they forced us to come back here."

"Please don't blame Sarah," Josh said. "It's my fault for getting involved with Mike's gang in the first place. I swear this isn't what I wanted. They told me we would steal cars, sell them, and share the profits. Not hurt people. I should have left after the first attack at the lake, but I was a coward. I knew it was wrong, but I stayed anyway."

Gideon arrived behind Riley, and Josh's eyes showed his pure terror as he looked up into the face of the angry gargoyle.

Gideon leaned down closer to Josh. "Do you regret your actions? Tell me the truth. If you are lying, I will know it."

Riley noticed how Gideon was holding himself much higher to intimidate Josh into speaking the truth.

Josh lowered his head. "I will regret everything I've

done until the day I die. I can't sleep at night because I still hear the cries of some of the people we've hurt. I'm sickened by what I've done. But I swear I did it for my family. I never kept a penny for myself. It was all for the others."

"Please believe me, Gideon, when I say that Josh isn't bad," Sarah begged. "It's true, he's been doing this for us." She lowered her head. "I know you won't take me and Josh with you, but will you take the others? They deserve a better life than what we can give them."

"Sarah, no!" Jill cried. "If you're not going, I'm not going."

"We're not going without you," Robbi said.

"Going where?" Josh asked.

Sarah was about to speak when Riley held up a warning finger. "Don't say it." She looked over her shoulder to Mike and the others.

Sarah nodded. "I really am so sorry I caused this."

Gideon inhaled deeply. "The fault is theirs, not yours, Sarah." He studied Josh closely, and Riley had the feeling he was gazing into Josh's soul. Finally, Gideon straightened. "You are welcome to join us."

"Gideon?" Riley said.

"It is all right, Riley, he is speaking the truth. He may come."

"I—I don't understand," Josh said.

"And you won't, not for a while," Riley said. She looked back up to Gideon. "Are you sure he's safe?"

Gideon nodded. "He is."

"Thank you, Gideon," Sarah said as she started to weep again.

When that was settled, Riley and Gideon walked back to her mother.

"Now what?" Riley asked.

"Now," Beverly said, looking at everyone in the room, "we go."

They had wanted to give Gideon more time to recover, but Sarah's actions changed all that. While Mike and the gang remained tied up in the living room with Maggie standing guard over them, the others scrambled to get the last of the items into the vehicles.

When the final bag was carried out, Riley returned to the lounge with Maggie's cloak. "We're ready to go."

Mike was watching them closely, and Maggie turned to look at him. She pulled back her lips and snarled. "Perhaps I should have a quick snack before we go, just to keep up my strength."

Mike started to panic and scream through his gag.

"Maybe not," Maggie finally said. "He might ruin my digestion."

Riley reached out and squeezed Maggie's hand. She knew exactly what her friend was doing. "Good decision. C'mon, let's go."

As everyone darted through the house for a final check, Riley looked around. This had been her childhood home. All her memories were here. And yet she felt no sadness in leaving. This final realization revealed that a house was just a house, and furniture was just furniture. It was family and memories that made it a home. Since everyone she loved was going with them, there was nothing left here but stuff.

Her mother walked back into the living room with Gideon. "We're ready." She looked at Mike and the others. "We're going now. When I feel we are far enough away from you, I will call the police and let them know you are here. If you tell them what you've seen . . ."

Mike shook his head wildly.

"Or," Gideon added as he opened his wings threateningly, "if you do not surrender yourselves to them as promised, I will find you and you will wish that you had done as you said. Do you all understand me?"

Mike and the others nodded quickly.

Riley took Maggie by the hand. "C'mon. Let's go home."

12

BECAUSE RILEY AND ALFIE WERE BOTH feeling dreadful, they traveled in the motor home with the Atlanteans. Beverly was in the driver's seat and leading the way.

Danny was driving the rental car behind them with the six members of Jill's family plus as much clothing and items as they could fit in it.

With Josh traveling with them, there were extra drivers for the car, which took the pressure off Danny, but as for the motor home, Beverly planned to drive it all the way.

There was still snow all around them, but the roads were clear as they drove away from their neighborhood and headed toward the highway, out of Denver.

Riley was seated at the small kitchen table beside Maggie. Alfie, Bastian, and Miss Pigglesworth were seated opposite them on the bench seat. Mary and Pea were up in the berth area above the driver while Gideon was forced to lie down on one of the beds at the rear, as he was just too big to stand or sit in the motor home.

Riley pulled back the blinds on the window and peered out. The road around them was empty. She checked the time and saw that it was almost eleven in the evening. They planned to drive through the night as far as they could before they needed to stop and rest. A two-thousand-mile journey lay before them, meaning it would normally take them four days. They hoped to do it in two.

Because they were so rushed to leave, they hadn't worked out sleeping arrangements. The motor home was big, but it wasn't big enough for everyone. But at the same time, there was never any talk of hotels.

This was going to be a long and stressful trip. Added to that was the fear for the Atlanteans. Mike's arrival put a lot of needless stress on them, and it wasn't good for their health. Maggie was feeling worst of all. After a short time, Riley had to get up and help her back to the bed, opposite Gideon.

Gideon raised his head when they arrived. "Are you all right, Maggie?"

Maggie nodded. "Just a little tired. It's been a dreadful evening."

"Indeed it has," Gideon agreed.

When she was settled down, Riley covered Maggie in a blanket and leaned down and kissed her on her warm, fur-covered cheek. She felt Gideon's eyes on her, and when she glanced over, he smiled and whispered, "She'll be fine when we get her back to Atlantis."

"I hope so," Riley whispered back.

She returned to her seat and settled down for the long drive. As her own headache was slamming, Riley dozed off. When she awoke again, it was light out and they were still moving. Alfie and Bastian were leaning on each other and sound asleep.

Riley got up and walked a few steps forward, taking the seat beside her mother.

"Good morning, sweetheart, how are you feeling?"

"Rough," Riley said. She looked out the window and saw the change in landscape. There was a dusting of snow, but not nearly as much as there was at home. "Where are we?"

"Kansas."

"Already?"

Her mother nodded and then yawned. "You, Alfie, and Bastian were down for the count. You didn't move when we stopped for gas."

"We stopped for gas?"

"Uh-huh. Josh has taken over driving the car."

"How about you? Do you need a break?"

"I'm okay for a while longer, but I wouldn't say no to a coffee if you would make one for me."

"Sure, I'll make it a double." Riley got up and moved farther back to the small kitchen. She put the kettle on and while she waited for it to boil, she checked on Maggie and Gideon.

Gideon had turned at dawn and was lying on his side, curled up. She patted his arm and felt the cold stone beneath her hand.

"He is well," Maggie said softly.

"I'm sorry, I didn't mean to wake you," Riley said.

"You didn't, I've been awake for some time."

Riley sat down on the edge of Maggie's bed. She reached out and stroked her head, feeling the heat radiate through her fingers. "How are you feeling?"

"I'm fine," Maggie said. "Just a bit feverish and my head is . . ."

Riley nodded. "Pounding. Mine too. I'm sure we'll feel better when we get back."

Maggie nodded, then sighed. "I am sorry we have to go back. I shall miss your world. I think I will especially miss a stove and oven and how easy it is to cook. I think I've become spoiled."

Riley grinned. "I won't mind going back if it means we can all stay together and be healthy. And I promise you, things won't be the same in Atlantis. We won't let them put you back in your cloak, no matter what. And I'm going to fight Beresford if he tries to make you and the other Cloaks stay outside during a Red Moon."

"Please don't endanger yourself for me," Maggie said.

"I will if I have to. That's one of the big things that I really hated about Atlantis. The discrimination against Cloaks."

"I can almost remember a time when cloaks weren't worn."

"Yes, I saw pictures of that in one of Pea's books. It looked a lot happier back then. And I know it will be that way again."

The kettle started to sound. "Can I make you a cup of tea?"

Maggie smiled. "Thank you, dear, not at the moment." She settled down and closed her eyes.

Riley walked back into the small kitchen area and prepared the coffee for her mother. She wanted to look out the rear window to see how everyone was in the car behind them, but the blinds were closed to ensure that no one could see in.

With the coffee in her hand, Riley walked past Bastian and Alfie, who were still sleeping on the bench seat. Miss Pigglesworth raised her head weakly as she walked past. Riley bent down and stroked her. Miss Pigglesworth was as feverish as Maggie.

Taking the seat beside her mother again, she handed her the coffee. "I hope we can get there quick. Maggie really isn't doing well."

"I know," her mother answered. "And you don't look great either."

"Trust me, I feel worse than I look." Riley faced forward and watched the long road ahead.

They continued without stopping for most of the day, making it through Kansas and well on their way to Missouri. They stopped several times to refuel and to give Beverly a break—each time they stopped, they ensured they were far enough away from other motorists not to be seen.

After one break, Danny offered to drive the motor home while Beverly could sleep, but she wouldn't have it. When Pea offered to drive, it gave them the laughter and break they needed. After a couple of hours of rest, they were on the road again.

As night fell, they pulled over at a deserted rest stop outside St. Louis and waited for Gideon to rise. Everyone piled out of the vehicles to stretch their legs. The Atlanteans donned their cloaks to be safe, but they enjoyed the break and the cool, fresh air.

As always, Chrissy ran over to Pea the moment he climbed out of the motor home. Despite feeling dreadful, playing with Chrissy always managed to cheer him up. Pea insisted that her young laughter was better than any medicine.

Josh and Sarah were still feeling very guilty for the events at the house and were quiet and hanging back, away from Riley's family. But when Gideon emerged from the motor home, he went over to them.

Riley couldn't hear what he was saying, but at the

end of the conversation, Sarah embraced the gargoyle tightly and Josh was nodding.

While the younger members of the group ran around and played, Beverly called the police and explained about Mike and his gang being tied up in their house. She went into details about the home invasion and how they had been terrorized by the gang but had managed to fight them off and gain the upper hand.

When the detective asked Beverly why they left and where she was, she explained that she was taking her family away for a while because of the attack. She ended the call by saying she could be reached by phone if necessary.

Riley wasn't sure it would satisfy the police, but with luck, they would be in Miami or maybe even at sea before they needed to speak with the police again.

With Gideon safely awake, they hit the road again. At midnight, Chrissy was brought into the caravan to sleep in the berth above the cab with Mary and Pea. At two in the morning, they reached the half-way point of their journey. Riley's mom explained that driving the long hours wasn't too different from working on-call shifts at the hospital.

That said, by dawn, she was struggling to stay

awake, and they had to stop again. She walked to the rear berth and shared the bed with Maggie. It was tight, but Beverly was too tired to care and fell asleep the moment she lay down.

Three hours later, Beverly's phone rang and woke everyone in the motor home. When her mother answered it, Riley watched her face change from tired to instantly alert.

"I told you, after the loss of my husband and the police investigation, then with what Mike and his gang have put us through, we needed a break—my children needed a break. We're headed down to a friend's place for a couple of weeks. . . . I can give you a full statement when we get back."

After a few more minutes Beverly exclaimed, "He's a dangerous criminal, surely you can't be listening to him. . . . No, we're not . . . Yes, because he's terrorized us. . . . You couldn't protect us, so we left."

Riley, Alfie, and Bastian got up and walked to the back to better hear what Beverly was saying. From a friendly conversation at the beginning, it changed quickly to something completely different. Her mother was defensive and insisting that Mike and his gang were making up stories.

Hearing that, Riley was instantly on guard. It didn't take a genius to realize that despite Gideon's warning, Mike and the others had told the police everything.

"So you're taking the word of a known criminal over mine, a respected doctor," Beverly said.

Whatever the reply was, it was enough to make her disconnect the call. She was shaking badly. Riley wondered if it was from exhaustion, anger, or fear. "Mom, what it is? What did they say?"

Beverly got up from the bed. "Go wake up everyone in the car and get them in here. We have a problem."

"What is it?" Mary asked as she came down the aisle.

"It's Mike. He's told the police that we've abducted the Decker children and I think they believe him."

13

WITHIN MINUTES, EVERYONE WAS PILED into the motor home as Beverly explained her conversation with the police.

"They've ordered us back to give a statement." She looked at Sarah, Josh, and their family. "They think we've abducted you."

"But you haven't," Sarah insisted. "We wanted to go with you."

"I know. But I never told them you were with me. Mike did. He said that Josh was part of his gang and that we threatened him, so you all had to come with us. They've twisted everything around, so it sounds like we've abducted you. He told them we were using scary monsters to control you. All the gang members said the same thing, so whether they believe them or not, they insist we come back to clear it up."

"What if I spoke to them?" Sarah said. She looked at her brother. "Or Josh. We could explain."

Riley said to her mother, "It's worth a try."

Beverly reached for the phone and called the police back. She explained that Sarah and her family had been staying at their house for protection after Mike became violent toward Josh. When she offered to put Sarah on the line, Beverly handed the phone over.

"Hi, I'm Sarah Jane Decker," Sarah started. "I'm Josh's sister, and I'm here with my brothers and sisters. We're safe, thanks to Beverly and her family. After what Mike did to Josh, we were really scared, but then Beverly invited us to go away with them for a few days. We didn't tell anyone because we were hiding from Mike."

Riley stood back with the others listening to the call. Just like with her mother, Sarah's tone changed as she argued with the officer.

"But our mother is gone. She left us months ago—we have no one!" Sarah cried. "If it wasn't for Beverly's kindness, I don't know what would have happened to us. . . . No, I couldn't, they would have separated us and put us into foster care. We're safe here. Josh can tell you, he's right beside me." She handed the phone to her brother.

When Josh got on the line, the conversation became even more confrontational. "I know I was there," Josh was saying. "And I know I've committed crimes and I'm sorry for everything I've done. I should have left Mike at the beginning when I saw what he was doing. But I was weak. I've done so many terrible things, but I had to, to protect my family. But when I finally had the guts to stand up to him, he beat me up and then came after my family. He found us at Beverly's house. That's the truth, not whatever crazy lie Mike is telling you."

There was a long pause, and then Josh spoke again. "No, we can't. I just need to keep my family safe and together. You don't get it. Mike has more gang members than you know. They'll come after us again. . . . Seriously, you can't protect us, not as long as they're out there. Please just find them all and we'll come back."

Josh held the phone from his ear and looked at Beverly, mouthing the words *They won't believe me.*

Beverly took the phone back. "Look, I know I should have told you about the Decker children before, but they are desperate to stay together. We both know that the social care system is stretched to breaking. I'm doing the best I can for them. You just sort Mike and his gang out, and we'll gladly come back. Then I can file the paperwork to become their legal guardian."

Riley couldn't hear what was being said at the other end of the line, but she had a pretty good idea by her mother's posture.

"I know—but—wait, why? I haven't done anything wrong. How can you suggest such a thing? No, I can't . . ." Just like last time, Beverly disconnected the call. She shook her head in frustration. "They won't listen. Now they're saying because I didn't register as your new guardian, I'm in trouble. I've been ordered to bring you back, or they'll put out a warrant for my arrest."

Riley's heart was pounding. Mike was the criminal, but now they were in trouble for doing good.

"We're endangering you and everyone in here," Josh said. "We have to go back."

Jill was shaking her head. "I'm so sorry we got you into this."

"I'm not," Beverly responded. She looked at all of them. "You all deserve a good home, and from what Riley and Alfie have told us, Atlantis will be perfect for all of us. We just have to get there."

"But—" Sarah started.

"No buts," Beverly said. "We're not going to let Mike, or anyone, change our plans. Now, get back to the car. We're heading out."

Josh stepped forward and said, "We can't. We have to abandon the car."

"What?" Riley said. "Why?"

"Because if the police issue a warrant for Beverly, they're going to be looking for her—for all of us."

"What does that have to do with the car?" Pea asked.

Josh looked at everyone. "You know I've done some really terrible things with the gang. One of those was stealing cars. But we never touched rental cars because they have several trackers built in. Right now, that rental car back there will tell them exactly where we are. Then there's your credit cards. If the police think you've kidnapped us, they'll be tracking your card use as well, and with all the stops we've made, again, they'll know where we are. They'll probably be on the lookout for our license plates too. We're gonna have to replace them."

The color drained from Beverly's face. "Oh lord, I never realized."

"I wouldn't have either, until I met Mike," Josh said. "He taught me these things. Right now, if they start looking for us, they'll find us unless we change how we go."

Pea looked fearfully around. "What are we going to do? I don't want to be put in a zoo. I'll never survive."

"Me neither," Maggie agreed. "We won't survive much longer if we don't get back to Atlantis."

Josh looked around. "It'll be tight, but we can all move in here." He looked at Beverly again. "How much cash do you have on you? I have thirty."

Beverly shrugged. "I don't know. A couple hundred, maybe. I planned to take out more, but then Mike got involved . . ."

Josh paused and looked guilty for a moment and then finally said, "I really am sorry about all of this."

"Now's not the time for apologies. We need to think," Danny said.

Josh nodded. "You're right." He turned to Beverly

again. "We're going to need more cash for gas. After today, we can't use your cards again, since they'll be tracking them. We're not far from St. Louis. I suggest we fill up with as much gas as we can, and then find an ATM and take out as much as you're allowed. Then after that, we'll only use cash to buy fuel. We can all do without food for a bit."

"We have plenty of food here," Riley said. "We packed lots, just in case it took us a long time to find Atlantis."

Josh looked at Beverly's phone and reached for it. "And these," he said, holding it up. "Those of you who have a phone, take out your battery. They can track phones, too, sometimes even if they're turned off."

Riley hadn't been sure about Josh joining them, but listening to him talking about what they needed to do to stay safe, she was suddenly grateful he was here. She had to ignore the fact that it was because of him that they were in this predicament.

"All right," Beverly said. "First, disable your phones. Then let's go empty that car; we've got to get moving. Josh is right—as of now, we are going completely off the grid."

Everyone felt the pressure of time as they started to unpack the car and carry things back to the motor home. While items were delivered to the door, Pea, Mary, and Maggie found places to stash them. Chairs and beds were covered in layers of clothes. The cupboards were stuffed full of things. In the end, with careful packing, nothing was left behind.

Things only became tight when everyone piled into the motor home. There were not enough seats, so Robbi and Pauly sat on the floor. Chrissy remained in the berth over the cab with Pea and Mary, and Sarah lay down on the bed beside Maggie. Josh sat on the floor near the front while Danny sat in the passenger seat opposite his mother. Despite Beverly's early protests, she finally agreed that the driving would now be split among all of them, as they were not going to stop to rest until they reached Miami.

"Are we ready?" Beverly called as she started the motor home.

"Yes," Riley said, along with everyone else.

They were soon on the road again. When they reached the suburbs outside of St. Louis, they filled the motor home with as much gas as it could take, then parked up at a shopping center and found a bank machine. Beverly was able to draw her daily limit of cash from her debit card. But when she tried her credit card, it was declined.

"This is unbelievable. They've stopped my credit card!" Beverly announced when she returned to the motor home. "We needed this to pay for renting the boat!"

"If they've canceled your cards, you can bet they're looking for us," Josh said knowingly. "They might even bring in the FBI because we're kids."

"What are we going to do?" Danny asked.

"We keep going," Beverly said. "Tony at the marina knows we're coming. I'm sure we can work something out."

Before leaving St. Louis, Josh suggested they change their Colorado license plates to Missouri ones. He explained that it was all about blending in. If the police were looking for a motor home with Colorado plates, they wouldn't find it.

"Won't someone notice their plates missing?" Mary asked. She was leaning heavily on Alfie, but despite how she was feeling, she still wanted to be part of the discussion.

Again Josh nodded. "That's why we have to find a vehicle that's not really being used. Like at an airport's long-term parking or something like that."

"All right," Beverly said as she moved to the driver's seat. "Let's head to the airport."

They wasted no time finding the St. Louis airport. It was still early, and the heavy traffic hadn't started yet. They parked away from the long-term parking, and Danny and Josh headed out with tools from Pea's new kit.

They returned less than an hour later. After removing their Colorado plates, they replaced them with Missouri ones.

"Those'll work fine unless a cop enters the plate numbers into their police mobile computer," Josh said. "Then it will give the make and model of the car and we won't match. So we can't do anything to draw attention to ourselves."

"Right," Beverly said as she pulled away. "I'll keep it to the speed limit."

They drove for the rest of the day through Missouri and then crossed over into Tennessee. Danny offered to take over driving, but Beverly said she was too keyed up to just sit. By late afternoon, they reached

Nashville, where they bought maps and found their way to the international airport. Once again, they switched license plates on their motor home to match the Tennessee plates.

"You're getting good at this," Riley said to her brother as he and Josh finished changing the plates.

"Don't go getting too used to it," Beverly called from the front as she drove the motor home away.

"Yeah." Danny laughed. "I'm sure there are a lot of parking lots in Atlantis!"

As nightfall came, they didn't pull over to allow Gideon to wake. Instead they kept moving. They crossed into Georgia as the gargoyle started to stir. Riley was at his side, stroking his arm.

"It's all right, Gideon, you're safe. We're all here." She watched his breathing grow deeper as the wings on his back started to move and fold tighter.

"I am awake," Gideon said. He opened his eyes and looked up at Riley. "Is all well?"

Riley looked over to Sarah and Maggie on the bunk opposite them. Finally, she said, "Not exactly. But we need you to stay calm."

"I am always calm," Gideon said.

"You might not be once I tell you what's happened."

Because of the tightness in the motor home, Gideon had to keep lying down as Riley, Sarah, and Maggie told him the events of the day. The gargoyle raised his head and glanced down the aisle to see Robbi and Pauly sitting there, looking back at him. Josh was farther down, near Beverly at the wheel.

"So we are all in this vehicle?"

Riley nodded. "We didn't want to be traced through the car."

"And Mike did this to us, after I warned him what I would do if he told?"

"Yes," Riley said. "Please don't be too mad. You need to stay calm in here."

"I am not mad," Gideon said. "I am disappointed. But this is further proof of why we gargoyles removed ourselves from the world of humans. With a rare few exceptions, you cannot be trusted."

This stung Riley to hear, but Gideon was right. A lot of the time, people couldn't be trusted. Mike and his gang were a good example. "I'm sorry," Riley said.

"Me too," Sarah agreed.

"This is not your fault," Gideon said. "Though I can assure you, Mike *is* going to be very sorry he betrayed us."

Riley saw a cold hardness in his eyes that she'd never seen before. "You—you're not going to leave us to get him, are you?"

Gideon's eyes softened as he reached out and patted her hands. "No, Riley, I am staying right here to see everyone back to Atlantis safely. But after I am fully recovered . . ."

He stopped speaking and Riley didn't want to ask what he planned to do. Instead she said, "Mom says we'll reach Miami tomorrow. But there's a problem. Because the police shut down her credit card, we can't rent a boat."

Gideon smiled. "Do not fret, Riley. I am sure we will all think of something."

Riley sat on the floor between Gideon, Maggie, and Sarah for several hours until she couldn't keep her eyes open anymore. Her body clock was all messed up because of the strange hours they'd been keeping, which made her headache so much worse.

She looked down the aisle and saw that Robbi and Pauly were asleep on the floor while Alfie had his head down on the table. Bastian was sleeping against Miss Pigglesworth.

"Riley, take my place and lie down." Sarah got up

from the bed. "I'll go sit with the others. You need to rest."

Riley was too tired and too weak to argue. She gratefully lay down on the bunk beside Maggie, and right before she drifted off to sleep, she felt Maggie's arms wrap protectively around her as she whispered, "Sleep well, my love. . . ."

14

WHEN RILEY WOKE AGAIN, SHE LOOKED over and saw that Gideon was stone. But though it felt like she'd only just closed her eyes, somehow most of the night had passed.

She sat up and looked beside her. Maggie was sleeping. Riley reached out and stroked her head and felt the heat emanating from it. It was almost as hot as when she had that bad spell at home.

"Maggie?" she said softly as she shook her. "Maggie, wake up." But Maggie would not awaken.

Riley looked down the aisle. Her mother was asleep on the floor, and Josh was driving the motor home. Riley got up and went down to her mother. "Mom, wake up."

Her mother raised her head. "What's wrong?"

"It's Maggie, her big fever is back."

Beverly climbed to her feet.

"Is everything okay?" Danny called from the passenger seat.

"Just keep your eyes on the road," Beverly said. "I'm going back to check on Maggie."

Her mother tried to wake Maggie, but she couldn't. She looked at Riley. "This isn't good. Get me a bottle of water—we've got to cool her down."

While Riley ran to the small kitchen area and reached for a bottle of water, her mother called, "Sarah, Jill, Pauly, open all the windows up there— we need some fresh air moving around."

Riley reached her mother with the bottle of water. It was opened and poured all over Maggie. "Get me another one, we need to soak her."

After two bottles of water were poured all over Maggie, Beverly reached behind the blinds and opened the window beside the bunk. "Open Gideon's window, too, we need to cool it down in here." She called forward. "Josh, turn up the air-conditioning!"

Riley had to climb carefully over the sleeping gargoyle to reach the window. When she opened it, she felt the warm breeze blowing in. She called forward, "Danny, where are we?"

"Northern Florida," her brother answered. "How is Maggie?"

"She's getting worse." Riley took a few steps down the aisle and called up to the berth over the front of the motor home. "Pea? Mary? How are you doing up there?"

"Not great," Mary called down. "We're both roasting."

Riley grabbed another bottle of water. She hated to use it, as there were only two left, but Pea was more important. She stepped carefully around Robbi and Pauly in the aisle and then forward to the bunk.

"I've got some water—wet him down. You too," Riley said.

"Good idea," Mary said.

Riley opened the bottle so Mary wouldn't have to struggle with the seal and then handed it up. Before Mary started to pour the water, she asked Chrissy to get down so she wouldn't get wet.

"No, stay with Teddy!" Chrissy screeched.

"Leave her," Sarah said. "She's all right. If she gets wet and wants down, I'll take her."

As Mary poured the water over Pea and herself, Riley looked at Bastian. His face was flushed and his forehead hot. She stroked his head. "How are you doing?"

"Hot. My head really hurts and I'm dizzy. Miss Pigglesworth is worse."

"I am too," Riley admitted. She left Bastian and Alfie and made her way back to Maggie. Her mother was brushing Maggie's fur in the opposite direction to raise it and get air to it.

Beverly looked up at Riley. "I'm really worried. This is worse than the last time. Her breathing is much shallower."

"What can we do?" Riley asked helplessly.

"I don't know," her mother said. "I don't know what's wrong with all of you. I just pray we reach Atlantis before it's too late."

Riley felt chills go through her. The expression on her mother's face was one she'd never seen before. Did she know more than she was saying? Was Maggie going to die? What about Pea, Mary, or Bastian and Miss Pigglesworth? The thought of losing any one of them was a dagger to her heart.

"Stay with her," her mother said. "I'm going to take

over driving. We need to get there—now. Just keep brushing her fur the wrong way, it will cool her down."

Her mother walked forward while Riley took a seat on the bed and did as she was told. With each backward stroke of Maggie's fur, she said, "Stay with me, Maggie. Please don't die."

Each mile seemed endless as the motor home made its way farther south. By midmorning they were passing through Orlando, then went on the toll road heading to Miami.

Three hours later, Danny called, "We're on the home stretch. Just fifty more miles to Miami!"

Everyone in the motor home clapped their hands and cheered. But Riley didn't feel the excitement. She was too scared. Maggie was still dangerously hot, even after being drenched by two bottles of water. Riley peered up the length of the motor home and saw that Pea and Mary were both lying down and not reacting to the news. She felt her own fever climbing. The Florida heat certainly wasn't helping.

Just over another hour later, they were driving past Miami and heading toward Grove Harbour Marina. Riley bent over and peered through the blinds on the back window. Blazing afternoon sunshine struck her eyes, and she saw the palm trees lining the roads.

When they reached Grove Harbour, Riley heard a heated argument up front. She left Maggie and walked forward.

"Please, Beverly, trust me," Josh was insisting. "Drive past it and we can walk in. At least until we know what's going on."

"We don't have time to waste," Beverly was saying. "Maggie and the others are critical. We have to get moving."

"Yes, we do!" Josh said. "But we won't be any good to them if the cops are there and arrest you!"

"Mom," Danny put in. "I think he's right. Let's just drive past it a bit and we can walk back."

Riley's mother hesitated and then nodded as the motor home sped up a bit. "All right, I'll just park up the street."

When the motor home stopped, Riley walked forward. "Mom, I think Danny and I should go in."

"What?!" her mother cried. "No. Your dad and I have known Tony for years. Even if my credit card is canceled, I'm sure we can make some kind of arrangement."

"But what if the police are there?" Riley said. "They might have found out that you've reserved a boat down here and could be looking for you. I don't know if they'll know Danny and me." Riley realized that her face was all over the news a few weeks ago. But her hair was styled differently, and her clothing had changed. With luck, no one would remember.

"I could go too," Jill said. "No one knows me."

"No, I'm sure it will be fine," Beverly said. But there was hesitation in her voice.

"Beverly," Mary called down weakly. "Let Riley, Danny, and Jill go. We need you here. Pea isn't well."

"Please, Mom, let us scope it out first and make sure it's safe," Danny insisted.

Finally their mother nodded. "All right. But if you see the police, promise me you'll get out of there and we'll figure something else out."

"I promise," Riley said.

"Hey, Shorty, I'm coming too," Alfie said.

Riley looked at her cousin. He looked just about as bad as she felt. But they'd gone so far together, he should be here now. "Sure, let's go."

They left the motor home and walked back toward the marina. Within a few steps, Riley was sweating and exhausted. Not so much from the weather—Florida in early winter was lovely. It was her own fever spiking. The sunshine made it even worse.

"You okay, Riley?" her brother asked. "Do you want to go back and sit down? It might help."

Riley shook her head. "No, the only thing that's going to help is getting back to Atlantis."

"If we're not too late," Alfie said.

Riley wanted to snap at him to tell him not to be so negative. But she was feeling the same, so she remained silent.

They finally made it to the entrance of the marina. There were cars and people everywhere. The smell of barbecue was in the air, as people on boats were having parties. That smell always made Riley's mouth water. This time, it was making her feel queasy.

"There's the sales office," Danny said.

The last time Riley and Alfie were here was when they arrived at the marina after escaping Atlantis. The *Moon Dancer* was too big to come in under her own power, so a towboat came out to meet them and brought them in to dock.

Her mother and Danny had been waiting for them and had cleared the way with the dockmaster,

Tony Zamora. Their arrival had been a big event, and Tony, his assistant, Cristina, and all the staff were there to meet them and welcome them home.

There were loads of questions, especially about how they managed to survive the wreck of their boat, the *Event Horizon*, and the months away at sea, but Riley's mother had handled everything perfectly.

Walking through the parking area, Alfie pointed. "Hey, look, there's the *Moon Dancer*!"

"That's the *Moon Dancer*?" Jill asked. "It's beautiful!"

Riley followed his finger and saw the magnificent antique sailing yacht moored at one of the larger slips. Even from this distance, she could see the big warning sign on it telling people not to trespass. She stopped and stared, remembering what it was like to sail on her.

"Earth to Riley," Danny called.

Snapped out of her memories, Riley caught up with Danny and Alfie. They finally reached the sales office.

When they entered, the blast of cold air from the air conditioner was a welcome relief from the heat and her fever.

A man was seated by the window, reading a newspaper. He peered around the paper at them, then looked back to what he was reading. At the reception counter, Riley saw Cristina's smiling face. Her hair was shorter than the last time Riley had seen her, and the streak of white that ran through the front was styled neatly to the side, looking very distinctive. She had the same surname as Tony, but they weren't related. That was always a source of fun for them.

When Cristina saw them there and realized who they were, her smile dropped, but then came back.

"Hi, Janey, Richie, Susan, and Tim, what can I do for you? Don't tell me. The Janottis are playing their music too loud again and your dad sent you in to complain?"

Riley frowned at Cristina and wondered if she had them confused with someone else. But she'd known Riley and Danny for years.

"No, we, um . . . ," Danny started.

"Oh, wait, yeah, of course, Richie," Cristina said. "Sorry, you needed to see Tony, didn't you?"

"Uh, yeah," Danny said.

She nodded over to the man seated by the window. "I'll be right back. I'm just gonna take them to see Tony. He's been waiting for them."

Riley glanced at the man at the window. He nodded at Cristina and then went back to reading his paper. Riley noticed how his posture was stiff and he was wearing heavy black polished leather shoes. Everyone at the marina always wore sneakers or deck shoes.

Suddenly her senses were on full alert.

"This way, guys," Cristina said lightly. She was sounding strange and unusually friendly.

They reached Tony's office and Cristina didn't bother to knock. She pushed open the door and ushered them in.

Tony was seated at his desk, wearing his usual gray sweatshirt. It didn't matter the temperature outside; he always wore sweats. His salt-and-pepper hair was cut short, just like his beard. When he saw them standing there, he stood up. "Close the door, Cristina."

Tony crossed to Riley in three long strides and whispered tightly, "What on earth is going on with you guys? The police have been crawling all over this place. They said your mom has kidnapped a family and they're looking for her."

Riley gasped. Josh was right. The police were here. It felt like they were closing in.

"We haven't kidnapped anyone," Danny insisted. "It's all a big misunderstanding."

"Yeah," Jill said sincerely. "We haven't been kidnapped. We wanted to come."

"Then what's going on?" Tony said. "They've canceled your mom's reservation for the boat. They're waiting for her to show up."

"These guys are serious," Cristina said. "That guy in the reception area is an FBI agent. He's been here since yesterday."

"Tony, please," Riley said. "We can't tell you everything, but we really need a boat. Can you help us?"

"I can't," he said. "The police and feds are watching us like a hawk. They'll arrest me if I help you."

Riley looked at her brother and then pleaded with Tony. "It's a matter of life and death. If you don't let us have a boat, I'm going to die. So are Alfie and some good friends of ours." She leaned closer. "Here, feel my head. Alfie and I have a bad fevers. We're getting sicker by the moment."

Tony reached out and felt Alfie's forehead while Cristina felt Riley's. "You're burning up!" she cried. "You should be in a hospital."

"A hospital can't save us," Riley said. "But we know

of a place that can. And we need a boat to get there."

"Where?" Cristina asked.

Riley shook her head. "I'm sorry, I can't tell you. Not now."

"But we're friends," Cristina said. "You can trust us."

Tony looked at her. "You'd better go back out there before that G-man gets suspicious and comes back here. I'll tell you what's happening."

Cristina was reluctant to go, but finally nodded.

"Remember, keep it light," Tony warned.

When Cristina was gone, his expression became even more serious. "All right, guys, talk to me. What's going on? You say you need a boat, but none of the marinas around here will rent one to you, not with that warrant out there for your mother's arrest. Why are you here and not in a hospital?"

Riley looked at her brother and then Alfie. She'd known Tony all of her life, as her father had kept the *Event Horizon* here long before she was born. Finally she said, "We have to tell him."

15

THEY ASKED TONY TO SIT DOWN AS Riley and Alfie quickly told him the story of their arrival and subsequent escape from Atlantis. Riley felt sick telling him, like she was somehow betraying everyone there. But they had no choice. Tony needed to understand the seriousness of the situation.

When they finished, he shook his head. "Atlantis? Really."

Riley could see that he didn't believe a word of their story. "I know it all sounds unbelievable. But it's true. Somehow, spending time in Atlantis changed us. Now we can't survive away from it. We're sick, but there are others with us who are much worse."

Her voice softened. "It might even be too late for one of them. . . ."

"Riley, Danny, I've known you for all of your lives," Tony said. "But I have to say, this is impossible to accept. Every mariner knows the story of the lost city of Atlantis. But it's just a story. Like mermaids and the Loch Ness monster."

Riley looked at him. "Mermaids are real," she said. "They're in Atlantis too. They're the ones that controlled the storm that took us there."

"And the monster, the Leviathan that sank your boat," Tony repeated. "Are you saying they controlled that too?"

"Yes," Alfie insisted.

"Look, Tony," Danny said. "You don't have to take our word for it. We can prove everything we just told you."

"How?" Tony asked.

Danny looked at Riley and Alfie. "We have to show him Maggie and the others. He needs to understand how serious this is." He turned back to Tony. "Come with us. We can show you some Atlanteans that are much sicker than Riley and Alfie. If you can't help us, they'll all die."

Riley could see that Tony still didn't believe a word they said. "Mom is parked not far from here. Come with us and we'll show you."

"I don't know, kids," he said reluctantly.

Danny stood and leaned closer to him. "This is the most important decision you'll make in your life. Please, just give us five minutes. If after you've met the others, you don't want to help, fine, we'll have to find another way. But after all these years, can't you just give us five minutes?"

Tony looked at each of them in turn. "Five minutes. No more than that."

Several minutes later they left Tony's office. They were all laughing, and Tony was saying, "I can't believe your dad just did that. How many times have I warned him about it?"

"I know," Danny said, "but you know Dad."

They walked forward through reception past Cristina and Melissa, who was also working there, and straight for the door.

The FBI agent didn't even look up as they breezed past him.

Riley felt like she was going to throw up when

they hit the Florida heat again. This time it wasn't just her headache or the fever—it was the terror from walking past the FBI agent.

They kept smiling and laughing as they moved away from the sales office and through the parking lot.

"Nice and easy," Tony said. "I don't know how many cops are here, but there are a few."

Riley painted on a smile but was frightened that the fear in her eyes would give them away as they walked through the parking area and back out onto the public streets. The motor home was two blocks away, but this felt like the longest walk of her life.

They turned down the street where everyone was waiting. As they approached the motor home, Tony said, "Tennessee plates?"

"We kept changing them as we came," Danny said. "But we were nearly caught stealing new plates in Georgia, so we left these ones on."

"That's smart," Tony said. "I heard they were looking for your RV, but with the Colorado plates." He paused and looked at Jill. "You're sure you and your family want to be here?"

Jill nodded. "Yes. If we can't go, they're going to

separate us and put us in foster care. We don't want that."

"What about your mother?"

"Mom ran away and abandoned us. We want to go to Atlantis where we can all stay together."

Once again doubt rose on Tony's face as he turned to Danny. "Guys, it's one thing to believe in Atlantis, but, I mean, they think you've kidnapped these kids. Do you have any idea what could happen if you're caught? You could all end up in foster care and your mom in prison."

"We're not going to be caught," Alfie said. "We're going to Atlantis."

When they reached the door, Riley paused. "You might want to call Cristina and tell her you're going to be late coming back. Once you meet everyone, you'll understand."

"How about I see what you mean first, and then I'll call. I'm really curious to see this sleeping gargoyle."

Riley pulled open the door and invited Tony in. He walked up the steps and saw everyone jammed in there. Then his eyes landed on Gideon in the back berth, and he stopped.

"Like I told you, he's stone during the day," Riley said.

"Tony," Beverly called. She left Maggie and walked forward. "I'm so glad to see you." She embraced him warmly. "I assume the kids have told you about Atlantis. We really need your help. It's Maggie—if we don't get her home—well, it won't be good."

Beverly drew Tony back to Maggie. "None of us knew that once you've spent time in Atlantis, you can't leave. Maggie is very old and has been there the longest, so she is suffering the most."

Tony stood staring at Maggie for several minutes without speaking. He reached down and touched her arm lightly. Then he lifted one of Maggie's hands and inspected the claws at the end of her fingers. He pulled at the skin and gasped. "This isn't a costume. . . ."

"No, Maggie is very real, but very sick," Beverly said. "All my medical training and I can't help her."

"Tony," Mary called as she climbed down slowly from the upper berth. She walked unsteadily down the aisle. "It's good to see you again."

Tony gasped at the sight of the talking spider monkey walking toward him. "I—I—" he stammered.

"It's me, Mary Evans," Mary said. "I'm Andrew's sister. We met earlier this year when we took out the *Event Horizon*. Of course, I looked a lot different then."

Tony gasped again. "Mary?" He looked from Mary to Maggie and then to Gideon. "I'm dreaming, aren't I? This is just a dream."

"It's becoming a nightmare," Riley said. "If you can't help us get hold of a boat right now, we're all going to die."

"I—I just don't understand," Tony said. "How is any of this possible? Atlantis doesn't exist—it can't, it's just a myth!"

"It does exist. I know because I'm from there," Pea called. "Sarah, would you help me down, please?"

Sarah walked to the berth up front and lifted Pea down. She carried him to Tony. "I don't know if Jill told you about us, but my brothers and sisters and I want to go to Atlantis with everyone. We haven't been kidnapped."

"But the police are looking for you," Tony said.

"We don't want to be found," Jill added. "I told you, we all want to go."

"They will be treasured in Atlantis," Pea said. "I

am Pea; it is a pleasure to meet you. Please forgive my appearance, I am rather unwell. They've been wetting me down to ease the fever and I am quite unkempt."

Tony's mouth hung open as he looked at Pea. "You're a, you're a . . ."

"Koala," Riley said.

"No, I'm a ship's carpenter," Pea corrected.

"You're a seaman?" Tony cried.

Pea nodded. "I was for a great many years. But now, this is me. I must beg you on behalf of everyone I love, please, help us get back to Atlantis."

The color drained from Tony's face as he looked at everyone in the motor home. Finally, he turned back to Riley. "Okay, you got my attention. First, I'm calling Cristina and letting her know I won't be back today. Then I want you to tell me everything again."

Riley and Alfie repeated the story of their experience in Atlantis. This time with Pea and Mary's help. When they finally finished, Tony sat down on the edge of Maggie's bunk and shook his head.

"You can't get back there," he said softly. "There isn't a boat in Florida that you can hire. Your cards have all been canceled. The moment you try to go anywhere to get one, the police will arrest you. And even if you did manage to get hold of a boat, unless it's a sailboat like your old one, which would be too slow, would you know how to drive it? And then there's the built-in GPS, which could be used to track you. Will you know how to disable one?"

"We're desperate, Tony, we have to try," Beverly said. "Even if I have to stay and go to jail, I will not let them down. We need a boat, and if I have to steal one and break the GPS, so be it."

"You're not going to jail, Mom," Riley said. "You're coming with us." She turned back to Tony. "You said the new high-tech boats have GPS and tracking stuff—what about older boats?"

"No, not usually, unless the owners put them in. Why?" Tony asked.

Riley looked at her mother and then at everyone in the motor home. "There's only one solution. We have to steal the *Moon Dancer*."

"What?!" Tony cried. "You can't take the *Moon Dancer*! It's been federally seized. The court case determining its ownership is this week, and once it's decided, everyone's going to be all over it."

"Who do you think is going to get it?" Alfie asked.

Tony shrugged. "My money will be on the family. They'll have to pay back the insurance company because it paid out after the *Moon Dancer* was declared lost at sea all those years ago."

"But they're not the real owners of the *Moon Dancer*." Riley pointed to Bastian. "He is. That's Sebastian Fleetwood. He's the son of Adrian Fleetwood, who owned the *Moon Dancer*. His parents are gone, so by rights, shouldn't the *Moon Dancer* belong to Bastian?"

Tony stared at Bastian for several heartbeats. "You're Sebastian Fleetwood?"

When Bastian nodded, Tony shook his head. "How is this possible? When you guys brought her back, I read the history of the *Moon Dancer*. She's famous. She disappeared in 1929 in the Bermuda Triangle and was declared lost. That would mean you're . . ."

"Really old," Alfie finished tiredly. "We know."

"And I am not lost," Bastian said. He reached down and stroked the dog. "Neither is Miss Pigglesworth. We've been on Atlantis all this time."

Tony gasped. "That's Miss Pigglesworth? I read about her too. She was Sebastian's governess."

"She still is my governess," Bastian said. "She might have changed a bit. . . ."

"A bit," Tony choked. "She's a dog! What happened to her?"

"I told you," Riley said. "After a *really* long time in Atlantis, the people start to change. They turn into animals."

"Or if you spend too long in the Forbidden Zone," Mary added, "the change is much quicker. I still think it's ground zero for some kind of radiation. As you can see, I turned into a monkey in a matter of months. My brother, Andrew, is still in Atlantis waiting for us."

"Andrew is alive!" Tony cried.

"Yes," Mary said. "But he's a dolphin."

"A dolphin? This is just so hard to accept," Tony said.

"Whether you believe it all or not," Alfie said, "the *Moon Dancer* belongs to Bastian. So we're not really going to steal it—we're just returning it to its rightful owner."

Tony shook his head. "Look, I'm really sorry for all of you, I truly am. But you can't take the *Moon Dancer*. She's locked up tight and chained to the dock—I don't have the key. The feds do. And we have cameras everywhere. You'll be seen and caught."

"We don't have a choice," Beverly said.

"If there's a lock on that chain, maybe I can break into it," Josh said.

"No," Gideon announced as he came fully awake. "I will break the chains and free the boat."

Riley didn't realize how long they'd been talking. But if Gideon was awake, it was past sunset. She watched Tony's reaction to the talking gargoyle. If he'd been shocked by Maggie, Pea, and Mary, he was completely terrified of Gideon.

"Tony, it's all right," Riley said. "I told you, Gideon is a close friend."

"But—but . . . ," Tony said.

"Tony, please," Beverly said. "Gideon is no threat to you, but he's in danger here too. This world has no place for people like him or the others. We have to get them home. Will you help us take the *Moon Dancer*?"

"Or if you can't help us, will you at least stay out of our way?" Mary added. "Because one way or another, we are taking that boat tonight."

Tony looked at everyone jammed into the motor

home, from the hopeful faces of the Decker children to the pleading expressions of the Atlanteans. Finally, he looked at Riley and sighed.

"It'll cost me my job, and I'll most certainly end up in prison, but okay. Let's steal the *Moon Dancer*."

16

TONY STAYED IN THE MOTOR HOME AS they drew up their plans for the night.

"All right," he said. "The *Moon Dancer* is going to need more sails. You can't go out with just the one from your old boat, as you'll be too slow—I think I saw a delivery of sails come in for a client a few days ago. I don't know what's in there, but they're a start. Next, we're going to need a boat to tow her out of port."

"Oh no," Riley said as her spirits dropped. "I forgot about that."

"We obviously can't use any of the towing companies. Everyone around here knows the *Moon Dancer* and that she's been seized pending the court decision. No one will touch her."

"What can we do?" Danny asked. "Can we sail her out?"

Tony shook his head. "No, it's too tight in there. We need something else. . . ." He fell silent and looked down at the floor. It seemed like he had something very heavy on his mind or that he was trying to decide something.

"Tony," Gideon said. "Is everything all right?"

Finally, Tony looked up and sighed. "I have a boat."

Riley gasped. "You do?"

He nodded. "Before you get too excited, it's not big enough for everyone to fit on her, but being a scarab, she's powerful and fast and should be able to tow the *Moon Dancer* away from here. We move boats all the time—if it's me, there shouldn't be too many questions."

"Will you be endangering yourself if you do this?" Gideon asked.

Tony wouldn't answer for a long time, then said, "It doesn't matter. What matters is getting you all home."

"Thank you, Tony!" Riley cried as she threw her arms around him. "You've saved our lives."

They couldn't make a move for several hours, until the traffic at the marina settled down for the night. While they waited, Tony went out and brought back several pizzas as their last meal before departure.

Gideon was astounded by the taste of pizza and practically ate a whole pie by himself. "There are many things about this modern world that I do not like," the gargoyle said. "But pizza is not one of them. This is wonderful. Who would have thought that pineapple would be so delicious served this way with tomato and cheese."

"Yeah," Danny said. "This, I am going to miss, unless we figure out how to make it there."

"No more pizza?" Robbi asked as she was on her third slice. "But I love pizza."

"Nope," Jill said. "So eat slower and enjoy it."

Pea and Mary weren't feeling well enough to eat while Maggie remained unconscious. Her fever had come down a bit, but with everyone in the motor home, even with the air conditioner on, it was hot and stuffy.

Bastian and Miss Pigglesworth were also feeling terrible, but like Gideon, Bastian had a love of pizza and managed to eat a slice before needing to lie down again.

Tony was watching everyone and leaned closer to Riley. "They really aren't well, are they?"

Riley shook her head. "They're suffering a lot more than me or Alfie. I mean, we're bad, but they're so much worse."

Tony turned to Beverly. "And you have no idea what's wrong?"

"No," Beverly said. "But I can't do a full blood workup. I tried a while ago, but there were so many anomalies with Riley's, Bastian's, and Alfie's blood. It was causing too many questions we couldn't answer, so I had to stop. Without those tests, we have no idea what's causing this illness."

"So you don't really know if getting them back there will help," Tony said.

"Not completely, but I do know they're getting sicker. If leaving Atlantis is the cause of their illness, I hope getting them back is the cure."

"There was old text I found relating to it," Gideon added. "It said what would happen to those who left

Atlantis and that they should return. So we must assume everyone will recover when we do."

"Does that mean you'd get sick, too, if you moved away?" Riley asked.

Gideon shrugged his thick shoulders. "I do not know. We gargoyles have never spent any time away from Atlantis once we made it our home. But it seems logical that it would apply to us."

Tony checked his watch and stood up. "It's almost eleven. I'm going back to the marina to open up my boat. He handed Riley his cell phone. "I'll check the area out and see if the police have gone. When it's safe, I'll call, and you bring the RV onto the property. You've seen the *Moon Dancer* at the pier. Park the RV beside the warehouse, as that's the closest to it. Just know there will still be some people around and parties happening on boats, so act casual. We'll worry about getting the others on board later. Let's just get everything loaded first."

He opened the door a crack, peered out, and then left the motor home. "I'll call as soon as I'm ready."

When he left, Danny locked the door after him. "Do you think we can trust him? I mean, really trust him?"

"We don't have much choice," Beverly said. "We know what will happen if we don't. We won't get anywhere, and Maggie will . . ."

She never finished her comment, but Riley understood. If they didn't go soon, Maggie would die. Pea and Mary too. Not to mention Miss Pigglesworth and Bastian and then maybe even her and Alfie.

"He won't tell," Riley said. She looked back at Gideon. "I think he's too scared of you to do it."

Gideon shook his head. "That didn't seem to stop Mike or the others."

"But Tony is different," Riley said.

Gideon nodded. "Indeed he is. I can feel that he is a good man."

They did what little they could around the motor home to prepare to leave. But with so many people in such a confined space, it was difficult, so all they could do was wait.

Bastian was taking his turn on the floor, while Robbi and Pauly sat on the bench seat. Riley and Jill were seated on the edge of the bed beside Maggie.

Suddenly Bastian started to shout, "Miss Pigglesworth, Miss Pigglesworth! Wake up, please wake up!"

Tears filled his eyes as he looked at Riley. "Help me, please. I can't wake her!"

Riley and her mother rushed to Miss Pigglesworth. "Danny, help me lift her onto the table," Beverly said.

Moments later, Miss Pigglesworth was lying on the small dining table. "I was just talking to her," Bastian said. "Then she said she felt strange and passed out. Please, Beverly, please save her. I can't lose her. She's the only family I have left."

Beverly reached for her medical bag, pulled out her stethoscope, and pressed it against the dog's gray fur. "She's breathing, but her heart is slowing and she's burning up. She's just like Maggie." Beverly turned around and grabbed the last bottle of water. "She needs this more than we do."

Miss Pigglesworth was soon drenched in water. Though it cooled her down a bit, she was still very hot and unconscious.

Riley felt helpless as she saw the tears sparkling in Bastian's eyes. She couldn't imagine what it would do to him to lose Miss Pigglesworth. She reached for his hands and gave them a squeeze. "She won't leave you, Bastian. Miss Pigglesworth loves you and is strong. You'll see. We'll get her back to Atlantis, and she'll be fine." Riley looked up to her mother. "What's taking Tony so long?"

Almost as though he'd heard her plea, the phone rang. The caller ID said it was Cristina.

"Hello?" Riley said cautiously.

"Riley, it's me," Tony said. "I've opened the private gates leading to *Moon Dancer*'s slip. Tell your mom to bring in the RV."

"Sure, see you in a bit." Riley signed off. "Tony said it's time."

"Thank heavens." Her mother moved into the driver's seat. Just before they pulled away, Beverly called, "Josh, Sarah, Jill, Pauly, and Robbi, this is it. This is your last chance to change your mind. After this, there's no going back."

Jill was standing beside Riley. "I'm not changing my mind. I want to go."

"We all do," Josh said. He called forward. "We still wanna come."

"All right," Beverly called. "Everyone, sit down, and let's go."

17

RILEY WAS STILL HOLDING BASTIAN'S
trembling hands as they drove toward Grove Harbour
Marina. They turned in and slowed down as they
made their way toward the hangar-like warehouse. It
was here that the marina staff worked on boats to put
them in dry dock.

"She'll be fine," Riley said to him. "Miss
Pigglesworth is just sleeping, like Maggie."

Bastian raised his miserable eyes to her. "If anything were to happen to her . . ."

"It won't," Alfie snapped. "She'll be fine. We all
will."

Riley leaned over and gave Bastian a gentle kiss on

the cheek. "You'll see, we'll get on the boat tonight and she'll be up and running around in days."

Danny was in the passenger seat and called, "Mom, there's Tony over there; he's waving us in. Oh no, that's Cristina with him."

"I hope he hasn't told her," Alfie said.

"I hope so, too, but if he did, it's not going to change anything. We're leaving tonight," Danny said.

They were barely stopped before Tony was knocking on the door. Josh unlocked it and opened it up.

"Come on, let's start loading her," Tony said. "I've told Mario, our guard, to patrol the other side of the marina for a bit. We have some time, but not a lot. Cristina's here to help, so let's get moving before Mario returns."

Riley looked to Gideon. "We'll get the boat loaded and then you can come out. Would you be able to carry Maggie?"

"I will," Gideon said. "We will wait here until you say it is safe."

Jill and her family were the first off, and the frantic rush to get everything off the motor home began. While they were outside, Danny stood in the doorway as Beverly, Riley, and Alfie brought things to him to give to the others.

Bastian was still seated with Miss Pigglesworth, and Riley noticed how no one told him to get to work.

After the motor home was emptied, Riley and Alfie left it to join the others unloading the trailer they had towed.

Riley walked up to Cristina and embraced her. "Thank you for helping us."

"I don't understand what's happening. Tony says it's serious."

Riley nodded. "It is, very."

They walked to the trailer together and started to carry items. Riley was aware of how slow she and Alfie were working. Everyone else was moving at light speed compared to their slow pace. She was happy she could move at all, considering how bad she was feeling.

All the luggage and items were soon stacked up beside the *Moon Dancer*. Danny and Josh leaped up on board. "All right," Danny whispered tightly. "Start tossing stuff over."

No one among them dared speak in anything other than a soft whisper. Loud music was coming from a boat not too far from the *Moon Dancer*. When

Riley asked Cristina about it, she said, "Generally we don't allow people to spend the night on their boats. But we make exceptions for those who want to set off early in the morning, or if a crew from a bigger boat is preparing it for departure. I know for a fact the *Dragon's Breath* over there is heading out at six."

"We'll be long gone before then," Riley said. She saw the big FEDERAL SEIZURE warning sign that was hanging from the brass rail on the *Moon Dancer*. Then there was the thick chain holding it to the slip. Gideon was strong; she just hoped he was strong enough to break the chain.

Riley felt every second ticking by. Her heart was pounding as they worked to get everything on the yacht as quickly as possible. The hardest items to get aboard were the two treadle sewing machines in their stands. At one point, it was discussed leaving them behind, but in the end, they couldn't do it. They were a gift to Maggie, and they were going to be in Atlantis when she awoke from her coma.

After a few minutes, Cristina came back to Riley. "That's a lot of stuff you're taking. How long are you going to be away? And what's with those old sewing machines?"

Riley looked at her. Cristina had already helped them so much, including with the loading, that she deserved a bit of an explanation. "We're not coming back," Riley said softly. "And where we're going, there's no electricity."

"Where's that?" Cristina said. "I mean, even the remotest islands in the Bahamas have electricity."

"Not this place," Riley said. "It's extra special."

"It must be," Cristina said. "Tony's asked me to delete the security camera files after you go. You guys must be in big trouble if the FBI is looking for you and you're stealing this boat."

Riley nodded. "They think we've abducted my friend Jill and her family. But do they look like they're being kidnapped?"

They both turned and watched Sarah and Jill handing items over to Josh and Danny. Robbi and Pauly were doing what they could as well.

"Not at all," Cristina said.

Riley turned to her. "Their mother abandoned them, and they don't have a father or family. If we didn't take them with us, they'd go into foster care and be separated. They didn't want that—neither do we. So they asked to come with us, and we said yes."

"But where are you going that the authorities won't find you? There are very few places without extradition."

"I really wish I could tell you," Riley said. "But the less you know, the less trouble you can get into. Besides, you wouldn't believe me if I told you."

"Try me," Cristina said. "I've heard some pretty odd stories."

"Not this one," Riley said.

Moments later they heard the idling sound of a powerful boat getting closer. The area was lit with streetlights, and Riley saw Tony coming with his speedboat.

Alfie came up to her. "Shorty, do you see that? It looks way fast."

"I hope it's strong enough to tow the *Moon Dancer*," Riley said. "It looks so small compared to it."

"Oh, it's strong enough," Cristina said. "I just hope Tony knows what he's doing. He loves that boat. If we're caught, we'll all be prosecuted, and he'll lose it."

"If we're caught," Alfie said, "half of us will die."

"I still don't understand," Cristina said.

"It's better if you don't," Riley said.

The *Moon Dancer* was chained at the end of the

longest dock in the marina that was used only for the biggest yachts, so there weren't any other boats next to them. Tony positioned his boat in front of her bow.

Beverly came over. "We're almost ready to go. Would you and Alfie go get the others while we finish here?" She turned to Cristina. "I can't tell you how much we appreciate your help. But you'd better go—you don't want to see what comes next."

Cristina smiled but made no move to leave. "If I'm risking my job and possibly my freedom, I want to know why."

Beverly nodded. "If you insist. Will you help us load the last bits and pieces while Riley and Alfie go get the others?"

"There are more of you?" Cristina asked.

"Yes," Beverly said. "Come with me and I'll explain before you meet them."

While her mother and Cristina walked away, Riley and Alfie headed back to the motor home. When they entered, Riley called, "We're ready to go. Gideon, are you all right with Maggie?"

"I am," Gideon said as he struggled to move around in the tight confines of the motor home. He bent down and lifted Maggie in his arms gently.

Riley and Alfie walked over to Bastian and Miss Pigglesworth. As Riley stroked the unconscious dog, she asked, "How is she? Any change?"

Bastian shook his head. "No, and I'm so scared."

"Don't be," Alfie said. "We're leaving now, and she'll be fine." He turned to Riley. "Shorty, if you get Mom and Pea, Bastian and I will carry Miss Pigglesworth."

Riley nodded and walked farther forward. Pea and her aunt were still in the upper berth. "Are you ready to go?"

"I am," Pea said.

"So am I," Mary said as she climbed down.

Riley reached up and wrapped her hands around Pea.

"I am well enough to walk," Pea said.

"But I'm faster," Riley countered as she settled him in her arms.

Mary didn't argue as Riley picked her up. Her aunt was much heavier than Pea, but it wasn't a long journey to the *Moon Dancer*. She could feel the heat coming from both of them as their fevers climbed. She started toward the door and was the first one down the steps.

"Oh, that's much better," Pea said. "That motor home is so stuffy. But the night air is wonderful."

Next outside were Bastian and Alfie as they struggled to carry Miss Pigglesworth. "She's heavier than I thought," Alfie grunted.

"Just don't drop her," Bastian said.

They moved away from Riley and carried the unconscious dog toward the boat.

The motor home beside Riley started to rock as Gideon walked down the aisle. He was soon blocking out the light on the stairs as he dipped down and squeezed through the entrance with Maggie in his arms.

"It is so tight. . . ." Gideon grunted as he forced his large body through the doorway. Finally he was free and down on the ground. He opened his wings and gave them a flap before settling them on his back again. "That was not pleasant."

"At least you won't have to go back in there," Riley said. She stepped closer and stroked Maggie's brow. "She still has the fever. C'mon, it's this way."

They made it back to the *Moon Dancer* and saw that the Decker children were already on board. Beverly was working with Cristina, and Bastian worked with

Alfie and Danny to get Miss Pigglesworth safely aboard. When she was, they helped Bastian climb up on deck. "Ah, there she is," Gideon said. "I didn't imagine I would ever see her again."

"Me too," Riley agreed.

Cristina turned and her eyes opened wide at the sight of Gideon standing with Riley. She inhaled sharply.

Riley's mother said, "Cristina, don't scream, you'll draw attention to us. It's all right. I told you about Gideon and the others. Please, don't offend them."

"There would be no offense, Beverly," Gideon said gently. "Humans are never prepared for us."

"I—I'm sorry," Cristina stammered as she looked up at the immense gargoyle. "But when Beverly told me, I never imagined that you'd be so—so . . ."

Gideon chuckled, and Pea said, "So handsome? Gideon often has this effect on people."

Cristina's eyes shot to Pea. "You do speak!"

"Of course," Pea said. "It is a pleasure to meet you and I am grateful for your help."

"We all are," Mary agreed. Whatever her mother had told Cristina, it obviously wasn't enough. Riley added quickly, "Do you understand now why we need to take the *Moon Dancer*?"

"Ah yes, I do," Cristina said. She focused on Gideon. "But how do you know this yacht?"

"I was the one that helped the others fix her so they could take her away from Atlantis in the first place."

"Atlantis?" Cristina said. "You're going to Atlantis? It's real?"

"I hadn't told her about that," Beverly said.

"Oh," Gideon said. "My mistake. Yes, Cristina, Atlantis is very real. Now, if you will forgive me, Maggie isn't well, and I must get her settled on board." He opened his wings and flew gracefully onto the deck of the yacht.

Cristina watched him fly and then turned to Riley again. "Atlantis, really?"

Riley nodded. "It's hidden, but it does exist. Now that you know, please don't tell anyone where we're going."

"Who'd believe me?" Cristina said. "I hardly believe it."

Danny came over and reached for Mary. "I'll help you on board, Aunt Mary."

"Thank you, dear," Mary said. She looked at Cristina. "I wish we had more time to talk and explain, but we must go."

"Of—of course," Cristina said. "I promise you all I won't say a word. Now I understand why Tony wanted me to delete the camera files. I'll do that right after you go."

"Thank you, Cristina," Pea said. "Like Mary said, I wish we had more time to chat. That is, unless you wish to join us. There is plenty of room."

For the first time since meeting the Atlanteans, Cristina smiled. "Thank you, Pea, but no. I have family and friends here. But I appreciate the invitation. Besides, I have to cover your tracks once you go."

Moments later, Gideon returned. "Now, where is that chain?"

"I'll show you." Cristina led Gideon and Riley over to the thick chain that kept the *Moon Dancer* locked to the dock. "It's really thick."

Gideon picked it up and, with no effort at all, snapped the chain. He chuckled. "It's a shame I won't see the authorities' reaction to that." He took Pea from Riley's arms and turned to Cristina. "It was a pleasure to meet you, Cristina," He bowed elegantly and then returned to the *Moon Dancer*.

"Riley, come on," Alfie called softly from the deck. "We gotta go!"

Riley gave Cristina a final hug. "Thank you again."

"You stay safe, Riley," Cristina said. "And get them all back home."

Riley nodded. "We will. I hope you don't get in too much trouble."

Cristina grinned. "I'm like a cat—I always land on my feet."

18

RILEY MADE IT ONTO THE *MOON DANCER* and helped Gideon and her mother settle Maggie back in the same cabin she was in when they left Atlantis. Seeing her looking so frail and weak sent shivers down Riley's spine.

"Just hold on, Maggie, we'll be home soon," Riley said as she covered Maggie and kissed her on the forehead.

By the time she made it back on deck and walked up to the bow, she saw Danny and Josh securing the ropes that connected them to Tony's boat, which would tow the *Moon Dancer* away from the port.

"How's Maggie?" Danny asked.

"Not good," Riley said. "Neither is Miss Pigglesworth. Bastian's in his old cabin with her and won't leave it. I hope we get there fast."

"We're about to get underway," Danny said.

Most of the group gathered on the deck and felt the first jolt as the scarab revved its engines and started to tug the much bigger yacht away from the dock.

The sound of the scarab's engines worried Riley. They were so loud. There was no way they could hide them or the fact that the scarab was towing the *Moon Dancer*. Would those still on-site accept it? Or call the police because the famous yacht was moving?

"Come on, everyone," Danny said once they were going. "We have to get the sails Tony gave us up."

Riley didn't know whether it was the anxiousness of leaving or whether she was getting sicker, but she felt awful. Looking at Alfie and the way he moved, she knew he was just as bad, so the last thing she wanted to do was work. But she'd been practically raised on their old family boat and knew how to set the sails. This gave her no choice but to force herself to move.

While Robbi and Pauly held flashlights, the others opened the boxes and pulled out several sails.

They had been made for a different boat and didn't fit properly. Just like with the sail from the *Event Horizon*, they had to make do and get creative with the rigging.

Not long after they got the first sail laid out along the deck, there was a loud shout from the end of the dock. Mario, the security guard, was running the length of it, yelling at Tony to stop.

Riley and the others paused to watch. Tony said if he was asked, he would say they were moving the *Moon Dancer* to a new location in preparation for the handover to the new owners. But that wouldn't work now. They were beyond the marina and being drawn toward open water.

The guard was lifting his phone to his ear when they saw Cristina run up to him and snatch his phone away and toss it into the water. After that, they appeared to be arguing.

Finally, the guard stormed off. Cristina waved them forward, shouting, "Go, go!" before chasing after him.

"Perhaps I should stop him," Gideon said while watching Cristina chasing the guard.

"No," Beverly said. "We need you here to help

us get these sails up! Come on, everyone, let's get to work before he calls the Coast Guard."

Riley put her head down and worked with Gideon and the others to get the sails up. The job seemed unending and was exhausting, but finally they finished, and the new sails filled with wind, taking some of the pressure off the scarab.

When the work was complete, all the lights were extinguished, casting the *Moon Dancer* into complete darkness. They hoped it would make them harder to be seen by any nearby boats or ships.

As the night pressed on, the younger children were taken to bed in some of the cabins. Riley felt sick and dizzy but couldn't rest. She sat down on the deck, leaning against the cabin's outer walls, just hoping her head would clear.

"Are you bad too?" Alfie asked as he settled beside her.

Riley nodded. "I am so tired of feeling sick. The headache is worse than the fever. I feel awful."

"Me too," Alfie agreed. "I really hope it gets better when we reach Atlantis."

"It has to. . . ."

As they sat together, Riley gazed out over the black ocean, even though she couldn't see anything. Then she looked up at the stars twinkling above them. It was only then that she realized they were still being towed. "Didn't Tony say he was going to tow us out of port?"

"Yeah, so?"

"So we're out of port and he's still towing us."

Alfie paused. "You're right. He should've left by now."

Jill approached Riley and sat down on her other side. "I know why Tony is still here. I heard him and Beverly talking while you went to get Pea and the others from the motor home. He said if the Coast Guard chases us with their cutters, they'll catch the *Moon Dancer* really quickly. But with his boat, we can go farther and much faster, so it will be harder for them to find us. He said he'd stay as long as he could."

"That's so kind of him," Riley said.

"I just hope Cristina stopped Mario from calling the police or Coast Guard," Alfie said.

"They're going to find out anyway," Riley said. "Tomorrow morning, everyone is going to realize the

Moon Dancer is missing. I worry about how much trouble Tony is going to be in."

"Maybe he could tell them we held him at gunpoint or something," Alfie said.

"Maybe," Riley agreed. She leaned her head back and felt the world spinning around. In all her life, she'd never been seasick. But she felt it now and wished she hadn't eaten the pizza.

The night moved along at a snail's pace for Riley as she sat back, trying not to be sick. Her mother was at the helm, holding the wheel steady so the *Moon Dancer* wouldn't fight the scarab towing her farther out into the deep, dark ocean.

Riley tried to remember how many days it had taken them to get home from Atlantis. It was three or four. But then again, they only had the one small sail from the *Event Horizon*. Now the big yacht had several more, plus the tow.

They never really discussed it, but she worried now how they were going to find Atlantis. It wasn't on any charts, and the first time they went there, it seemed Atlantis found them, not the other way around.

She glanced over and saw Gideon standing at the bow. He must know the way to Atlantis, as he'd flown from there to find them. Was he guiding them back?

At some point in the long night, Riley dozed off. When she awoke again, she discovered she was curled against Alfie, and Jill was sleeping beside her. They were covered in a couple of blankets. Confusion filled her. Then she remembered. They had stolen the *Moon Dancer* and were heading back to Atlantis.

"Morning, sleepyhead," Danny called when Riley sat up.

Riley was stiff and ached all over from sleeping on the hard wooden deck. She climbed slowly to her feet but was quickly overcome with dizziness and fell down again, landing on Alfie.

"Hey!" Alfie complained, coming awake. "Get off!"

"Sorry," Riley said as she fought the dizziness.

Danny was at her side in an instant. "Nice and easy," he said, helping her up. "Not too fast."

With her brother's support, Riley made it to her feet. She looked down and saw that Alfie was already back to sleep. Jill hadn't moved at all.

"Guess I don't need to ask how you're feeling," Danny said.

"Not really." Riley was still dizzy and needed to hold on to her brother to stay up. She looked around and saw that they were far out in the ocean and there was no land around them.

"Any idea where we are? Have we entered the Bermuda Triangle yet?"

Danny shrugged. "All I know is we're somewhere between Miami and Bermuda. It's not like the Triangle has warning signs or stuff like that."

"Ha-ha, very funny," Riley said. She glanced forward and gasped.

Gideon was still standing at the bow. He was stone and looked like a strange figurehead, as one of his arms was pointing out over the water.

"Gideon was directing us when the sun rose and turned him," Danny explained. "It was so fast."

"That's how he got hurt in Atlantis," Riley said. "He was fighting a wildling and turned."

"Well, since we don't want another break, I've tied him to the railings in case that storm you told us about hits."

They walked up to Gideon, and Riley saw the determination on the gargoyle's face as he led them toward Atlantis. Then she looked forward and saw Tony still at the helm of the scarab. "I wonder when he's going to turn back?" Riley asked.

"I don't know," Danny said. "I don't know if he'll have enough fuel to make it back. He said his boat held four hundred gallons, but it has two engines and towing us is using a lot. I just hope he brought extra."

Riley looked at him sharply. "That means he could be stranded out here."

"I know," Danny agreed. "But he does have his phone and radio. I'm sure he'll be fine."

Riley was tempted to call out to Tony, but the roar of the twin engines would be too loud for her voice to get over. "I hope he knows what he's doing."

Laughter erupted on the deck behind them. Riley turned and saw Robbi and Pauly chasing little Chrissy. They were running around playing an easy game of hide-and-seek and would duck behind a mast and then reappear, sending Chrissy into fits of giggles.

"They seem really happy," Riley said. "I hope they like Atlantis."

Danny looked back and smiled when Sarah appeared on the deck and joined the game with her siblings. "If they're together, I'm sure they'd be happy anywhere."

Riley noticed the look in her brother's eyes as he

followed Sarah while she played. It was obvious he really liked her.

"Then I hope *you'll* be happy there," she said, knowing full well what his answer would be.

"I hope so," he said lightly.

Riley shoved him playfully. "Yeah, right."

Danny blushed and said, "What . . . ?"

There were plenty of food rations on board, but Riley couldn't face eating. Neither could Alfie or any of the Atlanteans when they awoke. Instead they stayed on the deck, trying to find relief as their fevers raged.

Bastian, however, remained in the cabin with Miss Pigglesworth. When Riley visited, she found him lying on the floor beside the bunk. He was asleep but moaning softly, as though he were in pain.

Riley pulled down an old pillow and gave it to him. Then she covered him with a blanket. She stroked his hair back from his eyes and felt the heat on his forehead. Just like hers, his fever was climbing.

She considered waking him to check that he was all right, but then changed her mind. There was nothing anyone could do until they reached Atlantis. Riley gave him a soft kiss on the cheek and then left.

Back on deck, Riley sat down again with Pea and Mary. Pea was in and out of sleep as Mary kept a protective arm around him.

"How is he?" Riley asked softly.

"The same," Mary said. "I hope we get there soon."

"Me too," Riley agreed.

They fell silent and sat together, gazing out over the water and praying that they reached Atlantis in time.

Riley was unaware that she'd dozed off. But when Danny shouted, "Mom, they're coming!" she woke with a fright. Struggling to her feet, Riley followed Danny's pointing arm, and in the distance she saw two large boats heading right for them.

"It's the Coast Guard!" Beverly called. "They've found us!"

One hundred years ago, *Moon Dancer* had won awards for her trans-Atlantic speeds. She was the fastest of the age. But that was in the days before Coast Guard cutters. Even with Tony's scarab pulling them, they were nowhere near fast enough to outrun the cutters.

A bullhorn sounded from the closest cutter. "Cut your engines and lower your sails! We're coming aboard."

"Mom, we can't do it!" Danny cried.

Jill and all her family ran to the railing and started shouting for them to go away and leave them alone.

But still the cutters came closer.

Instead of surrendering, they heard the scarab roar as Tony pushed the twin engines to full throttle to haul the sailing yacht even faster.

One of the cutters went for the *Moon Dancer* while the other raced forward and cut across the scarab's bow, forcing Tony to slow down. He couldn't stop fully because the *Moon Dancer* was right behind him, and with her sails still up, she was moving at a good speed and risked hitting him.

Riley was close to panic when the cutter closest to them moved alongside their yacht. It was much smaller than the *Moon Dancer* and didn't come all the way up the side, so the sailors couldn't see everyone on board their yacht. But the cutter was powerful and fast. They couldn't outrun it. "I said lower your sails!" they commanded. "Stop the boat!"

"What's happening?" Pea asked weakly.

"It's the police," Riley said. "I'm so sorry, Pea. They've found us."

19

RILEY FELT TEARS OF FEAR AND FRUS-
tration stinging her eyes. They'd tried so hard and
been through so much to bring everyone home. But
to fail so close was painful beyond imagining. She
checked the sky, and dusk was coming. Gideon would
turn soon, but then what? Would the Coast Guard see?
Would they shoot Gideon, thinking he was a monster?
She considered moving Pea and Mary belowdecks, but
it was pointless. They would be found.

"Go away!" Robbi shouted down at the cutters.

"Leave us alone," Pauly and Jill added.

"Pull in your sails," an officer shouted up at them.
"We're coming aboard."

"Shorty, it's over," Alfie said softly.

"It can't be," Riley wept. "It just can't be. . . ."

They were all too emotional to notice the dark, scudding clouds rising on the horizon. But when the wind picked up suddenly, Riley turned and inhaled sharply.

"Creep, look at the sky."

The clouds were moving at an incredible speed, becoming fuller and darker and heading straight at them. Reds and greens appeared among them, and Riley realized what it meant.

"They found us!" Alfie cried.

"What is that? What's happening?" Danny called.

"It's them!" Riley shouted. She staggered over to her mother. "Mom, look at the sky. The mermaids are doing that, they're coming for us. Atlantis has found us!" She looked over at Jill and the others at the railing and yelled, "The mermaids are here! Call out to them, ask for their help!"

Soon all the Decker children were shouting for help.

"We're coming," one of the sailors on the Coast Guard cutter answered. "Don't worry, kids, we'll save you!"

Riley approached the railing and shouted at the Coast Guard officers. "Not you." She pointed at the darkening sky. "That storm is for us, it's going to bring us home. Please, get out of here before you get hurt!"

The sailors on the cutter looked at the changing sky. Fear was rising on their faces as they stared at the growing maelstrom.

"Please, go now!" Riley shouted at them. "Save yourselves and go!"

Beverly was standing at the wheel, struggling to hold the *Moon Dancer* steady as the waves around them swelled and started to break. "Danny, Josh, Sarah, Riley, and Alfie, pull in the sails. Robbi and Pauly, take Chrissy inside and stay there!"

"I wanna see the mermaids," Robbi complained.

"You will," Riley promised. "But not now. Go inside!"

"And take Pea and Mary with you!" Beverly added.

The first time Riley went through the storm was terrifying because she didn't know what it meant. This time, it wasn't quite as bad because she knew what was happening. But it was still very imposing as the sky swirled around them in colors unimagined for a storm. The ocean swelled and made the old yacht creak and moan as it was lifted and then lowered in the heavy waves. Soon they started to break over the *Moon Dancer*'s deck.

Riley and Alfie worked with the others to pull in the sails before the boat was tipped over in the winds.

"What's happening?" Danny shouted.

"It's the mermaids, they control the storm," Riley called. "Soon the Leviathan will come." Riley had just spoken the words when there was loud, frightened shouting coming from the Coast Guard cutter crossing Tony's bow. All the sailors on board were pointing at the water.

Riley struggled back to the railing and called down to the cutter resting alongside them. "You must go now. It's too dangerous for you to stay here. They don't want you, they're here for us!"

"You must come with us!" one of the sailors called.

"No!" Riley shouted back. "We're going with them. Please leave before it's too late!"

A loud roaring filled the air. Josh screamed and pointed, "What's that?"

"It's the Leviathan," Alfie called. "He's cool, he's on our side!" Then he softly added, "At least I hope he is."

Hidden behind the roaring of the Leviathan and the howling of the winds, Riley heard a sound that was pure music to her troubled head. She struggled to the bow of the *Moon Dancer* and stood beside Gideon.

"Riley, get away from there!" her mother shouted. "Get inside."

"Mom, it's Galina!" Riley called. "Can't you hear her singing? If Galina's here, Dad might be too!"

"Dad's here?" Danny cried. He joined Riley at the bow. Soon Alfie, Sarah, and Josh were with them.

Riley searched the surface of the breaking waves, looking for movement. Then her eyes landed on breath being shot out of a blowhole. "There!" she shouted. Riley started to jump up and down and wave. "Dad! Daddy!"

"Riley!" a high-pitched voice called back.

"Danny, look, there's Dad!" Riley cried joyously.

"Dad?" Danny called as the dolphin broke the surface.

"Danny Boy, I'm so glad to see you!" the dolphin squeaked.

The singing grew louder as Galina surfaced and commanded the Leviathan. The massive creature moved away from Tony's scarab and started to shove the Coast Guard cutter farther from the *Moon Dancer*.

"Galina, tell the Leviathan not to hurt them. Just move them away from us." Riley ran back to the railing near the cutter. "Please, listen to me, you don't understand what's happening. You must go—there's a sea monster. . . ."

Just as she spoke, the Leviathan's head rose above the surface and reared high over the cutter. It roared and snapped at the boat but didn't attack it.

"Go, now!" Alfie warned. "Before it attacks you!"

The sailors on both cutters were shouting in terror. Finally they started to move away at full throttle.

The skies around the *Moon Dancer* and scarab grew even darker and more enveloping. The winds whipped Riley's hair across her face, and the clouds seemed to be touching her cheeks. Yet despite this, she couldn't have been happier.

"Mom!" she shouted excitedly as she ran back to the wheel. "We've done it. We've made it back to Atlantis!"

20

THEY CONTINUED IN THE BLOWING STORM as the waves crashed in all directions and the wind howled and moaned, making the folded sails flap and dance.

Riley stood at the railing near the bow and saw Galina waving. The siren was also looking at Gideon.

"I'm so happy to see you!" Riley shouted down to her. "I have missed you so much, and I have lots to tell you." Riley patted the gargoyle's arm. "Don't worry about Gideon—he's fine. Thanks to you, we're all fine now!"

Just as suddenly as it started, the wind stopped, and the water calmed. The dark clouds cleared, revealing a brilliant blue sky. Directly ahead lay Atlantis. From the ocean, Riley realized it was much bigger than she'd imagined. Even from far away, they couldn't see from one end to the other. Gideon always mentioned the various territories, but somehow, Riley thought they'd be closer than they were.

Riley turned and searched the water behind them for the cutters, but they'd vanished. Or perhaps, she thought, the *Moon Dancer* had been the one to vanish.

A horn blared from the scarab and Riley suddenly realized Tony was still with them.

"Why didn't he go with the Coast Guard?" Alfie asked as he moved up beside Riley.

"I don't know. He's trapped here now."

The rest of the Decker children emerged from the cabins and ran forward. They pointed at Atlantis and started to cheer as they gazed out over the massive island.

"Riley, where's your mother?" her father called from the water.

With the water now calm, she could see her father clearly. All traces of the man he once was were gone. He was a dolphin now. "She's at the wheel," Riley answered.

"Would you go get her? I need to apologize for everything."

Riley nodded and trotted back to her mother. They embraced tightly. "We did it, Mom, we're home!"

"We sure did," her mother responded. Her eyes were huge as she gazed at Atlantis. "It's so beautiful."

Riley nodded. "It really is. Mom, Dad's here and he wants to see you. He's at the bow with Galina."

Her mother hesitated for a moment.

"Mom?" Riley asked. "Are you okay?"

Riley's mother looked uncertain. "I—I don't know if I can see him like that. When we were in Colorado and I saw the video he made for us, it was all right. But somehow now that we're here and he's a—he's a . . . "

"He's a dolphin, Mom. I know it's going to be hard to see him like that. It still is for me. But it's Dad and we'll get used to it. Just like we got used to Mary and what she turned into."

"I'm not married to Mary," her mother said.

"Just talk to him," Riley said. "Close your eyes if you have to. He's asking for you, Mom. Please, try."

Her mother shook her head. "I have to stay here and steer the ship."

Riley moved to take the wheel from her. "I've got this—just go talk to Dad."

Her mother smiled and tilted her head to the side. "Who's the adult here?"

Riley grinned. "Right now, I am. Go—"

"All right, hold her steady." Her mother kissed Riley on the cheek.

Riley watched her mother walk hesitantly toward the bow of the ship. This was the first time in Riley's life that she'd seen her looking uncertain. She was always so confident and sure.

When Beverly reached the railing and looked down, Riley saw her shoulders starting to shake. Danny walked away from the railing and ushered the others away as well, so their parents could talk in private.

Riley knew it would take more than one conversation to heal the rift between her parents. Her mother had been badly hurt when she learned that her husband had chosen to stay in Atlantis instead of coming home.

"Hey Shorty," Alfie said as he came up to her. "How are you feeling?"

"Fine," Riley said automatically. Then she realized she really did feel fine. The fever had broken, and her headache wasn't half as bad. "I can't believe it," she cried happily. "I really do feel fine!"

Alfie grinned. "Me too!"

Tony continued to tow the *Moon Dancer* closer to Atlantis. Just before they reached the shore, the tow line was disconnected. The scarab turned and came alongside the *Moon Dancer.*

Danny dropped the anchor to keep the yacht in place as Tony climbed up the rope ladder onto the deck.

He was shaking his head and staring at Atlantis. "I—I just can't believe it! I mean, I see it, it's right there in front of me, but I just can't believe it! What happened back there with that freaky storm?"

Riley was grinning. "The mermaids did it; they control the storms. They let us through, but not the Coast Guard cutters."

"Mermaids?"

"We told you," Alfie said. "Atlantis has real mermaids."

"But—but that sea serpent . . ."

"The Leviathan," Riley said. "We told you about him too."

"Yeah, but when you said it was big, I never imagined it would be that big!" Tony looked back at his boat. "I was so worried about getting away, I forgot to disable the GPS on my scarab. That's how the Coast Guard found us. It was a stupid mistake and could have been a disaster. I'll disable it now, so they don't find us."

"I don't think they can," Alfie said. "From what I saw, I think we have to be invited in."

"Still, I'm not going to risk it."

Beverly came up to him. Her eyes were red from crying, but her shoulders were back proudly, and her confidence returned. "Tony, why didn't you go with the Coast Guard?"

"I couldn't," Tony said. "When that strange storm hit, just like you said from before, I realized I couldn't leave. I needed to see Atlantis for myself. What mariner could turn away from such an opportunity? I mean, Atlantis. The real Atlantis."

"But you're trapped here," Riley said. "You can't go home."

"Do I look unhappy?" Tony said lightly. He turned back to the island rising above them. "I can't wait to see it all. This is the adventure of a lifetime!"

Pea appeared back on deck. His fur was still a mess from being soaked in water for his fever, but he was moving much better, and his eyes were brighter. He looked at Atlantis and his small shoulders slumped. "So, we're back. . . ."

"Yes we are, Pea." Riley went down on her knees before the koala. "But I promise you, it's going to be different. No more cloaks, no more Red Moons outside. If they try to treat you the same, we'll just come back to the *Moon Dancer* and live here."

Pea brightened. "Do you mean that?"

"Absolutely," Beverly said. "We're family, Pea, and no one does anything to hurt a member of my family."

Before they left the *Moon Dancer*, they untied Gideon and made certain the gargoyle would be safe for the day. Riley looked at the golden sands of the beach spreading before them. This was it. It was time to disembark and see if they would be accepted in Atlantis.

21

IT TOOK SOME TIME TO GET EVERYONE to the beach. Things were especially difficult with getting Maggie and Miss Pigglesworth off the *Moon Dancer*. They had to wrap each of them in blankets and lower them carefully over the side with ropes and into the scarab.

Bastian was feeling a bit better and climbed in the scarab to help with Miss Pigglesworth.

"Nice and easy," he said as the dog was lowered by Josh and Danny. "That's it."

When Miss Pigglesworth was safely on shore, they repeated the process with Maggie. When she was on the scarab, Riley helped settle her carefully.

Her father's head bobbed at the surface. "How is she?"

"Mom thinks she's in a coma," Riley said. "We've all been sick with terrible headaches and fevers, but it was worse for Maggie."

"Gideon told me," her father squeaked. "That's why he went for you. He knew you were in danger."

"Gideon risked his life to save us. We owe him so much."

"He loves you, Riley," her father said. "We both do."

As they idled toward the shore, Riley explained to her father about Jill's family and how they came to be with them. "I'm sure everyone here will love them."

"I'm sure they will," her father agreed.

When they reached the shallows, Tony stopped the boat. He looked down on Andrew in the water. "When Riley told me about you, I couldn't believe it."

"I know, it took a while for me to adjust," Andrew said. "But now, with my family here, I couldn't be happier."

Tony looked at the island before them. "So, I'm going to turn into an animal?"

"We all are," Riley said. "But it takes a really, really long time. Hundreds of years."

"Hundreds?" Tony gasped.

Andrew squeaked, "That's if you don't go into the Forbidden Zone. There it happens really quick. Mary and I turned in a matter of months."

"That's what she told me," Tony said. "I think I'm looking forward to living for a few hundred years!"

When the scarab was stopped, Tony and Riley climbed into the water and gently lifted Maggie down.

"Wake up, Maggie," Riley said as she walked beside Tony, who was carrying Maggie up onto the beach. Bastian was waiting for them onshore and helped settle her down.

"You're home now, Maggie. Please wake up," Bastian said.

When Maggie was resting on the beach, Tony took the scarab back to the *Moon Dancer* to get another load.

Several trips later, everyone was on the beach. "I suggest we go into the Community first," Bastian offered. "We need to get Miss Pigglesworth and Maggie to the doctor. We can come back for the supplies later."

This was the part that had Riley nervous. How would they be received by the Community? Everything was counting on the next few minutes. "Good idea," she said. "I just hope Beresford lets us stay."

"He will," Bastian said confidently.

Riley turned back to the water and saw her mother was standing waist-deep, talking to her father. She hated to disturb them, but they needed to go. "Mom, I'm sorry—we're taking Maggie and Miss Pigglesworth to the Community."

"Coming," her mother called. She said a few more words to Riley's father and then treaded out of the ocean.

While Bastian and Alfie carried Miss Pigglesworth, Tony lifted Maggie up again. Though Pea was feeling better, he was still weak and accepted a ride from Riley while Beverly carried Mary.

"Wow," Jill was saying as she walked beside Riley. "This place is so pretty."

Robbi and Pauly ran up to a vine leaf that was much bigger than they were. "Sarah, look!"

"That's amazing!" Sarah said. She was carrying Chrissy and walking beside Danny, taking in all the sights.

"This whole place is amazing," Josh said as he glanced around, wide-eyed.

Riley looked over to Alfie and could see he was probably thinking the same thing she was. How they felt the first day they were here. Though the situation was very different then. At the time, they thought their parents were still lost at sea. This time, everyone knew this was their new home.

Walking through the trees, Riley smiled as they came upon the same path she had followed so many times before. This led straight to the Community. And again, just like their first time, they walked forward and were faced with the orchards and vegetable gardens. The Crucible rose in the far distance, sparkling like diamonds in the sky.

"What is that tower?" Tony asked.

"That's the Crucible," Alfie said. "The gargoyles live there."

After a few more paces, Riley saw Kevin working among the people in the orchard. She put Pea down and ran forward, waving and calling, "Kevin, Kevin, over here!"

The rhino looked up and made his strange sound. Then he charged toward them at full speed.

Tony panicked. "Everyone run, that rhino is charging!"

Riley ran—not away from Kevin, but toward him. When they met, Kevin did his happy dance at seeing her and leaped around like an excited puppy. Riley threw her arms around his thick neck. "I have missed you so much!"

It was then she noticed deep and angry scars on the rhino's back. "Kevin, what happened to you? Was it a Red Moon?"

The rhino nodded.

"I'm so sorry," she said, hugging him again. "That will never happen again!"

Moments later, a stunned Lisette arrived. "Riley? Is that really you?" She looked over to Alfie and then to Bastian. "You have returned?"

Alfie nodded and waved his arm back to show the others. "Us and a few more."

Bastian nodded. "We are happy to be back, but please, Lisette, we need to take Miss Pigglesworth and Maggie to the doctor's hut."

"But—but how?" Lisette demanded. "How did you get away? And how did you come back?"

"The mermaids let us return," Riley said. She

motioned her family forward. "Mom, Danny, everyone, this is Lisette. She assigns the jobs here."

Beverly came forward. "It is a pleasure to meet you, Lisette. Riley has told me so much about you."

Lisette's mouth was hanging open. "You are Riley's mother?"

Beverly nodded. "And this is my son, Daniel. These other children are the Decker family. They are looking for a home and we hope that you might accept them here."

Everyone from the gardens gasped, and Riley heard comments like "More children . . ." and "They brought more children. . . ."

"You brought these children with you?" Lisette asked.

Riley nodded. "And my mom's a doctor. So now, if you want, Atlantis has two."

Moments later, Beresford and Shane arrived. Their stunned expressions matched Lisette's.

"I do not understand," Beresford said. "How were you able to leave?"

"And how could you come back?" Shane demanded.

"It's a long story," Riley said. "But right now,

Maggie and Miss Pigglesworth need help. We must get them to the medical hut."

"You want us to treat them, after you betrayed us?" Beresford said. Then he looked at Pea and frowned. "Why are you out of your cloak?"

Riley bent down and picked up Pea again. "We didn't betray you. We needed to get home to get our family. You knew how close we were; we never lied about that. And Pea doesn't wear a cloak anymore. Neither does Maggie. They live free, just like it used to be here."

"What are you talking about?" Shane demanded. "Cloaks have always worn . . . cloaks."

"No, they haven't," Riley said. "Don't you remember? It only started when Walston Greeves arrived here. Before then, everyone who was changing lived among you like normal. They were as much a part of the Community as you all were."

This caused gasps and sounds of shock from the others.

Lisette snorted. "You have just returned and already you are telling us lies."

"No, I'm not," Riley insisted. "I've seen pictures of the Community from before. It's in a book that Adam made before he became Mada."

There were more gasps from the gathering as Riley spoke Mada's old name.

"It's true, you've just forgotten," Riley continued. "In the past, everyone lived together in harmony. There were no territorial boundaries. No cloaks, no separation. And when the Red Moons came, everyone was protected on the *Queen*."

Riley heard shocked muttering among the others behind Lisette.

Moments later, the meal bell started.

"What's that?" Danny asked Riley.

"The lunch bell," Riley said. "It's calling everyone to eat."

Beresford looked at Riley doubtfully, but then he gazed at the children behind her. He opened his arms wide. "This isn't the time to discuss such matters. We must make these newcomers welcome! Come, come, children, everyone. Join us for a meal."

A woman Riley barely knew stepped up to Sarah and took Chrissy joyfully in her arms. "Oh my, I haven't seen a child so young since . . ." She paused and then frowned. "I don't know how long it's been."

Others came forward and introduced themselves to Jill's family and to Danny. Many offered their hand to Beverly and Tony and welcomed them to Atlantis.

"Come," Beresford repeated. "Join us for a meal—all are welcome."

Everyone walked forward, and once again Riley saw the reactions on her family's faces that must have mirrored how they looked when she and Alfie first arrived.

They headed toward the Community, past the boat houses and strangely colored stone buildings.

When Riley's family walked around the bell tower and saw the large cruise ship, *The Queen of Bermuda*, they stopped.

"Wow!" Danny cried. "It really is a cruise ship!"

"Told ya," Alfie said. "We had cabins on board."

"How?" Tony demanded as he jogged up to the *Queen*. He peered up her side. "This is impossible. We're in the middle of the jungle. How did it get here?"

"The Leviathan," Pea said. "It dragged the *Queen* to shore, and we all set it here. Though it was a very, very long time ago and I was a much different person." The koala looked at his hands. "I had much bigger hands back then."

While everyone was gazing at the *Queen*, Bastian said, "Please, Miss Pigglesworth."

"Of course," Beverly said. "Where is this medical hut?"

"It's this way," Bastian said.

Beverly turned to Riley. "I'll stay with Bastian and Tony, and we'll look after Maggie and Miss Pigglesworth. Would you please get the kids to lunch? They could use a good meal." She handed Mary over to Danny. "We'll join you when we can."

"Sure," Riley said. "But Mom, don't be too shocked by the medical hut. I told you before, it's . . ."

"I know, it's basic and holistic," her mother said.

"Exactly." Riley went up to Bastian. "She's home, Bastian. Miss Pigglesworth will be fine, I'm sure of it. I mean, you're feeling better, and so am I. It will be the same for her."

"Indeed she will," Pea said, patting his arm. "She is a strong one."

Fear lingered in Bastian's blue eyes. He nodded but didn't speak as he carried Miss Pigglesworth forward.

Riley really wanted to go with him, but the others were waiting to be led forward to the dining area.

When they reached the clearing, the Atlantis children were already seated at their table. Soraya squealed with joy when she saw Riley. She charged forward and gave Riley and Pea the biggest hug. Then she laughed even more when she met Robbi, who was around her age.

The two girls were soon locked in excited conversation as Soraya invited Robbi to sit next to her.

Ellis and John came up to Pauly and they started talking animatedly.

As always, the twins, Victoria and Elizabeth, couldn't have been more disinterested and kept to themselves.

When Riley approached the table and saw Kerry sitting there, she smiled. "Hi, Kerry, it's nice to see you again."

Kerry looked like she'd just bitten into a lemon as her face screwed up with anger. This almost reassured Riley. Some things never changed.

Alfie walked forward and introduced his mother, then Danny and the Decker family, to the others at the table. There was a lot of laughter and loads of questions. Watching them all together, Riley realized bringing Jill and her family was the best thing for all of them.

As there were now more than double the children in Atlantis, a second table was moved and set up with the others.

Everyone took a seat. Riley was aware of the mutters and tutting she received when she gave Pea the seat right next to her and Mary sat with Alfie.

"Perhaps I should go," Pea said nervously.

"If you go, I go," Riley said to him. "I told you, we're family, Pea. Whatever they try to do to you, they do to all of us."

"Exactly," Danny added. "We don't have to stay if you're uncomfortable."

Soon everyone at the table agreed, including the Atlantean children—everyone, that is, except for Kerry, who sat with her arms crossed over her chest in anger.

Pea lowered his head and Riley thought he might be tearing up. "Thank you, everyone. I can never express just how much you all mean to me."

Riley leaned forward and kissed him on the top of his head. "You mean everything to us, too, Pea."

When they were settled, Beresford stood up. "I'm sure you are all as surprised as I am to see Riley, Alfie, and Bastian returned to us. Not to mention those they brought with them. I do not know their names yet, but I'm sure in time we all will. Now, there are a lot of unanswered questions surrounding their mysterious departure and subsequent return. Or why the Cloaks are uncloaked and sitting among us. But for now, let us show these newcomers that they are welcome in Atlantis!"

Everyone in the gathering rose to their feet and cheered and applauded.

Jill leaned closer to Riley. "Are they doing this for us?"

Riley nodded. "They never get visitors, so all of you being here is a big deal for them."

"A *really* big deal," Alfie said.

Soon the servers arrived with a large cauldron of soup.

"I'm starving," Robbi said as she gratefully received her bowl of soup and reached for a bun.

Their table exploded in loud conversation as the Atlantis children bombarded the newcomers with questions.

"This is going well," Riley said, leaning down to Pea.

"Yes, it is," Pea agreed. "Though I am a touch

concerned about Beresford. There was an edge to his voice."

"I noticed it too," Alfie said.

"But this time, we're not trapped here," Riley said. "If they give us a hard time, we'll just go back to the *Moon Dancer* until we can build new homes for all of us."

"I'm sure it won't come to that," Mary said as she picked up the fine silver spoon and started to eat. "Mmm, this is delicious!"

"The food is great here," Alfie said.

Because Pea and Mary had been feeling so ill for so long, they hadn't been able to eat properly. But now that they were starting to recover, their appetites were back, and they enjoyed their meal.

At the end of it, Beresford and Lisette came over to the table. He smiled warmly at all the children.

"So now, tell me all your names."

One by one the Decker children introduced themselves. When they finished, Beresford said, "Vadin, John, Ellis, and Soraya, you are excused from your chores this afternoon. Would you please be kind enough to show the newcomers around and tell them about our ways?"

"We were going to do that," Riley said.

Again Beresford smiled, then shook his head. "I would much prefer to spend some time with you and Alfie. Perhaps understand better what has happened."

Riley felt a lump forming in her stomach. She looked at Alfie before saying, "Sure. It would be lovely to chat with you again."

"Wonderful," Beresford said. "Would you and Alfie please come with me?"

Riley looked at Jill and the others before getting up and leaving the table to follow Beresford and Lisette. They had only gone a few yards when Pea called, "Shall I come with you?" He trotted up to Riley.

"And me," Mary said as she joined them.

"No, that's fine, Pea, and . . ." Beresford frowned as his dark eyes landed on Alfie's mother. "I do not know you."

"Mary," Alfie said. He lowered his voice. "You might remember that name. This is my mother. You know, the one you said drowned and was buried. Obviously she didn't drown and was never buried. Instead she was put in the Forbidden Zone with

Riley's dad. Mom turned into a monkey and Uncle Andrew became a dolphin. He's here too. He talked to the mermaids and helped us come back."

Beresford gasped and Lisette's mouth dropped as they looked at Mary.

Mary nodded. "I didn't used to look like this. But that Forbidden Zone is potent. We turned in such a short time."

"I—I—" Beresford stammered, looking around nervously.

Riley leaned closer. "Don't worry, Beresford, we won't tell anyone the truth—that you lied to us about our family and created false graves to trick us. We're not here to cause strife. We just wanted to come back and share Atlantis with Jill and her family."

Beresford's eyes were wild, like a cornered animal. "I—I don't understand. Why would you come back after you tried so hard to leave? You obviously made it to your home."

"Yes, we did," Riley said. "But Atlantis changed us. It changes everyone. We started to get sick. If we didn't come back, we would have died."

"That's why Maggie and Miss Pigglesworth are so ill," Pea added. "I was, too, but I am recovering now."

"I have never heard that people who leave here die," Lisette said.

Riley turned to her. "Do you know of anyone else who's left?"

Much to Riley's surprise, Lisette nodded. "I did. Long ago. But they never came back, and I assumed they were happy away from here. Though, after that, the older ones in the sea made sure no one ever left again. That is why we don't understand how you did it."

"We had help," Riley said. "My father talked to the mermaids, and they agreed to let us go." Riley thought it best not to mention Galina or Gideon's part in their escape. "But I'll be honest with you. Alfie and I missed Atlantis and all of you more than we ever expected. What you have here is special. There are problems, but it's a lot better than out there."

Beresford's demeanor changed when Riley said that. "So you chose to come back?"

"Duh!" Alfie said. "We're here, aren't we?"

Riley looked at her cousin and wished he'd control himself. Beresford was softening, and they couldn't risk annoying him. "And it's not just because we were getting sick. This is an amazing place." She paused, wondering how much more she should say. Finally she said, "The reason Alfie and I wanted to go home in the first place was for our family. Not because we hated it here or missed the modern world. It was only our family. But now we're asking to be allowed back."

"And if we refuse?" Lisette asked. "Or if we let the youngsters stay, but not you? What would you do?"

"Well," Riley said, "Jill and Sarah and all of them are now part of our family. So if you don't want us to stay, we'll all leave together. Or if you try to force Pea, Mary, and Maggie back into cloaks, we'll simply go back to our boat and then we'll find somewhere else on Atlantis to live."

"Is that a threat?" Beresford said.

"No, sir," Riley said respectfully. "It's just our options. But I do want you to realize that you're not being fair. Pea and all the other Cloaks were members of this community—and even helped build it. They still do work here. It's not their fault that they're changing. We all are. So why do you discriminate against them and treat them like they are less than you?"

"We do not do that," Lisette said.

"Yes, dear lady, you do," Pea said sadly. "Lisette,

when you look at me, what do you see? Just an animal? Do you not recall who I was before, back when I was a carpenter? We were such good friends. Now you do not speak to me. Perhaps it is because I remind you of what is coming for you, and that I do understand. But what you don't realize is how lonely we are, or how much your rejection wounds us."

Lisette lowered her head. "I am sorry, Pea."

"And Kevin or Jeff," Alfie said. "You expect their help, but then you ignore them or, worse, lock them outside during the Red Moon when there is plenty of space on the *Queen*. You want them to die, and that's not cool."

"We do not seek their deaths," Lisette said quickly.

"You must, otherwise you'd let them on board," Riley said.

"No, we forbid them coming on board because it has always been this way," Beresford said. "And they have their own place to shelter."

"No, they don't!" Riley insisted. "They are exposed to all of it. Haven't you seen Kevin? Where do you think he got all those scars? He was attacked during the last Red Moon." She looked at Pea. "Tell them, Pea. Tell them that there's no place for you to hide."

"It's true," Pea said. "We are left to the mercy of the Red Moon and many of us are killed. Surely you must know this."

"But—but it's tradition," Beresford insisted. "It has always been this way."

"No, it hasn't!" Riley said. "It used to be different here, and I can prove it." She looked at Pea. "May I go to your house and get Adam's book?"

"Of course," Pea said. "If it's still there."

Riley said to Beresford, "Please wait here. I need to show you both something really important."

Beresford nodded. "We will wait."

Riley dashed away from Alfie and the others and ran toward Pea's house. It had been a few months since she'd been there, and the path was overgrown. But she knew the way perfectly.

Tearing through the vines and bushes, she made it to the fence surrounding Pea's cottage. She walked through it and entered the quaint home. Vivid memories of happy times spent here flashed back to Riley and she realized just how important the next few minutes would be to so many people.

Riley found the book exactly where it had been left and picked it up. She was out of breath by the time she made it back to Beresford and Lisette. Pea was wringing his hands, and Alfie was holding his mother in his arms.

"Here," Riley panted. "This book was created by Adam. Please look at it. I know you can't read, but there are paintings inside that show how Atlantis used to be—and could be again. It's from the time before Walston Greeves arrived and changed everything with his fear and prejudice against those who were turning."

Beresford opened the book, and he and Lisette started to look at the fine paintings on the pages showing the Community in a time before the Cloaks, when everyone lived together in harmony.

Seeing their reaction, others in the Community approached and gazed at the pictures in the book. There were gasps of surprise at the images of those who had turned into animals, walking arm in arm with non-turned Community members.

"See?" Riley said, loud enough for the others to hear. "Those who were turning didn't always wear cloaks. It wasn't tradition. It was the fear of one man who came here long after the Community had been established. He changed things. *You* can turn them back." She looked up at everyone. "You can heal the Community and unite Atlantis again."

"Where did you get this?" a man called.

Riley looked up and saw that it was Edward. She knew his name but hadn't really spoken to him before.

"Adam gave it to me," Pea said. "It was back when all the books were being burned. He didn't want this to be destroyed, so we hid it in my home. The gargoyles took away what they could, but everything else went into the fire." Pea turned to Riley and grinned. "I am so looking forward to reading it now."

Lisette gasped. "You can read?"

Pea nodded proudly. "Yes, Mary taught me."

Others in the crowd murmured, "Pea can read. . . ."

"You read too?" Lisette asked Mary.

"Of course," Mary said. "I could teach you, and anyone here who wants to learn."

Lisette looked at Beresford and then to the pictures in the book. "This looks so peaceful. Everyone is so happy."

Beresford snapped the book closed. "We are happy now."

"Yes, *you* are happy," Riley agreed. "But the Cloaks

aren't. Look, I don't want to cause trouble, but the Cloaks are suffering because you don't like them anymore. You've turned your back on them and it's not right. I just wish you could remember how it was."

"Please, Beresford," Pea begged. "You can't imagine what it feels like to have friends one day, but the next they are gone because of how you look, or because you have fur or scales. Perhaps that is why the Red Cloaks surrender to their inner predator, because you stop treating them like people."

That comment caused more murmuring from the crowd.

"Listen to him," Alfie said. "There is so much right about Atlantis, yet you discriminate against your own people when they start to turn."

Beresford looked at Lisette. "I believe we have much to discuss."

"I agree," Lisette said.

"I should like to keep this for a bit," Beresford said. "Study it further."

"As you wish," Pea said.

Beresford straightened his back and invited them to walk with him and Lisette, away from the others. "Now, what to do with all of you?"

"Well," Riley said, "I was kinda hoping that you would let us stay on the top deck of the *Queen* where I was staying. The suites up there have a lot of space. My family and the Deckers could live there without bothering or moving anyone on the lower decks."

"She's right," Lisette said. "There is plenty of room up there. We can't abandon those children—they need us."

"And you need them," Alfie added.

They all glanced over to the table where Jill and her brothers and sisters were laughing with the Atlantean children.

"I must say, they all do look happy," Beresford said.

"We're all very happy and grateful to be here," Mary said.

Finally Beresford nodded. "All right, we shall try this for a while. You may all settle on the top deck."

"That includes my mom, Pea, and Maggie, right?" Alfie asked.

"Cloaks on the *Queen*?" Beresford choked.

"Not Cloaks," Riley insisted. "People. Maggie, Mary, Pea, they're people, just like us. They only look a bit different."

"Besides, Miss Pigglesworth is there with Bastian," Alfie said. "She was once a Cloak."

"That is different," Beresford said.

"Why?" Alfie charged. "What's the difference between Miss Pigglesworth and my mom? Obviously they look different, but that's all. They're just like us."

Beresford sighed and shook his head. "This goes against everything I've been taught, but all right. We'll try it. You may all reside on the top deck. But if there is one hint of trouble from the Cloaks—I mean, from Maggie or Pea"—his eyes trailed down to Mary—"or you, I will reconsider this decision."

Riley couldn't keep herself from grinning. She threw her arms around Beresford. "Thank you, Beresford, you won't regret it!"

22

AFTER BERESFORD WALKED AWAY WITH the book, Lisette looked at Riley. "Are you prepared to go back to the sewing hut? You must still work to stay here."

Riley grinned. "Yep, and we have a surprise for you. One I'm sure you're going to like."

"What is that?"

"We didn't come back to Atlantis empty-handed," Riley said. "We brought loads of stuff. Clothing, tools, fabric, threads, and sewing supplies . . ."

"Seeds and gardening tools too," Alfie added. "So we can grow more vegetables. Especially tomatoes and squashes! Maybe we can make pizza."

"There are all kinds of treasures to be shared with everyone," Pea said. "I am sure you'll be pleased."

Lisette seemed genuinely surprised. "You brought these for us?"

Riley nodded. "I know you are all self-sufficient here. But we thought a few extras wouldn't hurt."

"I—I don't know what to say," Lisette said. "'Thank you' seems inadequate."

Riley grinned. "You once told me we're all in this together. And we are. So we wanted to help. But now we're going to need extra help to bring it all up here from the boat."

"Of course," Lisette said. "Tell me where your boat is, and I will arrange a group to meet you on the beach."

Before heading back to the *Moon Dancer*, they left Danny and the Decker family at the table with the others while Riley, Alfie, Pea, and Mary walked back to the medical hut.

Fear was sitting heavily in Riley's stomach. She'd hoped to see Bastian, Miss Pigglesworth, and Maggie before now. The fact that they were still there frightened her.

When they reached the medical hut, Riley was stunned to see her mother standing outside it, laughing with the doctor.

"Mom?" Riley called. "How are they?"

Her mother smiled at her. "Go in and see for yourself."

They entered the hut and saw Tony standing at the treatment table and talking to Maggie, who was sitting up.

Bastian was kneeling on the floor, talking to Miss Pigglesworth, who was lying down and panting lightly.

"Maggie!" Riley squealed. She ran over and embraced the leopard-woman. "Are you all right? How are you feeling? I've been so scared!"

"I'm fine, my love," Maggie said warmly. "And feeling much better, thanks to all of you getting me back here. Tony was telling me about the adventure you had."

Tony grinned broadly. "It sure was, but we're here now and I'm looking forward to getting to know the place."

"I would be delighted to show you around," Maggie said. "But I need to find my cloak."

"No, you don't," Riley said.

"It's true," Pea said joyously. "No more cloaks for all of us!"

"What? How?" Maggie asked.

Riley grinned. "We showed Beresford a book Pea had with pictures of Atlantis before you had to wear cloaks."

Alfie added, "Okay, so we might have blackmailed him a bit. We told him if they made you wear your cloaks again, we'd take the *Moon Dancer* and everyone and find somewhere else to live on Atlantis. I don't think they wanted to lose us kids."

"That was dangerous of you," Maggie said.

"No, it wasn't," Riley said. "We meant it. If they try to force you, Pea, and Mary into cloaks again, we'll leave. So we're giving it a trial period. I hope it changes everything for Kevin and all the other Cloaks as well."

"I do too," Maggie agreed.

Bastian stood up and Riley could see the relief on his face. She went over and embraced him boldly. "I'm so glad Miss Pigglesworth is all right."

"So am I," Bastian said, returning the hug. "I couldn't have gone on without her."

Riley bent down to the dog. "You had us really scared, Miss Pigglesworth."

The dog whined and licked Riley's face.

"She says she is feeling much better," Bastian said.

Tony watched the exchange in wonder. "I still can't believe you two can understand each other."

Maggie said, "It just takes time to learn the language."

Tony grinned. "From what I hear, I'm going to have plenty of time."

"Indeed you will," Pea said. "Now, everyone, we must get down to the beach and unload the *Moon Dancer* if we hope to get settled on the *Queen* before nightfall."

When Lisette said she would get help for the unloading, Riley never expected it to be practically everyone from the Community. They were all gathered on the beach, waiting for them.

Many were pointing at the large sailing yacht anchored just offshore, while others marveled at the scarab.

Jill's family and the Atlantean kids were running on the sand and playing tag. Some of the people stood back, watching the water nervously. Riley real-ized they were still frightened of the Leviathan. They didn't know about Galina or how she could commu-nicate with him. This bit of information Riley kept safely hidden.

Maggie was holding Riley's hand as they walked on the golden sand. The closer they came to the people, the more Riley felt Maggie's hesitation. Her hand was trembling, and it became worse as everyone around them gasped and tutted when they saw the leopard-woman walking uncloaked.

Riley could actually feel Maggie shrinking under their questioning stares. "Stand tall, Maggie," Riley said to her. "You are free, and maybe now they can see how beautiful you really are."

"Absolutely," Tony agreed. He stepped forward and spoke loudly. "So who's going to help us unload the *Moon Dancer*?"

Everyone cheered as they walked closer to the shore.

Danny, Sarah, Alfie, Jill, and Bastian climbed onto the *Moon Dancer* and tossed items down to Tony and Josh on the scarab to shuttle to the beach. Riley, her mother, and Mary remained on the sand

and organized the packages and those taking them to the Community.

With each new boatload, there were excited squeals from members of the Community. The mood on the beach was almost like Christmas as every package was opened and admired.

When Tony and Josh carried the first of the treadle sewing machines to shore, Riley grinned and drew Maggie closer. "We got two of these for you."

Maggie gasped. "Are these what I think they are?"

"Uh-huh," Riley said. She looked at the people eyeing the machine curiously. "These sewing machines are Maggie's. If you want to know how they work, you must ask her." Riley winked at Maggie and whispered, "Just think how envious everyone in the sewing hut is going to be when they see what you can do with them."

Maggie turned from the machine and gave Riley the biggest hug. "How can I thank you?"

Riley grinned at her. "By never getting sick again. You really scared me!"

Maggie smiled, showing her sharp, feline teeth. "I'll try my best."

A man Riley knew only by looks hesitantly

approached her. "Is that what it's like out there beyond Atlantis? Are all boats like that one?" He was pointing at Tony's scarab and looking green with envy.

Riley shook her head. "Not all boats. That's called a speedboat. It's built to go especially fast. It's so powerful, it was able to pull the *Moon Dancer*."

"It's beautiful," the man sighed. "I wonder if I might visit it."

Riley shrugged. "You'd have to ask Tony. It's his boat."

Load by load all the items were carried into the Community. As the items were piled up outside the *Queen*, Riley and her mother were stunned by how much they'd managed to bring in the motor home and trailer.

Lisette approached Riley. "You did say this was for us to share?"

Riley nodded. "Most of it. There are a few things for my family, but most of it is for everyone here."

Lisette's face softened. "Speaking on behalf of the Community, we are grateful."

Riley smiled. "I lived here, remember? You all shared everything with Alfie and me. I know how precious clothing is, so we brought as much as we could carry."

Her mother nodded. "I wish we could have brought more. Though we did bring a lot of medical supplies. I'll be working with Cameron to get the medical hut reorganized as we combine his treatments with mine."

"That is very kind of you," Lisette said.

When Lisette walked back to the pile of goods to help with the sorting, Riley turned to her mother. "Cameron?"

Beverly nodded. "Yes, the doctor. You were right, Riley. It is very holistic, but he seems to know his stuff. There is a lot we can teach each other."

"I guess so," Riley said. "So, we've been given the suites at the top of the *Queen* that I used to live in. Would you like to see them?"

Her mother grinned. "Absolutely. Let's grab some of our things before they're all gone, and you can show me."

23

THE FIRST NIGHT BACK IN ATLANTIS WAS completely different for Riley and Alfie compared to the first time they were here. Now her family was with her, and Riley couldn't have been happier as Maggie, Pea, Mary, and Miss Pigglesworth were allowed on the *Queen* with them.

There were actually four luxury suites on the top deck, each with their own private area that led out to the open promenade. The King and Queen suites had two bedrooms each, and the Prince and Princess suites each had three. Riley entered her old suite and saw that a few of her things were still in there.

Tony was given a cabin on one of the lower decks,

so the upper suites were principally for Riley's family and the Decker children.

After they settled in their cabins, they joined the Community for dinner and, after that, for the large bonfire that they had every evening. There the stories were told, and the singing began. But this time Danny brought his guitar and Sarah her violin.

Everyone around the fire was stunned to hear the same songs they'd sung for so long being accompanied by guitar. When they finished, everyone cheered and applauded.

After the sing-along, Danny and Sarah were asked to play something else. Danny went first and played and sang a country song he knew. This brought smiles and applause from the crowd. But when Sarah raised her violin and started to play, the gathering hushed and was carried away by the gentle and haunting melody.

Riley watched Sarah's face as she played and saw how she was lost in the music. Sarah was oblivious to the Atlanteans' reactions and didn't see the firelight sparkling in the tears in their eyes. When she finished and lowered her violin, everyone rose to their feet, crying and roaring with applause. Sarah looked around and blushed as though it was completely unexpected.

As the night drew to a close, a crowd huddled around Danny and Sarah and asked if they would play again on the following night. When they agreed, everyone headed back to the *Queen* happy and excited.

Just before they reached the *Queen*, Edward approached and called Riley aside. She'd never spoken to him before when she lived here. Now this was the second time in one day. He smiled broadly at her. "Riley, may I speak with you for a moment?"

"Sure." Riley turned to her mother. "Mom, I'll catch up with you later."

"Don't be too late," Beverly said.

Edward grinned. "I won't keep her long." He caught Riley by the arm and drew her away from the gathering. "So how are you?"

"Great, thanks. I'm so glad to be back."

"Of course you are."

Riley heard a trace of menace in his voice as his smile faded. "You think you are quite the little favorite here, don't you? Bringing all your gifts from the outer world and infecting us with your radical ideas."

"I—um . . . ," Riley started. She turned to look

back at her mother, who was walking with Cameron and talking very animatedly. Alfie and Jill were farther away, and she couldn't see Maggie or Pea or any of the others from her group.

"Don't look at them; they can't help you," Edward said as his voice turned hard.

"I'd better go." When Riley tried to leave, Edward's hand shot out and grasped her arm just above the elbow. She noticed that he was wearing gloves. In Atlantis, that only meant one thing: he was starting to change. Though there wasn't any trace of transformation on his face.

"Please, let me go," Riley said.

"Not yet. I will have words with you first."

Edward looked behind Riley and smiled as Shane walked by.

"Hi, Edward, Riley, that was fun this evening, wasn't it?" Shane said.

"It certainly was," Edward said jovially. "Wasn't it, Riley?" His dark eyes bored into her as his grip became brutal and warned of worse to come if she said anything.

"Yes—yes it was," Riley stammered.

When Shane moved away, Edward focused on her

again. "I don't like you, Riley. I never have, and I don't like any of those who you brought with you. I especially don't like how you've manipulated Beresford into allowing Cloaks to live on the *Queen* with us as though they have the right to be there. It's wrong. There is a large group of us that feels the same. We are not happy with this new situation."

"How can you say that when you're changing too?"

"What?" Edwards snapped. His grip became almost unbearable. "I am not changing!"

Riley realized she'd made a terrible mistake saying that. "What I mean is that we're all changing here."

"Not me!" His grip tightened further.

"Please, let me go—you're hurting me." Riley tried to pull his hand from her arm, but Edward's grip tightened even more.

"One move and I'll snap your arm like a twig," Edward warned.

Riley stopped struggling. "What do you want from me?"

"I want you to get that cat, monkey, and the rodent off our ship. The dog can stay, but the others must go."

"Pea is not a rodent," Riley said. "And Mary is Alfie's mother."

"I don't care. They all go!"

The grip tightened again, and Riley was sure she could feel her bone cracking. Edward was thin and lanky; how could he be so strong? "If you break my arm, I'll tell them it was you."

"If you say one word to anyone about this, your mother and brother might just end up in Red Cloak territory. You know how dangerous that is."

Riley gasped. She'd never been threatened by anyone in the Community before. Yes, Mada was dangerous, but he lived in Red Cloak territory. Edward lived in the Community and there could be no avoiding him. "Please," she said.

"Get them off the *Queen* and back into their cloaks and stop trying to change things, or I swear, you will regret it."

He released her arm, patted her on the head, and then smiled for the others walking by. "It was nice chatting with you, Riley. I'll *definitely* see you later."

When Edward walked away, Riley couldn't move. She was shaking too much. The cruelty in his eyes was terrifying.

Finally, the spell was broken, and she could move again. Not looking left or right, Riley ran straight back to the *Queen* before anyone could see the tears rising in her eyes.

Making it to the top deck, Riley ran to her suite. She was sharing the Queen suite with her mother, Mary, and Maggie.

Beside it was the King suite, her old home. That now had Danny, Alfie, Pea, and Bastian with Miss Pigglesworth, while the Decker children settled in the Prince and Princess suites.

By the time she arrived, everyone had gone to bed, but Riley was too frightened to sleep. She was in trouble. The look in Edward's eyes told her he meant every word he said.

Not wanting to disturb Maggie, who was still recovering, she walked through the living room and out onto the promenade.

Riley had spent so many evenings here, planning their escape from Atlantis and finding peace in looking out over the ocean. It was like a sanctuary for her. But now that was gone. Edward lived on the *Queen* as well and had easy access to the upper deck.

Suddenly all the joy of arriving back here evaporated. In just a few short hours her happiness had turned to fear. How could she tell Maggie and Pea to don their cloaks again and leave the *Queen*? Those cloaks were a symbol of discrimination, of separation.

She couldn't ask them to do it, even though she knew Maggie and Pea would if she told them what had happened. If she gave in to Edward's demand, what would be next?

When Riley reached the bow, she looked out over the ocean. Her father was out there somewhere. It had been such a busy day, she hadn't had a chance to go back down to the water to talk to him again. Now she really wanted to speak with him to get his advice, but the *Queen* was locked up tight for the night.

"Good evening, Riley."

Riley jumped at the voice and turned quickly to see Gideon landing on the deck. He chuckled softly. "I'm sorry, did I startle you?"

Seeing the large gargoyle there, Riley's tears started, and she ran to him. Throwing her arms around him, she cried into his chest. "Gideon, I'm in terrible trouble, and I don't know what to do."

"Riley, Riley, what's wrong?" Gideon said. "Talk

to me. What has happened? It's only been a day. Is it Mada? You are safe here on the *Queen*; he can't get to you."

Riley knew she probably shouldn't tell Gideon about Edward, but this was too big to keep in. Finally, she looked up at him. "I've been threatened, but it's not by Mada. It's someone here on the *Queen*."

"What?" Gideon cried. "By who?"

"He warned me not to tell anyone or he'd hurt my mother and Danny. But—but I can't do what he says. I just can't."

Gideon bent down to look Riley in the face. "Who is wanting you to do something against your will? What is it? Is it Beresford? Shane?"

Riley shook her head. "No, it's—it's Edward."

"Edward?" Gideon repeated in shock. "What does he want?"

Riley finally went into details about Edward's threats and what would happen if Maggie, Pea, and Mary didn't leave the *Queen* and wear their cloaks.

"How dare he!" Gideon boomed. "I shall certainly have words with him!"

"No!" Riley said. "Then he'll know I've told, and he might hurt Mom or someone else. He said he wasn't alone and that there were others who felt the same."

"Riley, you can't ask Pea or Maggie to go back into their cloaks. Not when strides have finally been made to heal Atlantis. It is a dangerous, backward step."

"I know," Riley agreed. "But we've only been back a day. I don't know who I can trust. Do I tell Beresford or Lisette? Are they part of it, or if not, will they be turned against us?"

Gideon rose to his full height. "I knew the Community had its problems. But I never realized just how deep the rivers of resentment ran."

"Neither did I," Riley said. "I'd never spoken to Edward before today. But he hates me and my family."

Gideon shook his head. "No, what he hates is himself and that he is changing. He thinks by removing Maggie, Pea, and Mary from his sight, it will bury the fear he holds. That by not seeing them, the change isn't real. But he cannot hide from the truth."

"What am I supposed to do?" Riley said. "I don't want to tell the others. Not when we've just arrived. But what else can I do? Move onto the *Moon Dancer*? Find somewhere else to live?"

"The *Moon Dancer* is lovely," Gideon said. "But

you can't live on it. She may not survive the next Red Moon, being exposed out on the ocean like that. She was protected from the worst of the Red Moon in the Forbidden Zone. I would not be comfortable with all of you on board for the next one."

"Then what?"

Gideon looked at her. "You are a very clever girl, Riley. What do your instincts tell you to do? Do you want Pea, Maggie, and Mary to wear their cloaks again and leave the *Queen*?"

Riley shook her head. "Of course not!"

"Then what?"

Riley thought for a long time. She sighed heavily. "Ignore Edward, I guess. I mean, he might be alone and not able to do anything against us. It could be an empty threat."

"That is true," Gideon said.

Riley kept thinking aloud. "I could tell Alfie and Bastian and we can make sure everyone we care for are always in crowds."

"Very good," Gideon said. "Anything else?"

"And I guess if we can make ourselves valuable to the Community, they might all defend us if Edward tries something."

Gideon nodded. "That sounds like a plan that could work."

"But what if it doesn't work?" Riley asked. "What if Edward goes after Mom or Danny or someone else?"

Gideon tilted his head to the side. "Should Edward try something against you, he will have me and all the gargoyles to answer to. We all want unity in Atlantis, and it is finally starting. We won't let it go backward."

Gideon stayed with Riley for a while longer. They walked along the deck and didn't speak most of the time. But just having him there made Riley feel safe. By the time he left, she felt more balanced and ready to take on the world again—or at least Edward.

The following day, Riley did tell Alfie, Bastian, Miss Pigglesworth, and Jill about Edward's threat. They were as furious as she was, and working together, they managed to keep their family always within sight of several people so that if Edward or his friends made a move, they couldn't succeed.

Despite Edward's threat, nothing did happen. Days and weeks seemed to fly by as everyone from the *Moon Dancer* settled in well to the Atlantis routine. Danny was given a job helping with building and repair work. Alfie worked with Bastian again changing the water on the *Queen*, and the Decker children were all assigned tasks based on their age and abilities.

Beverly was working with Cameron in the medical hut setting up her equipment and supplies. She was teaching the Atlantis doctor about modern medicine, while he taught her about the herbs and leaves he used to treat people. Working together with their combined knowledge, everyone would receive the best care possible.

Riley went back to her old job of sewing and repairs with Maggie. This time Jill was with her, and she was happily learning how to sew.

The hut wasn't big enough for the two treadle sewing machines, so a second sewing room was set up on the *Queen*. This room was once the crew's dining hall when the *Queen of Bermuda* was sailing. It had a large cutting-out table and plenty of shelf space for all the extra fabrics and sewing supplies that had been brought to the island on the *Moon Dancer*.

It was there that Maggie, Riley, and Jill worked.

They tried working in the sewing hut with the others, but some of the women were too uncomfortable with Maggie being without her cloak.

This insult really bothered Riley, and she wondered if those women were with Edward in their resentment toward Maggie, Pea, and Mary. Maggie seemed to take their attitude in stride, though she did grin when two of the women asked her to use her sewing machine on difficult repairs.

Riley saw Edward each night as everyone gathered together for the storytelling and singing. Maggie, Pea, and Mary joined in, and as the time passed, the other Cloaks were emboldened to come closer to listen to the music being played by Danny and Sarah.

Though Edward glared at Riley with fire in his eyes, he hadn't spoken another word to her or to her family. Riley realized that his threat, while scary, must have been an empty one—though she, Bastian, Jill, and Alfie weren't confident enough to stop keeping watch over their families.

After each working day, Riley, Bastian, Alfie, and Jill would go down to the slope leading to the water, where they met up with Galina. They would play and swim together. Many times her father would appear, and they would race.

On occasion, the Leviathan would show up. At first he was terrifying, but Riley and the others soon discovered that despite his size and appearance, the Leviathan was a sensitive, thinking creature that actually enjoyed playing with them.

The biggest adjustment for Riley was getting used to her father being a dolphin. But as the days and weeks passed, it became normal. At least as normal as it could be, having a dolphin for a dad.

Many times, Danny, Sarah, Mary, Pea, and Maggie would come. Danny, Sarah, and Maggie would enter the water and swim with them, but Pea and Mary preferred to stay onshore and watch, or in some cases, toss sticks for the Leviathan to fetch.

The one person always missing was Riley's mother. She would make excuses that she had work to do, but Riley knew the truth. Her mother was not dealing well with being married to a dolphin. Her father said he understood, but Riley could see the hurt it caused him.

"I'm sure they'll work it all out in time," Maggie said to her one evening as they walked back to the

Queen together. "Your mother has a lot to deal with. Not only the change in your father, but the choice he made in staying in Atlantis."

"But if he'd gone with us, he'd have been trapped," Riley said. "None of you turned back."

"True," Maggie agreed. "But your father didn't know that at the time. None of us did. He made his choice, and it was the ocean. Beverly knows that. And deep down, your father does too. He chose the water over her."

This gave Riley a lot to think about. Was this now the Atlantis version of a divorce? Would her parents get past this? Or was this the new normal?

Each day, just like she used to before she left Atlantis, Riley would wake early and rise before the dawn. She would tread quietly out on the deck and go for a walk. Occasionally Maggie would wake and join her, but most times Maggie left Riley to her thoughts.

Riley walked up to the bow of the *Queen* and watched the sun rise out of the ocean. It was going to be another beautiful day. But she never got bored of them. Things had turned out much better than she'd imagined.

She no longer kept track of days or time, as there was no need to. So she wasn't sure how long they'd been back. But since arriving, there had been no sightings of Mada or any Red Cloaks. Riley did ask Lisette about it one day, and though Mada hadn't been judged or banned yet, the tiger-man was staying away.

The sounds of the *Queen*'s outer doors being opened pulled Riley from her thoughts. She looked back toward her suite and saw Bastian and Miss Pigglesworth emerge from their room. Miss Pigglesworth saw Riley and charged down the deck at full speed to greet her.

Riley knelt down and embraced the dog as though they'd not seen each other in ages.

"Good morning, Riley," Bastian said brightly. "Up early again?"

"Always," Riley said, and grinned. She turned back to the ocean. "I love to watch the sunrise. It's just so beautiful here."

"It sure is," Bastian said.

Riley looked up and realized he wasn't looking at the ocean. She felt her cheeks flush as she rose to stand. Now that they were back in Atlantis, she found she wanted to spend more and more time with Bastian. And when she wasn't with him, she was thinking about him. Kerry was annoyed at first, but then her attention settled on Josh, and she actually stopped being mean to Riley. In fact, on occasion, she was actually almost . . . nice.

"Um, Riley," Bastian said awkwardly as he shuffled from one foot to the other. "Would, um, would you like to go to the bonfire with me tonight?"

Riley smiled. "We go every night."

"No—yes, well, I mean—what I mean is, would you like to go with me? Just you and me—uh—together."

Miss Pigglesworth whined, but her tail was wagging.

It took a moment for Riley to realize what Bastian was saying. Suddenly she couldn't look at him as her face felt hot again. "Um, sure, I'd really like that."

"Great!" Bastian cheered. He had a huge grin on his face and his eyes sparkled. "Wonderful, I'll—uh, I'll see you at breakfast!" Bastian leaned forward and gave Riley the sweetest, most tender kiss, then darted away before she could do or say anything.

Alone on the deck again, Riley felt like jumping, dancing, and running as her heart raced. She could still feel Bastian's brief kiss tingling on her lips and realized he had just asked her out on her first date.

Riley worked all morning as though she was walking in a dream. Instead of sewing, she was just sitting and staring out the ship's window.

"Earth to Riley," Jill said.

Riley snapped out of her reverie. "I—I'm sorry."

"Where were you?" Jill asked. "I called your name a few times."

Maggie was across from them, working the treadle sewing machine. She stopped and smiled. "I think I know where she was," she said softly. "And Bastian is behaving exactly the same way. Is there something you want to tell us?"

Riley felt her cheeks going hot again. "Nope, everything is fine."

Jill gasped. "You and Bastian?"

"And it's about time too," Maggie said.

The conversation was getting to be too much for Riley. She gathered up the finished garments and headed for the door. "I'm taking these back to the sewing hut and getting more for us to do. I'll be back shortly."

"All right, sweetheart, see you in a bit. Now don't get lost or distracted . . . ," Maggie teased lightly.

Riley turned back to her and saw the leopard-woman grinning. "I'll try not to."

Leaving their new sewing room, Riley carried her load to the stairs. Suddenly Atlantis was a small community, and everyone seemed to know everyone's business. Did the others know about her and Bastian? Was there anything to know?

Reaching the ground, she saw Lisette speaking with Tony. When they saw her, Lisette smiled broadly. "Well, hello, Riley, how are you doing?"

"Um, fine," Riley said quickly. "I have to get these to the sewing hut."

"Don't let us stop you," Tony said.

Riley nodded to them and kept moving. Tony had been spending a lot of time with Lisette, and she seemed much happier for it.

When Riley reached the sewing hut and walked in, everyone stopped speaking. Kerry was in her usual spot and for a change actually said, "Hi, Riley."

"Hi, Kerry," Riley said back. She carried the finished clothing to the completed basket and then went to the one with clothing needing to be repaired.

Picking up a load, she looked over and saw one of the women, Esme, glaring at her. Esme had always been the most difficult to speak with in the past. Since Riley's return to Atlantis, it was even worse. Riley stopped and challenged her. "What?"

Esme turned away and focused on her work again.

Just as Riley was about to say something, a horn blared. A horn that everyone knew but dreaded. A horn that cried, *The Red Moon is coming.*

Everyone put down their work and stood to leave. Riley returned the clothing to the basket and followed the others out of the sewing hut. They joined the stream of people heading toward the *Queen.*

This would be Riley's third Red Moon, the first one she'd experience from the safety of the *Queen.* The second was when they made their escape. On that occasion, the fog had moved in so quickly, they didn't make it to Pea's house before they couldn't see anything. Mada had been in that fog, waiting for them.

Riley shivered at the memory and knew that this time it would be different. This time her family was with her, and she intended to get all the Cloaks on board as well.

As the ladies from the sewing hut neared the loading ramp, Riley moved over to the side. It was here that Kevin and the other Cloaks had waited the last time they experienced a Red Moon. It was here the next revolution would begin.

Riley guessed that Alfie and Bastian were already safely on board, as their job kept them mostly on the *Queen*. She'd also seen her mother walking forward with the doctor and making it up the ramp. Not long after that, Danny, Sarah, and the rest of the Decker children arrived and climbed up. Danny paused when he reached Shane at the entrance and asked him a question. Shane shook his head and they both looked around.

Riley had the feeling that Danny was asking about her. To avoid being seen and called aboard before the Cloaks arrived, she ducked into the trees and crouched down.

Lisette stood across from Shane, helping get everyone on board. This was usually Beresford's job. It surprised her that he wasn't there. Though it might have made it easier for her to get Lisette to agree to let the other Cloaks on board.

As the crowd boarding the big ship thinned, Riley

prepared to stand, but then heard the snap of a branch behind her. She turned just in time to see a large dark bag descending over her head.

Just as Riley was about to scream, she felt a brutal blow. Her head started to spin, and then the world went black.

24

THE FIRST THING RILEY FELT AS SHE started to come to was pain. Her head was throbbing. For a brief moment she thought she was back in Denver, and this was the headache and fever she'd suffered with the others.

But then she remembered: she was back in Atlantis. And it was a Red Moon!

Coming fully awake, she opened her eyes and discovered that she was sitting on the ground with her arms tied back behind a tree trunk. The bag was off her head. When she looked up, she saw Edward standing above her with a self-satisfied expression on his face.

He was pulling the gloves back over his hands. Before they were covered, Riley saw dark fur and claws. But she couldn't tell what kind of animal he was turning into.

She struggled against the bonds. "Let me go!"

"I warned you, Riley," he said casually. "I told you what would happen if you didn't get those Cloaks off the *Queen*. But you wouldn't listen. You taunted me with your disobedience. Now you will pay for your defiance of my authority."

"What authority?" Riley challenged. "Beresford and Lisette are the leaders here, not you. You have no authority."

"Yes, well, we'll see about that."

Riley looked around and suddenly realized where she was. It was the beach in the Red Cloak territory where she'd first met Galina when Gideon had suffered his break. It was the same beach that sat right beside the land bridge from the Forbidden Zone that only appeared during Red Moons.

"Edward, please, untie me!" Riley cried. "The Red Moon . . ."

"You're right, it is a Red Moon," Edward said. "So I'd better get back to the *Queen* before the fog comes—or Mada and his Red Cloaks. You know, I've been speaking with Mada, and he is most anxious to see you again."

"Please," Riley begged. "You can't do this. It's wrong."

This set Edward off. "What's wrong is you, Riley! You and all the newcomers, with your strange ways and new ideas. You have made Beresford and Lisette weak. I told Beresford to stand up to you—to destroy that book you gave him and to cast the Cloaks out. But he wouldn't listen and continued to permit them to live on the *Queen*. He's even allowing more Cloaks to attend the bonfire and that's not right!

"But with you and Beresford gone, the Community will soon realize that they need a stronger leader. One who respects tradition and the way it should be—without change. I am that person. With Mada at my side, they will see that I am their only choice."

"You and Mada?" Riley cried. "But you hate Cloaks."

"I never said I hated the Cloaks. Only that they should know their place and remain hidden. They do have their uses. As servants, not equals. They lost their right to be considered people when they turned.

But you're trying to change a long-standing tradition and have turned Beresford around with your ideas of equality. That stops right now."

"But you'll work with Mada?"

"He is a means to an end. A way to remove Beresford once and for all. For some time, I've been thinking Beresford is too weak to rule. The Community needs someone strong, like Walston Greeves was. I am that man, and I have followers who agree."

"No, you're wrong. Beresford is strong. He'll stop you. They all will."

"Beresford can't do anything anymore," Edward said.

"Why? What have you done to him?"

"Me? Nothing. But I'm sure Mada or the wildlings will have some ideas what to do with him once they get here. Look, he's right over there."

Riley turned and saw that Beresford was also tied to a tree a few yards away. His head was down, and he was unconscious. "Beresford, no . . . Is he . . . is he dead?"

"Not yet," Edward said. "But he's the lucky one. He won't be conscious when Mada comes. Whereas you, well, Mada told me not to hit you too hard, so that you would be awake to see him. He's so looking forward to your special reunion."

Riley struggled against the bonds that tied her to the tree. "You can't do this—it's murder!"

"No, it's justice and a return to order!" Edward spat. "Walston Greeves was right when he subjugated the Cloaks and brought order to the Community."

"He ruined the Community!" Riley cried as she fought to break free of her bonds.

"Struggle all you want, but it won't change anything. You're stuck there—at least until Mada sets you free." He started to chuckle. "I'd say it's been nice knowing you, but I never lie. Excuse me now, I must return to the *Queen* before they lock her up tight."

Edward turned and walked away.

Riley couldn't believe this was really happening. She pulled against the ties, but all that did was bite into the skin on her wrists. Edward might have had animal hands, but he was good at tying knots.

The sun was still shining brightly, and the water was calm. The Forbidden Zone rose high across the channel, but it, too, seemed to have stilled as it waited for the fog to arrive.

She looked up the beach to the jungle. There

was no sign of Mada, but he could come at any minute. Turning back to the water, did she dare risk calling Galina? Would the mermaid hear her? And even if she did, could she crawl up on land enough to help her?

Or would Mada hear her and come?

It had been a long time since Riley felt this kind of terror. She was alone and trapped. She looked over at Beresford. His chin was down against his chest, but he was breathing.

"Beresford," Riley whispered tightly. "Wake up . . ."

But after several minutes, Beresford did not wake. If what Edward said was true, that would be a blessing for when Mada came.

She decided she had no choice. Riley gazed out over the water and started to shout, "Dad, Galina, can you hear me? I'm here! Please, I need your help!"

The water was strangely calm and looked more like glass. Riley had never seen it so peaceful. But then again, she'd never seen it at the start of a Red Moon and didn't know what to expect.

"Galina, Dad!" she called again. But still there was no movement on the smooth surface.

Riley kept calling, but she also started to wiggle and move, hoping that it might loosen the knots or even wear through the rope. But after a few minutes, all she'd managed to achieve was hands sticky with tree sap and making it to her feet. Her arms were still pinned back, but at least her legs were free. It wouldn't do much against Mada, but if he was going to get her, at least he'd know she put up a fight.

"Galina!" Riley shouted again. "Please, hear me! Dad?"

As Riley watched the water, she saw the surface start to move. For a moment she dared to hope it was Galina or her father. But then she realized the truth. It was the whole surface. The tide was changing, and the water was receding. Soon the land bridge between Atlantis and the Forbidden Zone would appear and the wildlings could cross over.

Riley finally realized there was no one to help her. She was alone. If she was going to survive this, she was going to have to save herself.

She tried to look back at the knots binding her, but the tree was blocking her view. Once again, she tried rocking her arms back and forth to wear through the ropes, but it wasn't working. The sap was just too sticky. But when she put more force into it, she felt the tree crack.

Riley looked up to the leaves and nearly cried with relief. Sticky sap and cracking. This wasn't a tree! Not a real one—it was an overgrown weed. Bastian had shown her all kinds of plants that grew here when she first arrived. He'd talked about these weeds, saying he'd once tried to climb one—but it broke!

With her heart pounding, Riley started to push back against the stem, then forward again. With each move, the stem swayed with her body. She could actually feel it starting to strain.

"Come on, Riley," she said aloud through gritted teeth. "Push!"

And she did. Harder and harder. Soon the stem was rocking so much, she didn't really need to use a lot of force, as the momentum was moving it. Then there was another crack, a loud one.

Riley pushed back harder than she ever had in all her life. Everything was riding on it. Finally the sound of cracking intensified. She looked up and saw the top of the weed starting to tip.

Suddenly the weed snapped, and Riley was pulled over with it and hit the ground hard. The rough edge of the break cut into the back of her legs, but she didn't feel it. All she felt was triumph.

Wiggling like a snake, Riley worked her way down until her hands slipped over the broken edge. In an instant, she was able to work her hands under her shoes and then up front.

Using her teeth, it didn't take her long to undo the knots. Her hands were sticky, and the sap tasted dreadful, but she did it.

Riley stood again, unsure what she should do. She could try to run for the *Queen* to get help for Beresford. But both her legs were hurt and bleeding—could she make it in time? What if she got there and they'd already closed the outer doors? Or what if Mada came for Beresford? What if the fog hit and she couldn't find her way?

There were far too many what-ifs. Instead she checked on Beresford. There was an angry bruise and swollen lump on his head. Edward had hit him brutally hard.

Riley went around to the back of the tree and untied his hands.

When he was free, she laid him down. "Beresford," she called softly, tapping him on the face. "Beresford, wake up!" No matter what she tried, his eyes remained closed. Riley worried that he might have a concussion.

Riley then inspected her own wounded legs. The broken weed had done a lot of damage, and her shredded calves were stinging. Whatever she planned to do, she'd better do it quickly before the real pain began.

Struggling to her feet, Riley soon realized she could taste salt on her lips. The last time that happened . . . She turned quickly and looked at the water. She gasped. A tall, solid wall of white was rolling in. It was the fog.

Loud roars and howling rose from the Forbidden Zone. Riley looked across the water and cried out. A monstrous wild boar with long tusks and coarse black hair was standing on the edge of the jungle, dipping his hooves in the water. But he didn't sink. Riley realized the boar was moving onto the land bridge.

There was no time to think, only react. Riley reached down and caught hold of Beresford. She started to haul him toward the water.

Pea and Maggie said they always climbed trees

during the Red Moon. Riley thought maybe she could. But what about Beresford? There was no way she could lift him, let alone carry him up into a tree, and she wasn't going to abandon him.

Instead she used what was left of her strength to pull him to the water. Maybe there were monsters in there—ones she didn't know about, or even ones she did, like Susan the alligator. But there seemed to be more land monsters than water.

The sound of snarling and fierce laughing made Riley look back at the land bridge. The boar was almost halfway across when a pack of hyena-like animals raced onto the bridge. They were making whooping, yelling, and growling sounds as they attacked it.

The sights and sounds were horrible as the boar fought to defend itself. But there were so many hyenas with their extra-wide mouths.

"Oh Riley . . . ," a teasing voice called.

Riley looked away from the attack on the land bridge and was sickened to see Mada emerging from the trees beside it. He was still wearing his filthy red cloak. Walking on his two back legs, he pulled off the cloak and cast it aside, revealing his tall, muscular tiger body.

"What are you doing, Riley?" Mada teased. "Where are you taking Beresford? Are you trying to steal my dinner?"

"Mada, stay back!" Riley cried. She tried to move Beresford faster, but he was so heavy. And with her wounded legs struggling in the sand, each step was both painful and slow.

"There is no one here to help you now, Riley. No Gideon, no mermaid with her pet water snake. It's just you and me." He paused and tilted his tiger's head to the side. "You know, I hate to admit it, but I have missed you and our little games."

"We don't play games," Riley grunted.

"Of course we do," Mada said teasingly. "Life is a game—a chess game, with strategy and cunning. But sadly, it's time for our game to come to an end. There are winners and there are losers. And I never lose."

Riley kept pulling Beresford. She reached the shore and split her attention between Mada and the fight on the land bridge.

"Look at me when I'm speaking to you," Mada snapped.

Riley realized that Mada was so focused on her, he was oblivious to the attack happening just a few yards away. But as she looked at the pack of hyenas, she saw two of them had locked their eyes on Mada.

"Mada, get out of here," Riley warned. She needed to keep him focused on her and not the land bridge.

"Or what?" Mada teased. "What will you do?"

"Not me," Riley said as she started to haul Beresford faster. "Them."

Finally, Mada turned and saw the boar breaking free of hyenas on the land bridge and charging right at him.

"Checkmate!" Riley shouted.

Mada had no time to move and was struck by the panicking animal. The tiger-man was knocked into the air and spun violently around as they both fell to sand. The boar gained his legs first and was able to dart away into the jungle. With their prey gone, the hyenas turned their attention to Mada.

Riley watched the hyenas advancing for a moment, but then the fog descended, and she could no longer see anything but white. But she could hear. There were yells, giggles, growls, hissing, and roaring as Mada was attacked.

Not knowing if they'd seen her or could smell her, Riley kept pulling Beresford toward the channel.

Soon her feet were wet, and it gave her the incentive to keep pulling. A bit farther and she felt Beresford become lighter as he was lifted by the water.

Riley wrapped her arm around him to keep him at the surface as she swam farther out into the channel.

The sounds from the beach were horrifying. But then an even bigger roar sounded from the land bridge. This was followed by stomping footsteps that were so heavy, Riley could feel the vibrations in the water. Whatever the new nightmare was, it was enough to scare the hyenas, as they let out shrieking squeals and laughed in the distance.

There were no sounds from Mada. If he survived the hyenas, did that bigger monster get him? Did he get away? Or was he coming after her quietly? Tigers liked water and Mada was an excellent swimmer. Was he entering the water right now and about to attack her? Riley had no way of knowing. All she could do was hold on to Beresford and pray.

25

RILEY SWAM A BIT FARTHER OUT UNTIL she could no longer feel the ground beneath her feet. Beresford was floating on his back as Riley held him close. Her heart was racing and her breath came in quick, silent gasps. She didn't dare make a sound.

When they were on the *Queen* for the first Red Moon, Pea had warned her to be silent so they wouldn't attract predators. This time Riley and Beresford were out in the open and exposed to every horror there was from the Forbidden Zone. If just one creature were to find them, there would be no escape.

Time stopped for Riley. The fog around her remained bright white, meaning it was still daytime.

But that didn't seem to stop the wildlings from cross-ing the land bridge. Each moment brought harsh sounds more terrifying than the last. Was it the fog playing sound tricks with her? Or were there that many snarling, barking creatures entering Atlantis? She didn't know. But at times it sounded like the monsters were right next to her.

Despite the air and water being warm, Riley was shivering. She had to keep her mouth closed to hide the sound of her chattering teeth. All the things that had ever frightened her in the past paled in compari-son to now. She wanted to cry, but she didn't dare.

Hour after endless hour, Riley kept Beresford at the surface as she treaded water. By now the others must have realized they were missing. Were they going to send out search parties? Probably not. This was a Red Moon; it would be too dangerous. They were on their own.

After a time, Beresford moaned and started to move. Riley slapped her hand over his mouth and leaned closer to his ear. "Beresford," she whispered tightly. "It's me, Riley. Don't move. Don't make a sound. Just float. We're outside and it's the Red Moon. Do you understand?"

Beresford nodded his head. He reached up, pulled her hand away, and spoke softly. "How?"

"Not now. We're in the channel beside the land bride. Wildlings are everywhere." Riley gave a quick answer and hoped that it would satisfy Beresford. It did. He nodded again and grasped the arm Riley had around him to hold him up.

Somehow having Beresford awake made Riley feel a bit better in the endless nightmare. She was holding on to him, and he was holding on to her—not speaking, just being together and sharing the terror.

Just when Riley didn't think she could be more scared, the fog started to darken. Night was coming. She had treaded water all afternoon and now she and Beresford were facing a night of it. She tried to take breaks and float to rest, but they constantly drifted to shore. Despite her exhaustion, she had to keep treading water.

Was this what each Red Moon was like for the Cloaks who were denied the protection of the *Queen*? Riley thought she could sympathize with them and understand how bad it might be. But until now, she never fully understood.

The arrival of darkness brought a new level of terror as more wild, ferocious calls started. Pea and the gargoyles called the sandbar that formed between the two islands a land bridge. Riley realized it should have been called a superhighway. It was constantly filled with nightmarish "things" moving to and from Atlantis.

Beresford held on to Riley tighter, and he was shaking even more than her. Not only were they enduring the Red Moon, Riley also realized that Beresford couldn't swim. All the Atlanteans had been taught to fear water. So as bad as this was for Riley, it must have been doubly bad for Beresford.

"We'll get through this," she promised quietly. "I won't let you drown. But you must not struggle. Just float."

"Leviathan," Beresford whispered.

"He's probably with Galina," Riley answered. And then she realized her mistake: Beresford didn't know about the siren. That was something Gideon asked her to keep secret. "I mean, he's probably in deep water."

Beresford tapped her arm lightly and nodded.

They fell silent again. If they could call it that, with all the wild sounds and horrors around them.

At some point during the seemingly endless night of terror, Riley heard sharp whinnies.

"Unicorns," Beresford said. He inhaled as though he was about to call out to them, but Riley slapped her hand over his mouth again.

"No, Beresford," Riley warned. "Don't make a sound; we can't be sure it's them. If it's not, we'll let the wildlings know we're here. We have to wait for the gargoyles. I'm sure Gideon will find us soon."

When Beresford nodded, Riley removed her hand.

"You know Gideon?" Beresford whispered.

"Yes, I'll tell you later," Riley said, and then fell silent.

It did sound like the unicorns. But then again, for the first Red Moon she'd experienced, the unicorns arrived at the *Queen* to protect it. Why would they come here? Would they drive the wildlings back to the Forbidden Zone?

The whinnies grew louder. Then there was splashing in the water just a few yards from where they were. This was followed by a soft, shrill cry.

Riley held her breath. Was it the unicorns? Or something else coming in after them? She could feel Beresford tensing as well. Something deep inside Riley told her to stay absolutely silent. Beresford must have been feeling the same because he didn't utter a sound.

More whinnying followed. Then suddenly, horns started to glow golden bright, and Riley knew for certain it was the unicorns. Because of the fog, she was unable to see them, but their glowing horns reminded Riley of lightsabers floating in the darkness. Several of them moved deeper into the water, and then two of them leaned down and Riley saw a golden spark.

After that the horns faded, and the unicorns became silent as they walked out of the water and drifted away.

Both Riley and Beresford were too frightened of the strange event to do anything. They stayed in the water, and both wished the night would end. But just a few minutes later, Beresford's legs shook.

"There's something touching my feet!" he cried tightly.

"Quiet!" Riley rasped. She treaded water and was still holding Beresford up, but she moved them a bit so Beresford didn't cry out. When she did, Riley also felt something soft brush against her bare arm.

At first startled, she reached out and felt a soft muzzle. Riley gasped. Touching along the head, her fingers grazed the start of a horn. Farther up were ears, and then a long neck with a short, bushy mane.

Riley suddenly realized it was a unicorn foal. She went back to the muzzle and, with one arm holding on to Beresford, used the other to grasp the foal's head and bring it closer. She put her ear to the muzzle and felt a soft, weak breath.

"Beresford, it's a unicorn foal," Riley whispered. "It's alive!"

Beresford started to say something, but then an especially loud roaring started on the beach. This was met by another roar and snarl, which was followed by the sound of a vicious fight.

Of all the sounds of the seemingly endless night, this was by far the worst. The snarling, growling roars followed by more sounds of fighting. Because of the fog and darkness, Riley couldn't be sure, but it seemed whatever was fighting, there were more than two. Finally, the fight ended with pain-filled screams and triumphant howls.

Riley wrapped her right arm around the foal's head and pulled it closer. She held on to Beresford with her left. All that remained were her damaged legs to work extra hard to keep them all at the surface.

The foal's soft muzzle was now pressed against Riley's neck, and she could feel its small whiskers move with each breath. Its breathing was weak, but it was even. She had seen the unicorn's glowing horns and knew they were used as a weapon. But she had no idea why they turned against the defenseless foal. She also remembered how one horn had been enough to bring down a charging Mada. What had a double dose of their power done to the poor baby? And why?

The night of horrors went on and on as Riley struggled to keep herself, Beresford, and the foal alive. Each moment that passed, she felt her energy ebbing as she forced herself to keep treading water. Her legs no longer hurt, they were completely numb. She prayed the gargoyles would come and drive the wildlings over the land bridge and back to the Forbidden Zone so they could rest. But still they didn't arrive.

Gideon had said he could feel her getting sick, which was why he came to Denver. So why couldn't he feel her now? She was in pain and terrified. Certainly if he could feel her emotions, he should have felt this.

Each moment became an eternity as Riley drove

herself to keep going. Finally, when she felt like she couldn't go on, the first raindrops started to fall. Bastian always said the rain started the morning after a Red Moon.

"Is it morning?" Riley panted.

"Not yet, it's still dark," Beresford said.

Riley was hardly aware of the fog fading as it was replaced by the rain. But then she felt the tide starting to turn, and she had to tread water even harder just to stay still.

"Get moving! Go. Leave here, it is over!"

Riley thought she heard a voice calling, but couldn't be sure if it was real or only in her dreams. But then the voice was followed by loud snarling and barking.

"Go, now!" a woman's voice commanded. "You are not welcome in Atlantis!"

"I command you to go!"

Riley recognized the second voice. It was Gideon. "Gideon . . . ," she tried to call. But she was so cold, and so weak from treading water all night, her voice was just a croak.

"Gideon!" Beresford cried. "Help us, please."

"Beresford?" Gideon shouted. "Beresford, where are you?"

"Here, in the water," Beresford answered.

"Gideon, there," the woman said. "I see them in the water."

Riley heard the sound of loud splashing. Then suddenly Gideon was beside her. "Riley?" he gasped. "What in the stars are you doing here? Have you been here all night? Priri, help me, please. Take Beresford."

Moments later, Beresford was pulled away from her. Then Riley felt Gideon's strong arms wrap around her. "The foal," Riley rasped. "Please, help me save the foal."

"What foal, Riley, I don't . . ." Gideon stopped speaking, then inhaled sharply. "Oh no, Riley, you can't save it. You must let it go."

"Please," Riley begged. "The—the unicorns, I think they tried to kill it. But it's just a baby."

"Riley, I can't. It's forbidden for us to get involved in unicorn business."

Riley felt sick and weak, but there was no way she was going to let the foal die. Not after everything they'd been through. "Fine, leave me," she said weakly. "I'll save it myself."

"You can't," Gideon said. "Riley, you are half-frozen."

"I won't let it die."

"You foolish child," Gideon said as he reached past her and caught the foal in one arm. "You have bewitched me, Riley. I can't deny you anything, even this."

Gideon carried Riley and the foal out of the water and laid them on the sand. The rain was coming down in sheets, and in the darkness, Riley couldn't see anything. But she felt the foal beside her and pulled its head into her lap. It was cold and shivering, but it was alive.

"Beresford?" she rasped.

"I am here," Beresford said softly.

"What happened?" Gideon asked. "How did you get here?"

"It was Edward," Riley said. "He—he attacked both of us. He tied us up here and left us to die during the Red Moon. He's working with Mada and wants to take over the Community."

Gideon inhaled deeply. In the dark, Riley couldn't see his face, but she had a pretty good idea of what it must be like. "I shall see to him later. So you have been out here since it started?"

"Yes," Riley said. "I didn't think it would ever end."

"It hasn't," Gideon warned. "Priri, will you stay here with Riley and Beresford? Keep them safe. I will take care of the wildlings."

"Be careful, Gideon," Priri said.

Riley felt someone move behind her and then the rain stopped hitting her on the head. She could hear the sound of it striking something, and it reminded her of rain hitting a tent. She reached back and felt a muscular leg.

"So you are Riley," Priri said. "Gideon has told me much about you."

"Are—are you a gargoyle too?" Riley asked through chattering teeth. She wasn't sure if it was from the cold or the realization that they might actually survive this.

"I am," Priri said. "And what you have there, that unicorn foal, is very dangerous for all of us. If the unicorns find out it lives, they will be enraged."

"Wh—why did they want to kill it?" Riley asked.

"When the light rises, you will see for yourself. It is imperfect and they do not tolerate imperfection, especially among their own kind. It's very small and its horn is malformed. It also has three white hooves. Meaning its power is diminished, if it has any at all. They destroy foals that are less than perfect. By the looks of it, I would say it was born this night."

Riley couldn't see it, but she could feel the young foal's head on her lap, and she stroked it. "That's so—so wrong. It's not this baby's fault how it looks."

"No, it's not. But they will not allow it to live and weaken their line."

"Well then, if—if they don't want it, I'll take it."

"You must not do that. If they find out . . ."

"I won't tell them. Will you?" Riley asked.

Priri stayed silent a moment. "No, of course not. It is a young life. But I just hope you know what you are doing."

"So do I," Riley said shakily. "So do I."

26

RILEY STAYED ON THE BEACH WITH Beresford, Priri, and the foal, listening to Gideon drive more wildlings across the land bridge. Her shivering was getting worse despite Priri shielding them from the rain with her wings.

After a while Gideon returned. "Riley, you are chilled. We must get you back to the *Queen* before the sun rises."

"A-and the foal?" Riley asked. "Please, Gideon, we—we can't leave it here. It will die."

Priri said, "Perhaps if we take it to the *Queen*, the unicorns will not know."

"Are you suggesting we save it?" Gideon asked.

"A life is a life," Priri said. "They are all precious."

Once again, Riley regretted not being able to see Gideon's face. His decision right there would make the world of difference to the foal, Riley, and how she perceived him. Finally he sighed. "All right, Riley. I am sure we're all going to regret this. But if Priri takes Beresford, I will carry you and the foal to the *Queen*. We will deal with the unicorns later."

Riley was too cold, wet, and weak to jump up and embrace the gargoyle. "Thank you, Gideon. Thank you, Priri. You don't know how much this means to me."

Gideon chuckled and said, "Pure witchcraft . . ." as he bent down and lifted Riley to his back, then reached for the foal.

"Gideon, look out behind you!" Priri shouted.

Riley felt Gideon turn. His wings flashed open and he leaped up into the air. Then he shouted, "Susan, Elijah, I told you both to go!"

Riley was standing on the gargoyle's tail and struggling to hold on as Gideon's wings flapped hard to keep him hovering. She couldn't see what was happening, but she had a pretty good idea. Susan was Mada's old love, and there was a portrait of her in Pea's book. She was once a beautiful woman, but now she was a large alligator. She must have tried to attack Gideon, or even her. But it wasn't just Susan—there were two of them!

Though she couldn't see, she heard hissing and snapping—and it sounded very, very close and very dangerous.

"I said, go!" Gideon shouted.

This was followed by more hissing and growling. Riley held tight to Gideon's neck as he moved. It felt like he was dipping down and kicking the alligators, forcing them to move away.

"Go!" Gideon commanded.

"You heard him!" Priri added. "Go!"

Finally Gideon touched down on the sand again as the sounds of the two alligators faded away and were swallowed up by the sounds of the rain.

"Have they gone?" Riley asked.

"Yes," Gideon said. "They are crossing the land bridge. Let's get you home." The gargoyle opened his wings and took off.

The journey back to the *Queen* was a short one. They soon landed on the upper deck just outside their suite. Riley saw the lantern lights were on despite the Red Moon.

Moments later, the door opened and Maggie appeared. She called back into the suite, "I did hear them! They're back!" She charged out into the rain.

When Riley climbed down from Gideon's back, her legs gave out from beneath her. He caught her just before she fell. Maggie reached Riley and held her up.

"She's been in the water all night," Gideon said.

"Riley?" Her mother ran up to her and helped support her. "What happened? We've been frantic!" They started moving back to the suite.

"The foal," Riley said as she reached back to Gideon.

"I have him," Gideon said. "Beverly, Beresford has been attacked. He is hurt, as is Riley. Her legs are cut. . . ."

"I'm all right," Riley said. "Take care of Beresford."

Riley was carried into their suite. She looked back and watched Gideon struggle to get through the door, carrying the small foal. This was the first time Riley actually saw the baby unicorn. He was adorable. All black with three white hooves. Priri was right, his horn was stubby and misshapen. He was limp in Gideon's arms, but very much alive.

"Shorty!" Alfie cried when he ran in. Bastian was right behind him with Danny. They pulled a chair over and helped Riley sit down.

"Where shall I put Beresford?" Priri asked when she entered the suite.

"My cabin is below," Beresford said softly.

"You're not going anywhere," Beverly said. "Put him on the sofa over there." She turned to Alfie. "Go find Tony and Lisette and tell them we have Beresford and Riley."

While Alfie darted out of the suite, Riley looked at the gargoyle and was stunned. Priri was almost as large as Gideon. She made Beresford look small in her arms. She had the same gray skin and large bat-like wings as Gideon, as well as the tall ears on her head. Yet, for as much as she looked like Gideon, she was definitely feminine.

"Whoa," Danny said when he saw Priri.

"Danny, this is Pr-Priri," Riley said. "Priri, this is my brother, Danny, and this is Bastian."

Priri lowered Beresford down on the sofa. In the lamplight, they could see the large swelling on his head. She looked up. "It is a pleasure to meet you, even under these circumstances."

Moments later, Alfie returned with Tony and Lisette. They both looked exhausted and stopped short when they saw the two gargoyles.

"Beresford!" Lisette darted over to the sofa. She looked fearfully at Priri, but then knelt beside Beresford. "What happened to you?"

"He and Riley were attacked," Priri said. "We found them treading water in the Red Cloak territory."

Lisette looked back at Riley. "What were you doing there?"

Beresford answered, "It was Edward. He attacked us. I must find him."

When Beresford tried to rise, Beverly put her hands on his shoulders and forced him to lie down. "You're not going anywhere. I'm sure you have a concussion."

"No, I must see to Edward. He's trying to take over. He tied us up in the Red Cloak territory so we would be murdered by Mada or the wildlings. I am certain there are others helping him." Beresford turned to Riley. "Riley saved me."

Lisette looked back at Riley, and Riley saw gratitude in her eyes the likes of which she'd never seen before. "Riley, I—I don't know what to say."

Riley was still shivering. "Just—just promise me you'll find everyone who tried to kill us so they don't try again."

Tony moved for the door, just as Jill and her family came through. "Don't you worry, Riley. No one else is getting in here tonight."

Danny and Alfie moved over to the door leading to the promenade and blocked it, while Bastian knelt beside Riley and held her hand. "We'll protect you," he said softly.

Jill ran over to Riley. "Are you all right? We've been looking all over for you."

Now that she was safe and getting warmer, Riley's shaking intensified. "I'm fine, I'm just a bit . . ." The world started to swim and then went black.

When Riley opened her eyes, she found herself back in her bed. She hurt all over and her legs were throbbing. Her head was pounding, and she felt like she was going to be sick.

The curtains were open, and she saw the heavy, post–Red Moon rain pouring down. Maggie was lying on the sofa across from the bed, and her mother was sound asleep beside her.

Riley tried to get up, but she couldn't move.

"Don't move, just lie still," her mother said, coming instantly awake. "Beresford's not the only one with a concussion."

"How is he?" Riley rasped. Her voice was gone, and her throat was burning. That was another complaint to add to the list.

Maggie was also awake and carried a glass of water to her.

"Nice and slow," her mother warned. "Not too much—you've taken in a lot of salt water; we don't want you to get sick again."

"Again?" Riley rasped.

Maggie nodded.

"I—I don't remember," Riley said. "Wait, the foal?"

"He's fine and so is Beresford," Maggie said. "The foal is in the living room with the others, and Beresford is in Beverly's bed."

Once again Riley tried to rise. "I want to see the baby unicorn."

"Not yet," her mother said. "He's been through an ordeal as well. There is a large burn on his back. He needs his rest. Gideon and Priri have brought some kind of milk for him and he's eating."

Riley sighed and lay back. "It—it was awful out there. . . ." She looked at Maggie. "How could you survive so many Red Moons outside? I thought I was going to die of fright."

Maggie smiled and kissed Riley's cheek. "I often wonder that myself. Now go back to sleep."

"But I want to see the baby."

"No, Riley," her mother said with a stern but loving voice. "Go to sleep. Doctor's orders."

The next time Riley woke, it was with a soft, warm bristle brush rubbing against her cheek. She opened her eyes and saw a black muzzle as the foal nuzzled her neck. "Hi," Riley said. She reached out and stroked his smooth face. "What are you doing in here?"

"There's no stopping him," Alfie said as he, Jill, Bastian, and Miss Pigglesworth stood in the doorway. "He's so determined and stubborn."

"Yeah," Jill said. "He's been trying to get in here for two days."

Riley frowned. "Two days?"

They entered the room and took a seat on Maggie's

sofa. Alfie nodded. "We didn't think you were ever going to wake up."

Riley still felt weak, and her legs were sore. But her headache was gone. "Neither did I. How is Beresford?"

"Just like you. He's in the next room and recovering slowly," Alfie said. "Edward got him good. His head's still swollen. But Beverly and Cameron have been taking good care of him."

"What happened to you?" Jill asked.

Riley continued to stroke the foal as she told them what she'd been through, starting with Edward hitting her, to getting free of the tree and Mada coming after her, to finally finding the foal.

Riley looked at Bastian and smiled. "It was you. You saved me."

"Me?" Bastian said. "I didn't. I'm so sorry I wasn't with you."

"But you were, in here." Riley tapped her head. "I remembered what you taught me about the trees and weeds that grow in Atlantis. Edward thought he'd tied me to a tree, but it wasn't. It was one of those tall weeds. If you hadn't taught me about them, I would never have known that I could break it."

"Wow, Shorty," Alfie said. "I don't know how you did it. I mean, you spent a whole Red Moon outside!"

"I didn't have much choice," Riley said. "I went into the water hoping Galina and Dad would find us. But they didn't."

Danny entered the bedroom. "Dad feels awful about it too. I saw him this morning. He, Galina, and the Leviathan were keeping the *Moon Dancer* safe from the storm. They had no idea you were in trouble."

"It's not their fault," Riley said. "It was Edward and Mada."

"Do you think that monster got Mada?" Bastian asked.

"I don't know," Riley said. "I couldn't see or hear him because of the fog. The last I saw, the hyenas were attacking him."

"I hope he was eaten," Alfie said.

"Me too," Riley agreed. "What about Edward?"

Danny shrugged. "We don't know where he is. We searched the *Queen* and couldn't find him. Shane thinks he got off somehow. That, or he never made it back here before they closed the doors, and he was outside for the Red Moon. All I know is that he's not on board."

"Lisette and Shane have been talking to everyone," Bastian said. "They are looking for traitors. So far two people have admitted to supporting Edward."

"Two?" Riley said. "I didn't think anyone would admit to it."

"I know, right?" Alfie said. "I sure wouldn't."

"What's going to happen to them?" Riley asked.

Bastian hesitated before saying, "It's already happened."

"What has?" Riley asked. She knew there were no prisons in Atlantis. What did they do to people who broke the law? Then she realized. "They gave them Memory Berries, didn't they?"

Bastian nodded. "I know how you feel about them. I feel the same. But in this case . . ."

"In this case, it's the only solution," Alfie said. "Gideon did have some other ideas, but they involved the Forbidden Zone."

Danny nodded. "That gargoyle is *furious* about what happened to you. He wanted them all taken to the Forbidden Zone and left there. But Pea and Maggie talked him out of it."

Normally Riley would have been horrified by the

use of the berries. "I guess the berries are better than the Forbidden Zone."

The foal was still nuzzling Riley's neck. She turned and looked at him. "So now, what about you?"

Jill got up from the sofa and knelt beside the foal and stroked his back. "I think he's adorable. What are you going to call him?"

"Call him?" Riley said. "I—I don't know."

"You could call him Red," Alfie said. "I mean, you did find him in a Red Moon."

"Or Moonlight," Danny offered.

Riley shook her head. "That's too many 'moon's. I mean, 'Red Moon,' 'Moon Dancer' . . ."

"What about Rainbow?" Jill added. "I had a cat named Rainbow and really loved her."

"Rainbow the unicorn?" Riley scrunched up her face. "Sorry, I don't think so. This boy needs a better name." She looked into the foal's dark eyes and started to smile. "How about Storm?"

"You're calling him Storm?" Alfie asked.

"Yep," Riley agreed. "He was born during a storm. He had the strength of a storm to survive the two horns touching him, and Gideon says the unicorns will be furious if they find out what I've done. So that's a different kind of storm. I think it suits him perfectly."

She lifted her head and kissed the foal's muzzle lightly. "Your name is Storm."

27

RILEY WAS INSTRUCTED TO SPEND ONE more day in bed. She was anxious to get up, but her legs were still weak and wouldn't support her, so she accepted her mom's orders. The breaking weed had done a lot of damage to her legs, but it was the night in the water that had done the most harm.

Storm settled in her room and spent most of the time with her. At one point, the foal leaped up on her bed and nestled down beside her, laying his muzzle on Riley's neck.

Riley loved it. Her mother didn't. So Storm was pulled off the bed and barricaded in a corner of her room. Riley then saw what Alfie and Jill meant.

He was stubborn and tried to get to her.

One of the first things Riley did when she could get up was visit Beresford. Because of the concussion, Beresford was recovering in her mother's bedroom instead of going down the stairs to his cabin. When Riley entered, she found him awake and sitting up in bed eating a bowl of soup. Maggie sat beside him after bringing him his meal.

"Thank you, Maggie," Beresford said when he'd finished. Then he saw Riley enter. "Riley, please, please, come in. Sit down."

Maggie got up and took the dishes away. "I will see you later, Beresford."

"Please don't go because of me," Riley said.

Maggie smiled brightly, exposing her sharp feline teeth. "No, dear, I have work to do. Please, take your time with him." She leaned closer to Riley and lowered her voice. "And make sure he stays in bed. He's as bad as you are."

When Maggie started to walk away, Storm trotted into the room. Maggie petted him on the head and then left.

"Please sit," Beresford said.

Riley took a seat in the chair Maggie had used,

beside his bed. Storm moved in right beside her and stood calmly.

"I see he's still with us," Beresford said.

Riley smiled at the foal. "You betcha. His name is Storm and he's already responding to it. He's really smart."

"Storm," Beresford repeated. "Somehow that suits him. Yes, the unicorns are very intelligent. Which is why I hope they don't find out he's here."

"Me too," Riley agreed as she stroked Storm's neck. "But we couldn't let him drown."

"No, we couldn't," Beresford agreed. "Now that we have some time, I want you to tell me what happened to us. And how do you know Gideon?"

Riley inhaled deeply. This was probably the first time she and Beresford had truly sat down together to talk without either someone interrupting them or his duties calling him away. She started explaining how she first met Gideon and then how he'd found them in Denver and helped bring them back. She ended with the terrible night of the Red Moon and all that they'd been through.

When she finished, Beresford lowered his head and seemed at a loss for words. "I—I just don't know what to say to you," he started. "You saved my life and exposed Edward's plot to take over the Community. How can words express my gratitude?"

"You don't need to thank me, Beresford," Riley said. "I know you would've done the same for me."

"But we were in Red Cloak territory," he insisted. "And instead of running, you dragged me all the way into the water and kept me safe."

Riley grinned. "If I'm being totally honest, I'm glad you were there. I think I would have freaked if I were alone."

Beresford also smiled. "Me too."

"But," Riley started, "if you really want to thank me, there is something you can do. It might be difficult, but it would mean so much to me and so many others."

"Name it," Beresford said.

Riley didn't know if this was the right time to address the issue, but it had to be said now, while Beresford was in a grateful mood and the memory of what they'd been through was still fresh.

"I, um, I'm asking you to allow all the Blue and Yellow Cloaks on the *Queen* for the next Red Moon and all the ones that follow. Now that you've been through one and seen for yourself just how awful it is outside of this ship, people like Kevin and Jeff and all of those who are changing don't deserve to be left to the mercy of the wildlings. They are members of the Community, and they work with us. It's only fair that they be treated like everyone else."

Beresford closed his eyes. "Do you realize what you're asking?"

"Yes," Riley said. "I'm asking you to be a great leader and to turn a good community into an amazing one. Where all the citizens are equal, no matter how they look or what they're turning into."

"If I do that, a lot of people are going to be very upset."

"Will they?" Riley asked. "Most are getting used to Maggie, Pea, and Mary being here and not wearing their cloaks—I mean, yes, a couple of the ladies in the sewing hut are still uncomfortable, but most of the others are fine and have asked Maggie to show them how to use her sewing machines. Think about it. Maggie was in here without her cloak and I didn't hear you complaining. And just this morning Alfie told me that a few people have actually asked Mary to teach them to read. She could even start a school for all of you."

"A school?" Beresford said.

Riley nodded. "Why not? You're the leader of this Community. If people see you accepting the Cloaks and treating them like people, I'm sure the others will follow your lead."

"I don't know," Beresford said. "People like Edward think I'm being too generous in allowing the Cloaks to remain here."

"Edward is a small-minded, prejudiced fool. He's changing and he's terrified, and he's trying to drive the Cloaks away so they don't remind him of what's happening to him," Riley said.

Riley couldn't let it go. She had to make him understand. "Beresford, don't you realize this is the perfect opportunity to heal the rifts in Atlantis that Walston Greeves started? You could be the one who brings everyone together again. And maybe if the other territories see what we're doing here, we could break down more barriers. Then if that happened, Atlantis would be practically perfect."

Beresford shook his head and chuckled. "And you really believe all that will happen if I just let the Blue and Yellow Cloaks on the *Queen*."

Riley shrugged. "And stop calling them 'Cloaks' and use their real names. Yes, I really do."

"Anything else?" Beresford laughed.

Riley grinned and nodded. "Well, you could also stop forcing them to wear cloaks."

"Is that all?"

Riley nodded. "Yep, that's all."

Beresford smiled. "All right. I will make no promises, but I will think about it."

It took longer for Beresford to recover than it took Riley, but eventually he was able to get up and walk around the Community again.

Lisette and Maggie stood on either side of him, supporting him as he walked. Riley had seen him walking just fine in their suite and realized he was doing this to show the value of Maggie and his acceptance of her help.

When Beresford caught Riley looking at him, he winked. She nodded back. The change might be slow and really wouldn't show up until the next Red Moon. But at least it was starting.

When they walked past her, Riley turned to go back to the sewing hut for another load of clothes to repair when Jill ran up to her. "You're needed on the *Queen*," she panted.

"What's wrong?"

"It's Storm—he's trying to find you and tearing the place apart."

Riley ran with Jill back to the *Queen*. After climbing all the stairs, they reached the top deck. Riley could hear Storm long before she saw him. He was making shrill whinnies and running amok.

"Storm," Riley called as she ran out on the open deck.

Storm was at the bow and stopped. He whinnied, turned, and started charging toward her. He stopped just before her and snorted and whinnied excitedly.

Riley went down on one knee and started to stroke his head and then his misshapen horn. "I was only gone for a few minutes—you have to calm down." She looked up at Jill. "I never knew foals could be so needy."

"I don't know if all foals are, but he sure is," Jill said.

Robbi and Soraya appeared on deck, approached Storm, and started to pet him. "He was running all over the place," Robbi said.

"He nearly knocked me over," Soraya said. "He was looking for you."

Riley continued to stroke the foal. "What am I going to do with you? I can't take you down to the ground; the other unicorns might see you."

"You might have to," Jill said. "He's really not happy up here when you go, and he starts to call really loudly. The others might hear him."

"But we have all those stairs. He can't climb them—he'll fall," Riley said.

"Well then," Jill said, "you're just going to have to stay up here all the time."

Despite early concerns with having Storm on the *Queen*, eventually everyone accepted his presence on the top deck. Every day the children would come up and play with him. Storm loved it and would run with the children and chase them all around the deck. Even some of the adults would find excuses to visit the deck and spend time with the young foal.

The downside of having the foal was that Riley could no longer leave the deck. It was just too upsetting and disruptive for Storm. Bastian and Alfie would bring up her meals and eat with her. Maggie and Jill started sewing on the top deck so Riley wouldn't be alone. But having Storm meant a big adjustment for Riley.

Most evenings Gideon and Priri would visit, bringing more milk for the foal, but also to spend time with Riley and her family.

"He is growing," Gideon commented one evening as he stroked Storm.

"That's because Riley is taking good care of him," Pea said.

"It's not me," Riley said. "It's thanks to you and Priri. He wouldn't have survived if you didn't bring the milk."

"Where does the milk come from?" Bastian asked. He was standing beside Riley with Alfie.

Gideon looked at Priri before answering. "Well, we do have some cowlike animals in our territory. But they are not domesticated as you know it. They live wild and free."

"Cows?" Riley said. "Really?"

Priri added, "We told a young mother about Storm, and she offered the milk you are feeding to him."

"You can talk to your cows?" Alfie gasped.

"Yes," Gideon said. "It is not as we are talking, but it is communication."

"Wow," Riley said. "Would you thank her for me?"

"I already have, many times," Priri said.

As they strolled along the deck, Riley paused and turned to Gideon. "I'm sorry if I keep asking, but have you seen or heard anything of Edward?"

"There is no need to apologize," Gideon said. "You are right to worry about Edward. I haven't seen or heard of him. He must have gone into hiding when he learned you and Beresford survived your ordeal. I haven't seen Mada either. Though from what you say, he might have been killed during the Red Moon."

Riley tried not to let her fear show, but knowing Edward was still out there somewhere really troubled her.

As though he'd read her mind, Gideon said, "Edward may still be free, but he would have to be a fool to come after you again."

Pea agreed. "Edward may be many things, but he is no fool." He reached up and took Riley's hand. "If he comes after you again, I will stop him."

"So will I," Alfie said.

"He won't come near you," Bastian promised. The intensity in his eyes made Riley blush.

After a comfortable pause, Riley looked at Gideon. "I know you told me never to look for the unicorns, and I promised I wouldn't. But would you tell me if they live very far from here? The only time they've come into the Community was during the Red Moon. But what about other times?"

Gideon tilted his head to the side. "Why do you ask?"

Riley glanced at Storm. He was looking up at her and his short, bushy tail wagged excitedly. "Well, I was thinking. It's not fair that Storm only stays up here all the time. He needs more exercise and room to run. And every time I try to leave the deck, he goes ballistic and really starts tearing the place apart looking for me. If he can't see me, he gets really upset."

Gideon smiled. "That is the price you pay for saving him. Storm has imprinted on you. He was a newborn when the unicorns drove him into the water. Their territory is actually quite far from here. So I must assume that his mother was working with the other unicorns against the wildlings when she went into labor. It's doubtful Storm even knew her. He smelled you when you were holding him up in the water, so you are all he has known. To him, you are his mother. And unicorn foals spend all their time with their mothers."

Riley considered this. "So if their territory is far away, do you think he'd be safe if we took him down to the ground? I just think he'd be happier if he had more room to run. But I'm scared the others might hear him and try to hurt him again."

Priri smiled at the foal and petted his head. "I do not think you need to worry about that. If you keep him here in the Community, and if he is with you, it is doubtful he will have cause to call out. And unless there is trouble, the unicorns tend to keep to themselves and their territory."

"So then," Riley said, "all we have to do is figure out how to get him down to the ground."

It was Bastian, Pea, and Danny who came up with the solution of how to get Storm safely on and off the *Queen*. Riley was grateful that they took time off their work schedule to build narrow ramps that lay over the stairs along the stairwell wall.

Along each ramp were stops. These pieces of wood ran across the ramp and would keep Storm from sliding down. The ramps were steep, but with Riley at the bottom of each level coaxing him along, and with Bastian, Alfie, and Jill there to help, Storm soon learned to use the ramps.

The first time Storm made it to the ground, Riley threw her arms around him and praised him like a well-trained dog. Storm seemed quite pleased with himself as he trotted around the area with his ears forward and head held high.

With Storm now able to follow, Riley regained some of her freedom and could join everyone for their meals instead of having to take them on the upper deck with the foal.

When the evening gong sounded, Riley, Bastian, Miss Pigglesworth, and Storm headed to the dining area. From the very first moment she arrived, Riley noticed a huge change.

Kevin the rhino and Jeff the gorilla arrived and took places at a table set up near the children's table. Soon more uncloaked animals arrived and also took seats at the table. When Jeff saw Riley, he rose and lumbered over.

"Riley," he said in his deep voice. "I, no—I mean, all of us would like to thank you."

"Me?" Riley said. "I didn't do anything."

"Oh yes, you did," Jeff said. "Beresford has been speaking to us. He told us what you did and how it was you who set us free." The gorilla reached out and pulled Riley to him in a surprisingly gentle embrace. "I shall be forever grateful to you," he whispered softly. "And I know that you are frightened of Edward coming after you again. I swear, I and all the others will not allow him to touch you. That is our solemn vow."

"Thank you," Riley said.

"No, child," Jeff said as he released her. "Thank you." He walked back to the table, and Riley saw all the other animals looking at her and nodding.

Riley glanced over to Beresford and saw that he was watching her. He nodded slightly. Riley grinned and nodded back. Then she mouthed the words *Thank you.*

Maggie and Pea arrived and took seats with Riley at the children's table. Her mother joined them, with Mary.

After the meal, everyone walked to the bonfire. Bastian shyly reached down and took Riley's hand as they went. Her heart fluttered with excitement as they took seats together.

For the whole evening, the storytelling and singing felt more like a celebration as all those who had been banned were now among them enjoying the music. Riley searched the crowd and didn't see any signs of resentment of their presence. Could this be the healing she was hoping for?

"You did it, Riley," Bastian whispered in her ear.

She grinned and looked at him. "*We* did it."

The next morning, Riley rose early as she usually did. With Storm at her side, the two made their way through the *Queen* and down the stairs. They arrived at the bottom just as the outer doors were being opened.

"Good morning, Riley," one of the men said as they secured the door open. "It's another beautiful day."

"It sure is," Riley agreed. "If my mom or anyone is looking for us, would you tell them we've gone to see my dad near Pea's house?"

"Sure will—have fun."

Riley grinned as she and Storm walked down the ramp to the ground. The air was fresh and clear, and the sun was peeking over the horizon.

Riley rested her arm on Storm's neck. "Come on, Stormy, I want you to meet my dad and my best friend."

They walked together through the Community and down toward Pea's old house. "This is where Pea used to live," Riley explained to the foal. "Before he moved onto the *Queen*. And just ahead is where he kept his boat."

They pushed through the jungle and made their way toward the water. Pea's boat was still tied at the shore. Riley remembered the last time they used it to escape Atlantis. She was glad it would never have to be used for that again.

Standing at the water's edge, Riley called, "Dad? Galina?"

Before she had to call again, Riley heard her father's light voice. "Riley!"

Riley ran into the water and greeted him as he darted forward. "Baby, I'm so glad to see you!"

"Me too!" Riley called as she embraced her dolphin father.

Galina surfaced beside him and sang her beautiful greeting. Riley grinned and threw her arms around the mermaid. "Boy, I've missed seeing you! But look."

Riley pointed to the shore where Storm was standing. The foal looked fearfully at the water.

"Dad, Galina, this is Storm."

"Alfie told us all about him," her father said as he tilted in the water to look at the foal. "I am so, so sorry we weren't there for you. It terrifies me to think of what could have happened to you."

Galina nodded and sang some notes.

"It's all right," Riley said to both of them. "You don't have to feel guilty. None of us expected Edward to attack Beresford and me. But at least I was able to save Storm."

Her father bobbed his dolphin head while Galina nodded. "He's beautiful. Knowing now what the unicorns do to their unwanted young, Galina and I will keep a watch on the shore for any more abandoned foals."

Riley grinned proudly. "That's great. If you do find more, just bring them here and we'll keep them safe on the *Queen*." Riley paused and kissed her father's dolphin head. "I have missed you so much."

"We've missed you too," her father said.

Moments later, Storm whinnied lightly and stepped into the water—one hoof and then the other, until he was neck-deep. Then he treaded carefully up to Riley.

Galina swam closer and reached out to the foal and stroked his muzzle. She laughed lightly as Storm nickered softly.

"Hey, wait for us!" Alfie called as he, Bastian, and Miss Pigglesworth appeared on the shore. They entered the water and were soon at Riley's side.

"You're up to your old tricks of sneaking off the *Queen* early," Alfie teased.

"Not this time," Riley said. "I told them where I was going."

Bastian grinned. "Yes, they told us."

Moments later, the Leviathan appeared. Its massive head rose out of the water, looming above them.

Riley put her arm protectively around Storm and pulled him closer. "Um, Galina," she said. "Would you please explain about Storm?"

"Don't worry, kiddo," her father said. "If Storm's with us, he's perfectly safe."

Galina looked back at the Leviathan and started to sing. The monstrous sea serpent ducked beneath the surface. When it rose again, Galina and Alfie were on its head.

"Whoa, whoa!" Alfie cried as he and the mermaid were lifted high out of the water. "You never said he could do this!"

Riley's father started to laugh in his high-pitched dolphin voice. "Hey, Galina," he called. "Want to race?"

Galina started to sing. Moments later, the Leviathan took off, moving swiftly through the water, carrying her and Alfie farther down the channel. Alfie held on tightly and started to whoop and shout as they raced the dolphin.

Riley watched the race and smiled as she recalled the dream she'd had not so very long ago. But this time there would be no Coast Guard boats with harpoons and nets coming after them. They were completely free.

With Bastian at her side and Storm in the water beside her, Riley watched the race. Bastian took Riley's hand again and turned to her. "Happy?"

Riley grinned at him and nodded. "Very happy. Everything is perfect."

"Not quite." Bastian leaned forward and kissed her lightly on the lips. Then he smiled. "Now everything is perfect."

ACKNOWLEDGMENTS

Before saying my thank-yous to those who so richly deserve it, I want to say that the feelings of being bullied never really go away. We learn to store them away in a place that doesn't haunt us all the time, but they are there, just waiting to come to the surface and remind us of the pain we suffered.

I was badly bullied at school. But not at every school I attended, and believe me, there were quite a few. When I was the victim of bullying, it hurt and scared me. So much so that when I went to another school and wasn't being bullied, I didn't have the strength to stand up to those who were being so painfully cruel to a girl in my class, Jill B. What was done to her was so much worse than what I endured. Jill was lovely and sweet and tried so hard to fit in. She would buy treats for the whole class, but still it didn't stop the relentless and cruel bullying.

I often think of Jill, and even now I can see her in my mind's eye. I wonder how she is. Is she happy? Did she survive and triumph? I hope so.

If you are being bullied, and I know I've said this

before, please tell someone. Don't suffer in silence, because there are a lot more people willing to help you than when Jill and I were going to school.

And if you are a bully and enjoy frightening people—STOP IT! Enough said?

Now, as always, there are some really special people whom I would like to thank. Veronique Baxter is my amazing agent, and I'm forever grateful for her support—as well as her awesome daughter, Remy, who along with her cousin, Eva, are wonderful fans, and I thank them for their extra-special support!

I would also like to thank Anna Parsons at Simon & Schuster for putting up with me. I'll miss you.

And here are some extra special thanks.

Tony Zamora and Cristina Zamora. These two wonderful people are real and they do work at Grove Harbour Marina. And it's also true that they are not related but have the same last name! (What are the odds of that happening?) I found them through my research, as I needed to understand what might have happened to the *Moon Dancer* if she were real. They gave me so much time and help, and it only added to the story!

Thank you, Tony and Cristina—I can't wait to meet you one day!

I would also like to send a special message to three lovely builders whom I had at my house. As writers, we always need names, so when these three brickies came and we had so much fun together, I told them I would put them in the book. They are Shane, Adam, and Beresford. Sadly, Beresford lost his fight with cancer a while ago, but he's still in my memories and now on the page.

You guys were the best!

And as always, I want to thank you, my readers. In these strange and uncertain times, knowing you are out there really helps me keep working. Please stay special and know that I love you all!